D0855623

Humbled

Humbled

Patricia Haley

www.urbanchristianonline.com

Urban Books, LLC
97 N18th Street
Wyandanch, NY 11798

ISBN 13: 978-1-60162-714-8
ISBN 10: 1-60162-714-9

First Printing March 2014
Printed in the United States of America

10 9 8 7 6 5 4 3 2 1

Distributed by Kensington Corp.
Submit Wholesale Orders to:
Kensington Publishing Corp.
C/O Penguin Group (USA) Inc.
Attention: Order Processing
405 Murray Hill Parkway
East Rutherford, NJ 07073-2316
Phone: 1-800-526-0275
Fax: 1-800-227-9604

Humbled

by

Patricia Haley

Praise for #1 *Essence* Bestselling Author Patricia Haley

and Her Inspirational Novels

"Phenomenal . . . Haley did an outstanding job on each person's outlook and how, without forgiveness, no problem can truly be solved."

— *Urban Reviews*

"Haley has a gold mine with this series. If I [were] a hat wearer, it would definitely be off to her. All I can say to her right now is, 'You go, girl!'"

— *Member of LVAAABC Book Club*

"Haley shared how God does choose the most unlikely person for ministry when we think there is no way. . . . A must read . . . Highly recommended."

—*APOOO Book Club*

"Haley engages one with subtle intrigue and touches of comedy. . . . An intriguing read with a subtle inspirational message woven into the story . . . Riveting."

— *Faygo's Report*

"A must read . . . highly recommend this book . . . promise you will not be disappointed."

— *Urban Christian Fiction Today on* Destined

Recent Reviews

"Haley showcases how God's word can be misinterpreted with greed, lust, and selfishness."
— *RAWSISTAZ™ on Chosen*

"The perfect blend of faith and romance."
—*Gospel Book Review*

"Haley has hit the mark yet again! I couldn't put this book down—the characters are believable and compelling."
—*Maurice M. Gray, Jr., author of All Things Work Together*

"The story grabs the reader from the beginning, drawing you in . . . and keeping you on the edge of your seat as the plot takes unexpected twists and turns."
—*RT Book Reviews on Let Sleeping Dogs Lie*

"Haley's writing and visualization skills are to be reckoned with. . . . This story is full-bodied. . . . Great prose, excellent execution!"
—*RAWSISTAZ™ on Still Waters*

"A deeply moving novel. The characters and the story line remind us that forgiveness and unconditional love are crucial to any relationship."
—*Good Girl Book Club*

"*No Regrets* offered me a different way, a healthier way based in faith and hope, to look at trying situations."
—*Montgomery Newspapers*

Humbled is also available as an eBook

Also by **Patricia Haley**

Mitchell Family Drama Series
(Listed in story line order)
Anointed
Betrayed
Chosen
Destined
Broken
Humbled

Other Titles
Let Sleeping Dogs Lie
Still Waters
No Regrets
Blind Faith
Nobody's Perfect

Humbled
is dedicated to my
Girls' Weekend sister friends,
a special group of women who keep me
laughing, encouraged, and humble.
Each year together we've grown older, wiser, and better.
Much love to my girls for always being there.

Rena Burks
Diedre Anise Campbell
Eddie J. French, III
Patricia F. Hill
Paulette Renée Lenzy
Tammy Jo Lenzy
Kirkanne (K.D.) Moseley

When pride comes, then comes disgrace, but with humility comes wisdom.

Proverbs 11:2 (NIV)

Chapter 1

Stability had been a stranger in Joel Mitchell's corner of the world for well over a year. He sat in Grant Park, situated in the heart of downtown Chicago, as the autumn breeze quieted his soul. So much had happened, too much to rehash, but he was certain getting a divorce was best in the long run. There was no question he was going to be better off ending a loveless marriage. He sighed, feeling an extra dose of relief as he anticipated how quickly the personal chaos in his life was coming to a close. He was finally going to be free, and it felt good.

One problem down, now he had to shift gears and concentrate on restoring his professional reputation. Spending a few days away from Detroit was the hiatus he needed. Joel intended to gather his thoughts and come up with a plan on how to regain his spot on the corporate scene. He clasped his hands behind his head, leaned back on the bench and sighed as he felt the noose of failure loosen, facilitating an inkling of enthusiasm.

A half hour or so later, Joel was disturbed by the buzzing sensation coming from the phone in his pocket. He must have fallen asleep. He was tempted not to answer, unwilling to frivolously relinquish the tranquility he'd scraped together just to answer an unwanted phone call. The ringing stopped, allowing him to relax again. When the ringing resumed, he was irritated but snatched the phone from his pocket.

"This is Joel." There was a lull on the line. He repeated his greeting, not sure if the person on the other end had heard him.

"Joel, it's me, Zarah."

Wow, his soon-to-be ex-wife was the one person he wasn't expecting a call from. "I thought you'd be heading home to India by now," he said, trying to balance his rising anxiety and concern.

"I'm not going."

Ha-ha, he thought, accounting for her accent shaving off some of the humor in her jokes. "Pretty funny, Zarah."

"Really, I'm not going," she repeated.

"What?" he fired at her. The blood drained from his face, along with a coherent response. His sampling size of tranquility took flight. Anxiety and pure fear rushed in, tackling his words ferociously. He struggled to speak but had to push something out to keep this train from derailing. "But we've already talked about this. After the divorce you're going to be better off with people who care about you."

"I'm pregnant," she blurted out.

"Excuse me? What did you say?" Joel asked as his body jerked forward on the bench.

"I'm pregnant," she said again. Joel experienced a piercing pain upon hearing those words. The park bench was twirling fast and faster. Joel couldn't hang on. He was in a whirlwind. Zarah rattled off something else, but he couldn't process what she was saying. Each cheery word out of her mouth was a dagger in his heart. She wouldn't stop talking. He repeatedly pulled the phone away from his ear and then brought it closer again.

She hadn't sounded this happy since their wedding five months ago. Words and thoughts were racing around his head but couldn't seem to connect long enough for him to create a rational statement. So he kept quiet.

"The gods have shown mercy on me and blessed us with a child."

Joel continued to struggle with formulating a coherent statement. Maybe he didn't know what to say, or maybe he did know what to say but wasn't comfortable sharing what was truly in his heart. Either way, the peace he'd realized earlier in Grant Park had evaporated. The sun, which had been dishing out the perfect amount of warmth to his face, was now feeling unusually hot and scorching. Joel couldn't breathe. If there was a way to escape, he would have jumped on it. But where was he going?

Sick with fret, Joel kept focusing on how this had happened. He had been careful not to mislead Zarah during their brief marriage and had intentionally avoided showing her too much affection. They'd spent less than five intimate nights together as husband and wife. This couldn't be happening. Divorce was one thing, but a baby was another. He was desperate for an out and wasn't willing to get worked up until there was undeniable proof that his world was crumbling. He needed confirmation, especially since Zarah was determined to remain his wife. Joel wasn't sure how far she'd go to keep him. His appeal was for her to accept the reality of their breakup and get on with life.

"How do you know you're pregnant?"

"I went to my doctor when you left. He thinks I'm about six weeks along. I'll have to wait for the official test results, but he's very certain."

Joel was clinging to the notion that Zarah was lying out of desperation, but hope was fading rapidly. From what he knew about her, she didn't seem to be the type who'd lie about something this serious. Since he was 100 percent sure there was no other man in the equation, certainty began choking the air from around him again. It was hard to believe that six weeks ago his fate had veered off course without his knowledge. As the shocking news sank in, Joel could think more clearly. He recalled the night with Zarah vividly. Right before her emotional breakdown, he'd felt sorry for her and comforted her as only a husband could; so much for his unselfish deed. Who was going to comfort his troubled soul now?

"When are you coming home?" Zarah asked.

"I'm not sure. I need time to wrap up a few matters here," he told her, which was partially true. The full truth was, Joel just didn't know what to do. The pregnancy had to be addressed. He just wasn't convinced it had to be right away. There were many months of pregnancy left, which offered him at least a few more hours, possibly weeks, to think.

"At least we aren't getting divorced anymore. We're a family now, and we must prepare for the baby. I'm very happy," Zarah said.

Joel was numb. Rushing home to the wife he'd planned to divorce as recently as an hour ago didn't elicit a fulfilling sensation. While nothing had changed for him emotionally, everything had realistically. He genuinely didn't know what to do. Overcommitting was definitely not the answer.

"Zarah, I'll call you tomorrow and let you know when I'll be in Detroit. In the meantime, you should take care of yourself. Maybe I'll see you soon."

"Yes, I will take very good care of our baby."

Joel let the word *baby* linger. This day would be burned into his memory forever. This moment marked the day when his reckless decisions of the past were marring the promise of a brighter future. Marrying Zarah Bengali with the intent of merging their companies was costing him dearly. He remained on the bench, clutching the shattered fragments of peace and freedom, not sure what was coming next.

Chapter 2

The hours passed as evening drew near, but for Joel time had stopped when Zarah uttered those words "I'm pregnant." He wasn't dead physically, but his hope of crawling out of his hole of despair had definitely died with the call, and Joel didn't know if there was a way to resurrect his personal or professional livelihood. The future appeared dire. He fumbled around his rambling thoughts a while longer before calling his mother, Sherry Mitchell, in search of a kind voice.

She was glad to hear from him. "How's your stay in Chicago going? Has it been helpful?"

He sighed. "Yes and no."

"You don't sound too good," she told him.

He repeatedly sighed. "I might as well tell you. Zarah is pregnant." He uttered the words like he was swallowing a nasty medicine, doing it quickly without dwelling on it.

"She is?" his mother yelled. "Oh my goodness, I am so happy for you. You're going to be a father."

Joel couldn't force himself to respond with glee, especially after making such a gallant attempt to conceal his true feelings about the ordeal.

"How do feel about this? You don't sound excited," his mother said after a moment.

His mother didn't need to hear his troubles. If she wanted to be the happy grandmother, he wasn't going to rob her of the special news. "It's a lot to think about. Remember, we are about to get divorced. The last thing

I expected was a baby to be in the picture. It's quite a shock."

"Yes, but a good one." He let her talk. There wasn't much he could add. This wasn't the time or place. "Look, Joel, unexpected situations happen. We just have to accept them and move on. This baby may be a blessing in disguise. Before this, you and Zarah didn't have anything holding the two of you together—"

Joel interrupted, "You mean like love?"

"Huh, love can be overrated."

He knew she was alluding to her marriage to his father. They'd been together twenty-five years before he died three years ago. She'd loved him totally, yet his father could only give half of his heart to her. The other half had always remained with his first wife. No matter how much love his mother poured into the marriage, she could never win his father's heart completely. At least that was what his mother believed. It was better for Joel to steer the conversation in a different direction and avoid the dead end that he was certain to confront when discussing a topic his family struggled to understand.

"Over the next couple of weeks or months we'll have to figure out how we want to raise the baby." The concept of becoming a parent pricked at Joel. "If we get divorced, then we'll have to agree on custody. Most likely, she'd be in India, which adds a slight complication."

"What do you mean? Come home and raise the baby."

"It's not that easy, Mom."

"You can't seriously be considering divorce, not now. Come on, Joel. You have to stay with your wife and raise your child. This isn't about Zarah. This is about your baby. Regardless of how the baby got here, your child deserves to have both parents while growing up."

"How can you say that? Dad left his four other children when he married you." His mother was quiet. He didn't want to hurt her by scratching the scab off old wounds, but Joel wasn't going to allow her to use guilt to convince him to stay in a failed relationship.

"All the more reason for you to stay with Zarah. Look at the turmoil your half sisters and brothers went through. You don't want that for your baby. Your child deserves a father who's present. Your child deserves you."

"Well, Zarah and I will figure this out. I promise."

"I hope so, and the sooner the better. When are you coming home?"

"I don't know yet."

"You're going to need a better answer than that one. If you ask me, the decision has already been made," his mother said with more directness than he was accustomed to hearing from her.

They ended the call. Joel wasn't as certain about the outcome as his mother was, by no means. When he'd driven his Lamborghini along I-94, heading west to Chicago, his concept of home had changed. The Zarah chapter had been closed. With the pregnancy, he was forced to reassess what *home* meant. So much would have to be considered. Should he return to his wife out of a sense of duty to the baby, or could he be a stronger influence outside of the troubled marriage? That was what he'd have to decide. He craved objective feedback, but there wasn't anyone who readily came to mind to supply it.

With no other outlet, Joel knew where he had to go for help. Zarah had repeatedly prayed to her gods for a baby. He didn't see any merit in her beliefs, but Zarah did. Maybe the time had come for him to pray to his God. Joel was lost since he couldn't ask God to reverse the process and make her un-pregnant. Direction and guidance would be the essence of his prayer, and he wanted lots of both. As soon as he reached his car, Joel planned on praying for the first time in nearly two years, which made him edgy. He aimlessly shuffled to the car, intentionally stretching out the short distance. God didn't need the extra time. Joel did.

Chapter 3

His mother was a piece of work, but Don wouldn't trade Madeline Mitchell for anyone else in the world. She was a rare gem and quite electrifying. There were no people or situations on earth that could rattle her, with the exception of his sister, Tamara, and Joel's mother, Sherry. The two women elicited unpredictable reactions from Madeline for different reasons, one driven by love and the other disdain. However, when it came to her daughter, Madeline's desire to appease seemed limitless. She didn't show nearly as much leniency to others, not even him. Don didn't mind. He understood their damaged history and his mother's attempt to make up for the past. Tamara understood too, but unfortunately, she wasn't as willing to extend such grace to Madeline.

Sherry, on the other hand, was as close to a nemesis as Madeline was going to get. Don couldn't see a time in the foreseeable future when his mother was going to accept Sherry into the Mitchell family. It had been almost thirty years since Sherry had married his father, but to his mother it seemed like yesterday. Regardless of the problems that had prevailed in his parents' marriage prior to the infidelity, Madeline was determined to blame Sherry for the rest of their days. In spite of his mother's vehement protests, Don had forgiven Sherry and had offered her a job not long ago. Madeline had pitched a fit, and needless to say, Sherry had ended up not working for Don at the Mitchell family's multimillion-dollar company, DMI. He hadn't bothered pleading her case on appeal. Don didn't have sufficient firepower. Even if he were accompanied by the entire United States Marine Corps, it wouldn't be enough force to change Madeline's mind. One day there might be total healing in his family, but it wasn't today. Yet Don wasn't complaining. Other than the discord with Sherry and a mild disregard for her offspring, Joel, Madeline, and the family were in a respectable place. Don relished the tranquility. It was rare in the Mitchell family and most likely fleeting.

"It's good to have you back."

Madeline moseyed over to the windows after tossing her bag onto one of the chairs situated in front of Don's desk. "It's good to be back." She folded her arms and leaned against the window frame. "When I agreed to walk out those doors a few months ago, honestly, I didn't know if or when I'd return."

Her voice dipped, and Don knew why. His mother had made one of the greatest sacrifices of her life. She'd agreed to step down from her executive position at DMI, the second greatest love after her children, and to leave the city of Detroit at Tamara's request. His sister had been estranged from the family and wanted to come home on her own terms. Her number one request was that Madeline couldn't be in town. Don actually had tried pleading his mother's case to Tamara, but the stubborn gene was too deeply rooted in her. His sister wouldn't bend. So, without fanfare or opposition, Madeline had quietly walked away. The few months she was gone were somber days for him, but the trauma was behind them. She was within arm's reach, exactly where his mother belonged.

"How are you and Tamara getting along?" he asked.

Madeline ran the palm of her hand from the front of her head to the back while peering at the floor. "We're getting there."

Don swung his chair around to face Madeline. "Well, it's going to take time, but at least the two of you are talking."

"I don't know how much time. She was gone fourteen years. You'd think that would be enough time," she said, clearly agitated, with her eyelids widened and her neck rolling. "At least she's staying with you, which makes me feel better," she added, seeming calmer.

"Uh, not any longer."

"What?" she shouted.

"She packed her bag and moved out last week." He'd begged her to stay with him longer, but Tamara wouldn't hear of it.

"And why am I just hearing about this?" she barked at him with her fists pressed against her sides. "Where did she go?"

"I'm not sure she wants me to tell you."

Madeline's concern was evident to him, but Don was afraid she'd zip over to the new place and start an argument with Tamara. He knew them too well to wonder what would happen next.

"I'm her mother. I have a right to know."

Don conceded a bit, hoping to ease his mother's concern without violating Tamara's privacy. "I can tell you that she moved not too far from her last building."

Madeline began pacing. "I know that crazy boyfriend of hers is long gone and no longer presents a threat, thanks to your uncle, but what was the hurry in her moving out? I don't understand that girl. She was safe with you," Madeline said, rubbing her face but not wiping away the worry. "What was she thinking, moving out?"

"I'm not sure, but I checked out her new place, and it seems okay." Don went to his mother and gave her a hug. "Don't worry and don't press her about this. Let her come to you."

Madeline pushed away from Don and walked back to the windows with her arms folded. “We’ll just have to see if that day ever comes when she lets me in on what’s happening in her life. I wonder if she’s ever going to let me be her mother again,” she uttered softly.

“Mother, give her time. You can’t push her. She has to work through issues at her own pace.”

Madeline meandered away from the windows, keeping her arms crossed. “But I don’t have forever. I’m sixty-five. I’ve already lived out most of my days. I have to get your sister back into this company.” Madeline leaned on the conference table located off to the side in Don’s office. “Your father and I built this company from nothing. I have poured my heart and soul into this place. This is your legacy,” she said, rapping her fingernails on the table. “You and Tamara are the rightful heirs. Both of you belong here, running this company.”

Don didn’t agree or disagree. So he let her continue without interruption.

“My dream is to have both of you here, together. I am determined to make my dream a reality before I die.”

“Nobody is going to die, Mother. Don’t you think you’re being overdramatic?”

“Nope. Somebody has to get this family on track and keep us from losing what your father and I have busted our behinds to build. If I ease up now, Sherry and Joel will whizz in here and snatch DMI right from under our noses like they own the place. You know it, and I know it. Heck, Joel already made his attempt to snatch the company, and he had it for several years. But right wins out every time.” She strolled over to Don and rested her hands on his shoulders, facing him. “He spun his little web and got caught up in his own mess. Now my children are in charge, just like it’s supposed to be. This is a good day for me.”

"Not so fast, Mother. Tamara hasn't agreed to stay at DMI if you're going to be here too. The original agreement was for you to stay away."

"I know, I know, but that was before we did our little reconciling thing," she said, with her hands moving in circular motions. "As long as she doesn't have to live with me, I'm sure she won't mind me being here in the office. Besides, I'm sure you need help around here. We have a lot of work to do. After your father's bumbling son lost half the company, our first step has to be getting the West Coast and Southern divisions back under the DMI umbrella."

The plan wasn't as clear for Don. A lot had happened. He needed time to sort out exactly where DMI was, where he was. "Wait, Mother. You're moving too quickly. First, we have to figure out how you and Tamara are going to work here together," he said, resting his arms on the desk.

"Oh, don't worry about your sister. I'll take care of her."

"That's precisely what worries me, Mother," Don said as he dropped his gaze and closed his eyes momentarily. He was praying for his words to be taken seriously by his mother, but the probability of that was low. "You can't push her, or Tamara will be on the first plane, fleeing the country. She's done it before, and if you push, Tamara might do it again. Is that what you want?"

"Of course not. I love my daughter."

"I'm not talking about love, Mother. I'm asking you to give her space. Can you do that?" Don could tell his mother was fretting, but he was okay so long as she was hearing him.

"What you're saying makes sense, but you have to understand how much the two of you and DMI mean to me. Having all of us here together is my dream. After your father passed, I vowed not to let Sherry and Joel get their hands on anything else belonging to me and my children.

I aim to keep my vow. If it means giving Tamara more time, fine. I think I can. But don't think I can wait forever. I don't have years to waste. Your father didn't, and who knows? I might not, either."

Don wasn't feeding into the mortality rant his mother was on. She was too stubborn and outspoken to go anywhere anytime soon. God had too many repairs left to do on her heart. She had time. They all did. He was convinced of it.

Chapter 4

Joel crept along Lake Shore Drive, unable to absorb the city view along the waterfront. He was too weighed down with confusion to concentrate on simple pleasures. He eased in front of a tall residential building and parked. Joel would have sat there longer, but the valet approached his door rather quickly, so he got out.

"Good afternoon, Mr. Mitchell," the valet said as Joel stepped around the car and went inside.

He received greetings and nods from both the doorman and elevator operator as he made his way to the penthouse suite. He reached the private lobby while being consumed with unrest. Joel stood in front of the double doors leading into the unit, not ready to enter. He gobbled up an ounce of solace, attempting to corral his thoughts. Partially successful, he knocked on the door. His friend opened the door, which was sort of surprising, since the butler usually answered.

"Why didn't you use your key?" his friend Sheba asked.

"Oh, I don't know. I wasn't even thinking," Joel said, plopping into the first seat he saw. "I'm sorry. I didn't mean to interrupt whatever you were doing."

"Come on. You're never an interruption. Surely you know that by now," she said, taking a seat next to him on the love seat situated in the long entryway.

Joel nodded in affirmation and let his head flop back.

"What's going on?" Sheba asked.

Joel didn't bother concealing his despair. Sheba was the one person with whom he could openly share his concerns without feeling pressure. She got who he was, both his complicated and simple characteristics. Their two-year friendship had seen him at the pinnacle of success during his reign as head of DMI. She'd also been Joel's source of compassion during his journey through the bowels of failure. She didn't judge. She didn't ask questions. She just didn't. Sheba was exactly what he needed when he needed it. When he sought professional advice, she was insightful, having successfully built an international chain of designer boutiques. He basked in her presence, soaking up each snippet of whatever it was she provided. Joel rested his forehead against the back of his hand and breathed heavily.

"Are you all right?" she asked with such sincerity that he had to respond.

"I have a situation that has come up with Zarah." He paused and then told her the news. "She's pregnant."

Sheba pulled away from him. "When did that happen?"

He couldn't imagine what she was thinking, but he figured it wasn't good. "I guess you're wondering why I asked Zarah for a divorce if she was pregnant." Joel buried his face in the palms of his hands and then let the fingers trickle down his cheeks until he could speak.

Before Joel said another word, Sheba rested her hand on top of his and said, "I'm not *wondering* anything." She squeezed his hand. "You're a good man. That's what I know for sure."

"Yeah, well, you might be the only person who thinks so . . . you and maybe my mother," he said, smirking. "I can't seem to dig myself out of this hole I've created. I was so close to breathing fresh air here in Chicago, and then, bam, here comes this situation." Joel clasped his hands together as his elbows rested on his thighs. "Boy, do I have a mess. How long do I have to keep paying for my mistakes? Is there no end?"

Rage attempted to rise up in him, but who would be the recipient? Not God, certainly not Sheba. Then who? There was no one else to blame, which forced him to calm down.

Joel rubbed Sheba's neck. "I'm sorry to dump my troubles on you. You're the last person I want to burden. You've been so good to me."

"*Mi casa es su casa.* Anytime you need a place to crash, I'm here." She squeezed his hand tighter. "You have your key. Come anytime."

Joel leaned over to give Sheba a peck on the cheek. "What would I do without you?"

"You'd be lost," she said, earning a heavy roar of laughter from him. "I realize things may be out of sorts for you right now, but you always land on your feet. You'll work this out."

"I wish I was as confident as you are." Joel leaned backward. "Not only is my personal life jacked up, but my professional one is too. I don't have a job. I don't even have a prospect lined up."

"Then I have some investors you should meet," she told Joel. "With your business mind, you could get a new venture off the ground in less than six months."

"Coming up with the seed money may be a problem," he said. "Remember, I sank so much of my personal assets into saving DMI after the merger with Zarah's father went sour. I'm strapped for cash."

"I'll gladly toss in twenty million as your first investor."

Joel laid his arm across Sheba's shoulder and gently pulled her as close as he could. "I can't have you give me any more money. I can't ask you for more. You've done plenty for me already. Just letting me crash here without any strings attached is more than I deserve."

"I believe in you."

He nodded in affirmation. She always had, which was what had drawn him to her from their initial meeting. Joel vividly remembered the day she walked into his office and handed him an eighteen-million-dollar donation to put toward the memorial library he was building in his father's honor. Ever since their initial encounter, they'd spent days upon days together, mostly talking and being open—no games, no pretending, and no maneuvering. This was one of those visits.

"I should probably head back to Detroit today, but I'm not going to. I'm not ready to face Zarah. I'll need a few more days to figure out my next step."

"I'm sure she's anxious to see you."

Joel stood and paced the room. "There's my problem. She wants to see me, but I'm not eager to see her. Nothing has changed as far as my feelings are concerned." He slid his hands into his pocket and hunched his shoulders. "I'd be lying if I said she's the one for me."

"But you are married and expecting a child. That could sway your vote."

"What's weird is that it doesn't. I just don't have the kind of passion for her that I want for my wife." Joel felt empty when Zarah's name rolled across his lips. There wasn't a sense of longing or love, or a desire to caress her in his arms. There was nothing, which was sobering. He stopped pacing. "I never had it for Zarah. You know that."

"Maybe not yet, but in time, you can grow to love her and have a wonderful family together."

"It's not easy. My mother and father loved each other, but it wasn't enough. I'm sure my dad tried loving my mother completely, but I know he never did. She knows it too. Staying with Zarah for the sake of a child isn't an easy decision. I'd basically be giving up my shot at happiness by settling into this arrangement."

"Well, it was an arrangement from the beginning," Sheba gently reminded him. He didn't take offense, because she was right.

"How can I forget? I married Zarah as a favor to her father so he'd sell me their family business. At the time, I was making a sound business decision, or so I figured. I didn't care if she believed in a totally different religion than I did. She worships a higher power, and it isn't the same one you and I know. Isn't that crazy? With my father being such a religious man, who loved God with his entire heart and built DMI on those principles, it's inconceivable for me to marry someone who worships many gods. What was I thinking? Really, what was I thinking?" He slammed the palm of his hand against his forehead. "This marriage couldn't help but to end badly." He chuckled and then abruptly stopped. "And you think I'm smart. Right? Okay."

Sheba went to Joel and hugged him. "Don't worry. The right decision will become clear for you."

"I hope so." Nearly half a foot taller than Sheba, Joel leaned down and hugged her in return. "There is some good that has come out of this already," he said. "Zarah forced me to say a prayer in the car while I was downtown."

"Really? My, my, my, now, that's good news."

Joel rested his arm on Sheba as they strolled into the living room, where the sea of windows displayed the untamed beauty of Lake Michigan. "Sheba, it's been a very long time since I actually prayed to God. He was probably thinking, *Joel who?* when I reached out to Him." The two of them laughed and laughed. Joel felt the heaviness melting slightly. He kept Sheba close.

"God hasn't forgotten you. You might not have spent much time with Him, but He definitely remembers you." She patted his chest. "Who can forget you, Mr. Joel Mitchell?"

Joel was amused. "I sure hope He gives me some advice."

"Don't worry," Sheba said, laying her head against his chest. "I know you'll do the right thing."

"Perhaps, if only I knew what the right thing was," he said, soaking in the warmth of Sheba's touch, the aura of the evening sky, and distancing himself from the problem Zarah represented. Morning would force its way in soon, but tonight belonged to him and Sheba exclusively. He wouldn't waste a single second.

Chapter 5

Thursday morning looked like Wednesday and Tuesday and Monday, and so on. Zarah sat alone at the kitchen table. She'd suffered through several mornings of nausea, but the inconvenience didn't compare to the joy blossoming within her. She was carrying Joel's child. It was like a fantasy come true. The marriage hadn't been good for him, but their troubles were going to fade. They were starting a family together. Zarah rested comfortably in her seat. Finally, she was going to be validated as a wife and a mother. She couldn't imagine any satisfaction greater than what she was feeling at this precise instance. She sipped her tea, wanting to remain calm.

"Would you like more tea?" the cook asked.

"No," Zarah responded as she traced her finger around the rim of the cup. "Excuse me," she said, practically leaping from the chair.

She grabbed the cordless phone from the kitchen island and made her way to the library. She was dialing the numbers too slowly for her satisfaction. Finally, after what seemed like forever, Joel was on the phone. His voice instantly began soothing her anxiety. "I'm very much looking forward to being with you. Have you decided when you're coming home?"

Joel cleared his throat. "Not yet. I have more business matters to handle here before I can get home."

She could feel her joy seeping out like the air in a punctured balloon and slowly dissipating. Zarah was desperate to cling to hope. Joel was coming home, and they'd be a family. They had to be because there weren't any other options for her. Returning to India as a divorced pregnant woman would garner too much shame for her to justify staying alive. She needed her husband. "I'll call you tomorrow and see if you have decided on a day. I really must see you so we can bask in this good fortune together," she said, resting her hand on her abdomen.

"Okay, but I have to go," he stammered.

Zarah was content holding the phone for hours if Joel was on the other end, but he wasn't. He'd said good-bye and ended the call. Tears formed in her eyes. She sat in the library, alone, unwilling to open the drapes and let light fill her space. She preferred to stay in the dark until her time of grieving had passed and Joel was home with her. She remained in the chair for a while, battling the thoughts swirling in her mind. Her heart echoed, *He'll be here. He will love this baby, and it will bring him home.* Her mind didn't agree. It said, *He's not coming. He doesn't care.* Her heart and her mind had equal strength in this battle.

She soon grew tired, and melancholy sank in. She desperately yearned for his assurance that he would return. Maybe one more call would make a difference. Zarah reached for the phone and then froze. She couldn't call Joel, not this soon. Her sorrow ruled. She begged for comfort, in fear of relapsing into her state of depression. She'd beaten it a few months ago with Joel's affection and wasn't ready for a second fight without him. The library walls were closing in on her. She had to find someone to talk to. Her former assistant had gone out of town for a short holiday after Joel fired her. There was only one other person who cared, her sister-in-law. She dialed the number. Tamara was a good friend, just what Zarah needed.

When her sister-in-law was on the line, Zarah calmed down. "I'm so glad you answered."

"Why? What's wrong?" Tamara asked.

"I went to the doctor, and it's confirmed. I'm . . . I mean we're having a baby."

"Yea! Congratulations!" her sister-in-law yelled. Zarah found it soothing that someone was excited about her pregnancy. "I know how much you wanted a baby with Joel. I'm not sure why you want a child with him, but that's another story. Anyway, how did my father's son take the news?" Zarah did not respond. "Are you there?" Tamara asked.

"Yes, I am."

"Did you hear me? I was asking how Joel feels about the baby."

"I'm sure he's happy, very happy to be a father," Zarah said, not feeling her best.

"Happy enough to rescind the divorce?"

"We haven't talked of the divorce. He's in Chicago, but I'm sure he will no longer want a divorce once he gets home and sees me."

"You think so, huh?"

"Yes. I believe he will be very pleased about being a father." She let her heart speak its truth, although her mind called her statement a lie.

"So pleased, but he isn't home yet? Come on, Zarah. You can't really believe he wants this baby or your marriage."

"I do, and he will. You'll see."

"The only thing I see is a woman who's waiting around for a man to make his decision about her life. Why are you so keen on letting him control you?" Tamara screamed. "I can't stand watching you do this."

"I need him. I can't raise a child alone. Joel is my husband. He has to come home."

"Millions of women in this country have raised babies as a single parent and do fine. You can too. I'll help babysit for you, including changing diapers. How's that for support?" Tamara was amused.

Zarah wasn't. "This is a very important matter."

"Come on. Lighten up. You're taking this 'stand by your man' thing too far. Move on, for goodness' sake. Within a few weeks, you could have plenty of good men interested in you. Why wait for a dud like Joel? He's totally worthless."

"I'm going to wait for him."

"How long do you plan on waiting?"

"As long as I must."

"You mean like a month, a year? What?"

"I'll wait forever, as long he allows me to keep my married name, Mitchell. It is what I will ask of Joel. He will respond kindly."

"How can you be so certain?"

"Since my father died earlier this year, Joel is my family. My life belongs here with him, not in India, or any other place. He is my husband, and I must make this marriage work."

"Excuse me, but I'm going to gag," Tamara said. A few seconds later, she continued. "Zarah, I have to go."

"So soon?"

"I have to get off this phone; because I can't stand to hear you sound so helpless when it comes to Joel. He's trifling," Tamara said.

"He's your brother."

"Technically, maybe, since we have the same father, but that's where the connection ends. Do me a favor. If you're going to pine over a man, make sure he's worth the hassle. Otherwise, you might get used to Joel making every decision for you and totally running your life. I can't imagine living that way and putting up with his crap, but this is your life, your choice. I respect your choice, and I'll leave it alone."

Zarah detected the disappointment in Tamara's voice and felt awful. "You'll see. This is for the best."

"Right, whatever," Tamara replied. "Look, I have to go," Tamara said, and then ended the call almost as abruptly as Joel had.

Sometimes Zarah couldn't figure out any of the Mitchells. Tamara and Joel were different but the same. Both contributed to her stress and forced her to question her future as Joel's wife. She decided to shake off the worry and stay positive. Soon the loneliness would be gone. She cherished the thought, confident in her decision. She sat in the chair a while longer, hoping Joel would walk through the door. Eventually, she dozed off, and Joel paraded through her dreams. It was the closest she'd gotten to him in weeks. She slept calmly in his arms.

Chapter 6

Tamara was fuming. She wanted to be mad at Zarah but didn't think it was fair to penalize her for being loyal and in love. Joel was the culprit. Too bad Zarah's dedication was wasted on him. Tamara's anger had intensified, and she was determined not to extend him the same grace. Who did Mr. Joel think he was? He'd moved his wife thousands of miles from her family, only to abandon her when she was pregnant. The more Tamara wrestled with his behavior and his flagrant womanizing ways, the less she was willing to let him get away without retribution. Obviously, Zarah wasn't going to speak up. Victims didn't. Tamara grabbed the phone. She would handle this.

After contacting Don to get Joel's number, Tamara eagerly made the call. Joel answered more quickly than she had expected. She hadn't quite figured out exactly what to say.

"Who is this?" Joel asked as she held the phone without responding. "Hello?" he said.

Forget about semantics, she thought. She was diving in. "Why are you being such a jerk to your wife?"

Joel chuckled. "And who is this?"

Her resolve was gaining momentum, and she was certain the words would flow freely. "Tamara."

"Okay, Ms. Tamara. This is a surprise. I wasn't expecting a call from you about my wife."

"Somebody had to call," she said, enunciating the words heavily. "You are a trip, leaving Zarah in Detroit alone when you know she's pregnant."

"Excuse me for one minute," Joel told her. She could hear his muffled voice as he spoke to someone else before he returned to the call. "Now, what are you going on about?" he asked.

"How can you leave your wife alone? She's pregnant, scared, and you are so insensitive that you can't come and check on her. What kind of a man are you?"

"Tamara, I don't see how this is your business. How did you get my phone number, anyway?"

"It wasn't difficult to get. We do know a few of the same people," she said, not feeling obligated to be cordial.

"Whatever. Like you said, this is between me and my wife. I'll take care of my business, and you handle yours."

His words resonated. She could back off and probably should have, but letting him off the hook wasn't sitting well with her. He was treating Zarah despicably. Zarah had said she was going to stand up to Joel, but Tamara didn't believe her. Unless she intervened, Joel was bound to get away with treating women as if they were disposable. No more.

The words came from deep within Tamara's soul, exploding by the time they reached her lips. "Who the heck do you think you are? You're a loser who has to pump up his manhood by walking over women." Tamara stood and shook her finger in the air, although Joel couldn't see it. "Look, buster, you've picked the wrong person to mess with, okay. Your women might fall for your crap, but I won't."

"Where is this coming from? You don't know me well enough to say anything about my marriage or any other woman in my life. You have some nerve."

Tamara felt herself overheating. Images of her eldest brother's brutal attack dashed into her mind, followed by memories of her ex-boyfriend's relentless stalking. She had to press those thoughts down in order to maintain control. She didn't intend on making Joel pay for every man's infractions. He deserved a thorough lashing, but only what belonged to him. So, she restrained herself just a little. "Since Zarah won't speak up, I'm doing it for her."

"What are you? Her new best friend?"

Tamara rested her hand on her forearm. "You could say that."

"I see," Joel said.

His cavalier response infuriated Tamara more. "You know, you don't deserve a wife or a child. You are too selfish and narcissistic. Why don't you do us a favor and keep your behind in Chicago, where you belong?"

"Tamara, I'm not going to discuss my marriage with you. This call is over. Take care of yourself, and maybe I'll see you in Detroit." He disconnected the call, leaving Tamara lingering on the line. Her anger cooled. Perhaps it wasn't her place to call him about Zarah. Then again, why not? Tamara set her phone on the table without regret.

Joel held the phone in his hand, staring into the room.

"Are you all right?" Sheba asked.

He rubbed his head. "Yeah, I guess so."

"You sure?" she said, her voice elevated out of concern.

"I don't know." He sighed. "That was Tamara Mitchell."

"Your sister?" Sheba sputtered.

"Right, my sister, or better put, Madeline's daughter." He rested the phone on his lap and used both hands to rub his head. "Madeline's children never considered me a brother. We might share the same Mitchell bloodline, but there's no love between us," he said, actually kind of disappointed.

"I didn't realize the two of you talked."

He gazed at her and roared, "We don't. She was calling to chew me out about not supporting Zarah during the pregnancy."

Sheba's eyebrows arched. "I see," she said. "I can tell that was awkward."

Joel lay back on the seat and pulled Sheba with him. He swiped his fingertips across his forehead. "It was, but you know, she has a point." Sheba rested her head on his shoulder. "I don't like Tamara calling me and barking out orders, but I respect her boldness." He wrapped his arm around Sheba. "There's something to be said about a woman who speaks her mind. Tamara is rough around the edges and, apparently, doesn't respect boundaries. She's definitely Madeline's daughter. Whew, for sure. My goodness; I feel sorry for Don, having to deal with both of them at DMI. Now, there's a job I wouldn't want," he said, finding the idea humorous.

Sheba patted his chest. "I'm glad she didn't upset you."

"Nah, I'm not upset. Confused, yes, but not upset. Maybe this is God's way of pushing me toward I-94 sooner rather than later. I guess it's time to go home," he said. "Heaven help me."

Chapter 7

If it wasn't Joel wearing on her nerves, it was Madeline. Tamara traipsed through the DMI lobby and took the elevator upstairs. With each step she second-guessed her decision about coming to the building. Her mother had called a few hours ago, before eight o'clock, and had asked Tamara to stop by. There had been a sense of urgency in the request, which made Tamara nervous. The last time they'd spoken, Madeline was being Madeline, trying to shove her plans down Tamara's throat. The impending tension blanketed Tamara, causing her to shiver upon exiting the elevator. Instinct said to turn around, press the ground level button, and get out of there while she had a chance. Tamara stood out in the open, completely vulnerable. Against her better judgment, she entered her mother's office, sure this was leading to doom.

"I see you made it," Madeline said, sitting at her desk. Don was in the office too.

"Oh my, the two of you together is probably not good for me. Is this an intervention?" Tamara asked, flinging her jacket and purse over the back of a guest chair located in front of the desk.

Don gave her a hug. Madeline was poised to give her one too, but Tamara dodged the gesture by tossing an air kiss in her mother's direction. It wasn't that Tamara had a problem with receiving affection from her mother. In this case, Tamara was determined to maintain her resolve and not let Madeline wear her down with words and gestures before getting out what she had to say. Her feeling of being in the wrong place was still there.

Madeline rushed over to Tamara and hugged her tightly. "Girl, get over here. The days of blowing me a kiss are long gone. You were gone far too long. I have a lot of years to make up, which means I'm going to hug my daughter every chance I get," she said, tightening her embrace. "You might as well get used to it."

What had made Tamara think her mother was going to let her slip into a chair at the conference table without incident? Tamara had to finally force herself free from the extended hug.

"Let's meet at the table," Madeline said. Don joined them.

"Okay Mother, let's cut out the small talk. Why did you summon me?"

"Have a seat. Can I get you some coffee?" Madeline asked.

"No," Tamara said, plopping into the seat clearly outnumbered. Don wasn't saying much, but he was there.

"What about tea?"

"No, Mother!" Tamara shouted. Quickly, she took a deep breath and harnessed her irritation. "I want you to tell me what is so important. Why did you want me to come in this early on a Friday morning?"

"All right, forgive me for being hospitable. My goodness, what's gotten into you? A little decorum from you would be nice. Common courtesies are still fashionable, my dear."

"Okay, ladies, let's take a break before this goes in the wrong direction," Don interjected. Right on cue, her brother was the consummate mediator. Thanks to the Mitchell family dynamics, he got plenty of practice in the role.

"I have a busy day ahead of me," Tamara said, which wasn't true, but she had to find some reason to cut this mini reunion short. Being around Madeline was a death wish. She had to get out. "I only have a few minutes to spare."

"Then let's get to the point. We need you here at DMI."

"Mother," Tamara said with a sharp edge.

"Wait. Hear me out," Madeline said, reaching over and caressing Tamara's arm. "Between the two of us, Don and I can maintain our family's presence in this place, but it's just not right unless you're going to be here too. Frankly, I don't want to run DMI with anyone other than you and Don. This is as much your company as it is ours. Besides, Abigail has resigned from her executive vice president position and is leaving in a few months, which will make our senior management team too lean."

"Good for her if she's really leaving," Tamara said, envying the freedom that Abigail would have once she left the Mitchell compound called DMI. But it was shocking that Abigail was actually leaving after being with DMI for more than eight years, having been hired as an assistant to Dave Mitchell after graduating from business school. From what Tamara could gather, Abigail had been loyal to the Mitchell patriarch, then to Joel, and now to Don. Apparently, Abigail's loyalty hadn't bought her any perks when it came to romance. She had to get in line behind the hordes of other women swooning over Joel, including his pregnant wife.

"Her departure does create a gaping hole in our executive team," Don added.

"A hole with your name on it," Madeline told Tamara.

"But I've already told you, working here isn't for me."

"Mainly because you haven't given this place a fair chance. What will it take to get you here?" her mother asked.

"Are you offering me the chief executive officer role?"

"Of course not. That's Don's job. But you can have any other role in the company, including mine as head of marketing. Whatever you want. Just name it."

Tamara let out a hearty laugh. "You don't get it, do you?" Tamara wrenched her hands before speaking again. "I don't want to work here. How else can I say this so you understand me once and for all? What other language can I use? Hear me good," she said with her voice marginally elevated but intentionally crisp. "I don't want a job at DMI, period, end of story, finito," she said, leaning against the edge of the table.

"Is it me?" Madeline asked.

Tamara let her gaze drop to the floor.

"Because we can work out our being here together. One of us can work from home or move to another floor. Heck, I'll rent you out a remote space with a small team to join you. I'm willing to do whatever it takes to get you into an executive management seat at DMI, where you and your brother belong." Madeline had a strange look. "Please don't let my years of fighting for DMI be in vain."

"I can't take this. You're not listening to me. This is a waste of time." Tamara stood and snatched her purse and jacket from the chair.

"Where are you going? We haven't finished." Madeline stood and rushed toward Tamara.

"Mother, let her go. She needs space, and we have to give it to her," Don interjected.

"Thank you," Tamara told him.

Madeline wrapped her hands around both of Tamara's arms. "Don't leave. I know we can work this out, if you give us a chance."

Tamara wiggled from her mother's clutches. "There's nothing to work out."

"I'll catch up with you later," Don told his sister.

Tamara gave a wave with her back to Don and Madeline as she crossed the threshold. The fog was lifting, and she began thinking more clearly with each stride.

"Well, that didn't go as planned," Madeline said, returning to her seat.

"I guess not, Mother," Don said. "You badgered her again. We keep having the same argument day after day. When are you going to accept the fact that Tamara has her own plans? You can't strong-arm her into returning. You just can't. When are you going to see it and leave her alone?"

"Oh, so now you're going to jump on me too?"

"It's not like that, and you know it Mother. But I am tired of this constant fighting. I want the best for our family. If she's happy doing something else, then so be it. Let her do something else. For our sake, let this go."

"Great. Both of my children are mad at me. I can't win."

Don walked closer to his mother and placed his hand on her shoulder. His glance locked with hers. "Mother, I know you mean well. I'm sure, deep down, Tamara knows it too, but you have to stop pushing. We're adults. You've done your job in raising us. Trust us to make our own decisions."

Madeline attempted to pull away. Why had she fought for decades? Defeat wanted to settle in. Madeline resisted, but her determination was weakening given the inevitability of the situation.

Don kept his hand gently on her shoulder. "We'll work this out. As much as you hate waiting, stand back and let God work out a plan for our family. That's what I'm going to do," he said.

"You're right about my hating to wait. I'm not willing to sit around for the heavens to make my dream a reality. I can handle this on my own."

"Good luck," Don said, chuckling as he walked toward her office door. "You're going to need it."

"Where are you going?"

"I'm running to my office for a few minutes. That should give you ample time to call Tamara and apologize."

"Apologize for what? For being a good mother and wanting the best for my daughter? I'm hardly going to apologize for loving my children."

"Fine. Then have it your way. Sit in here and pout while Tamara is out there making plans to leave town."

"Who said she's leaving?" Madeline asked as her eyelids widened.

"Nobody, but I know what she does. You push and she runs. You're both so pigheaded. Neither of you are willing to back down and let the other have her say."

Madeline grimaced. "Well, what do you want me to say?"

"That you'll call Tamara and apologize. It really doesn't matter if you're right or wrong as long as the two of you keep the lines of communication open and continue to nurture your fragile relationship. Wouldn't you agree reconciliation is the most important thing?" Don said and then left Madeline to meditate on his words and her dreams.

Chapter 8

Tamara darted down the street, not sure where she was headed but intent on getting as far away from DMI and Madeline as possible. The buildings were crowding her, choking her plans. She slowed down in front of a coffee shop, went inside, and found a seat in the corner. Tamara wanted to sink deeply into the seat and become invisible.

The waitress approached. "What can I get you?"

"Give me the largest latte you have with a double shot of espresso," Tamara said, placing her elbow on the table and resting her head on her tightly closed fist. She stared at the door while inhaling the rich aroma of brewing coffee, letting the distinctive flavor cleanse her emotions.

"Are you all right?" the waitress asked.

"I will be once I get my hands on my latte."

The waitress laid a couple of napkins on the table. "One supersized latte with an extra shot of caffeine coming right up."

The twenty-minute walk had helped reduce Tamara's outrage and frustration with her mother. It was evident Madeline wasn't going to stop pressuring Tamara into accepting a job at DMI. As recent as three months ago, Tamara would have jumped at a more senior role in the company. She'd craved the opportunity. Instead, she was given a junior marketing position. Tamara had performed the job to the best of her ability, but she had bigger plans than staying in a grunt-level role. Admittedly, working with Don had been quite pleasant, and she'd had an exciting couple of months. But she couldn't ignore a key contributing factor. Madeline hadn't been there. Her absence had been a requirement Tamara had demanded before agreeing to leave Europe and move back to Detroit. Madeline hadn't liked the request but had agreed without incident. If she could honor Tamara's request once, why not again? The more Tamara rehashed the spat with her mother, the more irritated Tamara grew. She let her head hang down in search of solace.

"Here's your latte." A half-filled mug the size of three or four regular cups was set on the table with another napkin. "This should give you a jolt and should fix whatever's bothering you, at least temporarily."

The waitress had offered her a kind word, and Tamara thanked her.

If only a magical mug of brew could solve her problems, she'd get a gigantic vat of espresso to handle her boatload of Mitchell problems. Tamara sipped her latte and stirred the foam on top for a while. She was in a calm space until her cell phone buzzed. It was Zarah's number. Tamara answered right away.

"Zarah, are you okay?"

"No, I'm not very good."

Tamara heard the agony oozing from Zarah and remembered the call she'd made to Joel yesterday. She'd gotten his cell number from Don, but what if Joel had blamed Zarah for the call? What if Zarah was mad at her for interfering? Blasting Joel had seemed appropriate in the heat of her anger, when her disdain was at the boiling point. Now that she was in a calmer state, her decision to interfere didn't seem wise, especially if Zarah was hurt in any way. Tamara prepared to apologize.

"What happened?"

There was sobbing before Zarah responded, "Joel isn't back."

"I know. You told me yesterday."

"I do not believe he is ready to come home."

"I guess not," Tamara said.

The sobbing continued, which drove Tamara crazy and her apologetic tone evaporated. There had to be zero tolerance for weakness if a woman was going to survive on her own. Zarah had to toughen up. Otherwise Joel was always going to have the upper hand. Being dominated was the pits. Tamara was too familiar with the feeling, having been overpowered by her eldest brother, Andre, then the nutcase of a boyfriend she'd fled from in Europe, and most recently Madeline. The reminders were overwhelming. There was no way Tamara could let her mother push her into a corner. No one could. She called the shots in her life, and that was final. Zarah had to grow the same emotional muscles if she wanted to last as a Mitchell and have a shot at independence.

Apparently, Zarah wasn't aware of the call Tamara had made to Joel. *Thank goodness,* Tamara thought, feeling relieved and recharged. "I hope you aren't planning to sit around and wait for him to come home. I wouldn't. You deserve better," Tamara said, consciously keeping her voice down while she was in the coffee shop. Just then the waitress came by to see if she wanted a refill. Tamara handed her the mug and nodded yes.

"He's my husband."

"So what?" Tamara blurted into the phone. "Is he acting like a husband? Stop giving him so much freedom to treat you badly. Stop doing this to yourself."

Tamara clicked her fingernails on the table rapidly as her frustration simmered. She was so irritated at Zarah for willingly settling for so much less than she was worth. Who was Joel Mitchell, other than a financially strapped spoiled brat? He wasn't the catch of the year. Yet he had Zarah groveling.

That notion had Tamara continuously stewing. That was why she wasn't settling for a second fiddle job at DMI. If her mother was so serious about having Tamara back, then why wasn't the CEO position being offered? She knew the answer. Because it was Don's spot. Honestly, Tamara didn't have any intentions of undercutting Don for the position. He'd been her hero for decades. When Andre went crazy and raped her eighteen years ago, it was her younger brother, Don, who came to her rescue. She'd never forgotten his loyalty toward her. As intriguing as gaining power was, backstabbing Don in the process wasn't worth it to her. Staying on the fringes of DMI and starting her own company was the best bet.

This wasn't the ideal time to approach Zarah about a business proposition, but with Joel in the picture, most of her days were going to be miserable. No sense waiting for a good day when each day was equally bad. Tamara had to get moving if she planned on purchasing the former DMI West Coast division from Zarah and moving to California. For starters, she had to talk Zarah into assuming leadership. It was a huge stretch but not impossible. She'd appeal to Zarah's sense of family honor.

"Zarah, you should think about taking control of your father's company. I remember you telling me how closely you worked with him. I'm sure no one else can run Harmonious Energy any better than you."

"I can't think of business today. It's not a very good day for me."

"I understand. Call me anytime, day or night," Tamara offered.

"I couldn't burden you."

"Yes, you can, and you will. I consider you a friend, and friends look out for friends. Zarah, don't hesitate to call me when you need help. Seriously, it's not a problem." Tamara didn't agree with Zarah pining over Joel, but she was motivated to support Zarah through her crisis. Maybe one day Zarah would return the favor by cutting a business deal with her. Tamara could only hope.

Chapter 9

Madeline had wanted to disagree with Don but couldn't when he was standing in her office, staring her in the face. Repairing her relationship with Tamara was her top priority. If only she could get some participation from her daughter. Madeline sat at the table, twirling her Montblanc pen and remembering. She'd fought many corporate battles, losing some but winning most. The difference between those struggles and the one she was facing with Tamara was that business didn't count. With business, she could walk away and sleep comfortably at night if the struggle became too great. She couldn't walk away from Tamara, no matter how much trouble her daughter caused. Her birth thirty-five years ago had been painful and not much had changed since then.

Yet Madeline wasn't going to let her daughter run off again without making every effort to keep her home. Pride was preventing Madeline from dialing the phone, but she eventually conquered it and made the call. Tamara answered.

"What do you want, Mother?"

"Do you have to answer in such a mean way?"

"Oh gosh, Mother, please! What do you want? Haven't you badgered me enough? I'm not working for DMI. What will it take for you to stop?"

"If you'd give me a chance to speak, you'd find out that I'm calling to apologize." Madeline could hear what sounded like Tamara fumbling with the phone. "Are you there?" More fumbling ensued. "Tamara, are you there?"

"I'm here. I'm sorry. I dropped my phone. I guess your apologizing was such a shock that I dropped the phone. Did I hear you right? You're apologizing?"

Madeline would have hung up on anyone else, but she remained on the phone. Tamara had more power than Madeline cared to admit. The bond of love was too strong to ignore and often too intense to manage effectively.

Just then Don walked back into her office.

Madeline let her gaze trace the edge of her shoe as she leaned against the desk. "You heard me," she said softly.

"What did you say?" Tamara asked. "I can barely hear you."

Madeline knew Tamara could hear perfectly well. She just wanted her to grovel. Madeline was reluctant, but if groveling kept Tamara in Detroit, she was willing to swallow a jumbo portion of her pride. "I apologize for pushing so hard with you earlier. I didn't mean to make you feel uncomfortable." Don gave her the thumbs-up. "I just wanted to . . ." she said before Don gave her the time-out sign. "Excuse me for a minute. Your brother is trying to tell me something." Madeline covered the mouthpiece and lowered the phone.

"Mother, don't rehash the discussion with her. It's bound to end up in a bad place."

Madeline pushed the mute button on the phone. "Can't I at least let her know why I'm so passionate about my proposal?"

"No."

"Why not?" Madeline whispered.

"Because she's heard it over and over. I mean no disrespect, Mother, but you should give it a rest. Apologize and leave her alone." Don took a seat in front of the desk.

Madeline was being double teamed. She wasn't going to win this round.

"Mother, I can't stay on the call much longer. What were you saying?" Tamara asked.

Madeline fumbled with the mute button before pressing it. "Nothing. I'm apologizing, and that's basically it." Tamara didn't respond as quickly as Madeline wanted. "Did you hear me?"

"Yes."

"Do you have anything to say?"

"Not really. I've heard you semi-apologize in the past. It never lasts, Mother, and you know it."

Madeline sat on a corner of the desk. "Look, young lady, I'm trying, so give me a break."

"You never give me one. What do you expect me to say? I could tell you the truth, but you don't want to hear what I have to say."

"Try me," Madeline said, latching her hand onto her hip.

Don grimaced.

"I'm starting my own company if Zarah will sell me the West Coast division."

"Hold on. Your brother is here. I'm putting you on speakerphone." He was the reason Madeline had overridden her better judgment and called Tamara, and that earned him the right to hear her nonsense firsthand.

"I'm putting together my business plan over the next few weeks," Tamara continued.

"If you're not going to work here, at least let me help you with a solid start-up plan. You can start a small business without the West Coast division," Madeline said.

"I won't need your help or your money. I'm getting the division on my own."

"Why are you being so stubborn?" Madeline asked.

"You call it stubborn. I call it being independent. I have to go, Mother. See you later, Don," Tamara said and hung up before giving them a chance to say good-bye.

After the call ended, both Don and Madeline sat quietly, neither reacting immediately to Tamara's revelation.

"See what I mean?" Madeline said, folding her arms tightly, breaking their silence. "Nothing I say or do sits well with that girl."

"This is crazy. We're both going after the same division, and she doesn't even know it. Why does everything have to be a fight for our family, especially when it comes to you and Tamara?" Don asked.

"I don't understand my child. She looks for controversy. I want to work with her, but you see how unwilling she is. There's no changing her mind about this. I am willing to give up on her working with us, but she can't have the West Coast division too. Tamara can't have everything she wants. The rest of us are making sacrifices. Shouldn't she?"

Don didn't have an answer. As a matter of fact, he didn't really want to think about the situation much longer. They'd spent too many precious years having fights, years that could have been lived in harmony.

Don shut his eyelids tightly and let his thoughts soar to the South African coast. The two years he'd spent there, while being estranged from his family, was a time he longed to repeat. The company he'd started, LTI, was based there. His special friend, Naledi, was there. His solitude was there too. If much of what he yearned to have was there, why did God have him here?

"What are we going to do with DMI?" Madeline asked.

"I'm not sure."

He'd engaged in numerous wars in the name of DMI, some with family members and others with outside foes. None had been simple, but Don was absolutely certain God had wanted him to return from South Africa last year and assume the leadership of DMI. Since then he'd grown to realize that his journey had nothing to do with the leadership of DMI. His role was to help restore the family. Nobody—not Joel, not his mother, definitely not Tamara, and not even Sherry—had made his task pleasant. Yet, for the Lord's sake, he had persevered. Last week it had seemed like he had accomplished the goal and was close to being able to relax. His mother and Tamara were speaking cordially, and Joel had left town. The Mitchell family was basking in a miracle. Needless to say, it was only the eye of a storm, the creepy calm before the second half hit land, threatening to do more damage than the first wave.

Don leaned back in his seat and chuckled louder and louder.

Madeline stared at him. "What's so funny?"

He continued chuckling, unable to stop. Madeline kept staring at him, then squinted. She probably thought he'd lost it. Maybe he had. It wouldn't be a far stretch. Their family could drive anyone batty. Finally, he was able to gain composure.

"Are you going to share the joke with me?" his mother said.

"That's it exactly. This place is a joke. We're like those gerbils running on a treadmill. They're huffing and puffing and getting nowhere. They're in the same spot after running for hours, days, years. In our case it's been decades. Regardless of how silly it looks, the little gerbil is going to keep running, because he doesn't have common sense. But you do," Don said.

"Well, when you put it like that, I sound like an idiot."

"No, Mother, you're not the idiot. *I* am, if I continue to stay on the treadmill with you."

"Don, don't second-guess your commitment. You've done an amazing job. You're the reason we're still in business. You've fought a good fight, and this is only the beginning. You belong here."

"I don't know how much is left in me." He glanced at his mother with reverence. "You are the best mother in the world, but you're the toughest to work with."

She grinned and folded her arms. "I can be tough, but you have to admit, I usually know what it is I want and go for it. And I want this," she said, slowly spreading her arms out and symbolically encircling the room.

Don pressed his fist against his forehead. "Is this what *I* want?" He sighed. "I have to figure out what God wants me to do at this point." With so much confusion smothering the place, he didn't know what direction to take DMI in. Whatever he decided, his next move wouldn't be hasty, and it wouldn't be based on emotions or pressure from anyone. He'd take his time and seek God, determined to get it right, or be forced to walk away.

Chapter 10

Friday was extremely intense, and Tamara was mentally exhausted from the events of the day. As defeated as she felt, Tamara couldn't help but think about Zarah. She was worse off, getting pregnant in the middle of a divorce. *Ugh,* Tamara thought. She was compelled to check on her, so she picked up the phone and dialed her number.

After a few rings Zarah answered. Tamara was kind of surprised. "I expected the housekeeper to answer. Has she gone home for the day?"

"She has. There's no one here except me. I'm alone."

Tamara could detect the sorrow, which was becoming commonplace when they spoke, but she didn't want to spotlight it. She tried to make the conversation pleasant. "I can't believe you're going to be a mother by next spring. Incredible."

Zarah didn't respond.

Tamara kept trying to lighten the conversation. There had to be something she could say to make Zarah cheer up. She'd keep trying. That was what friends did. "Remember a few months ago, when we spent the day together and went shopping? Let's take another day and hang out. I could certainly stand a day out, and you could too."

"No, I don't want to go far. I'm not well."

"Come on. Women have babies every day and survive. You will too, with or without a husband." Tamara would have gladly snatched the words back if it hadn't been too late. Her comment had already pierced Zarah's soul. The very topic Tamara had worked hard to avoid had slithered its way into the conversation. Joel was everywhere. She couldn't shake him. "You have to pull yourself together. How can you be a mother if you're sad most of the time?"

"I don't know if I'll be a good mother."

Stop with the nonsense, Tamara thought. Genuinely, she was fond of Zarah. Zarah was a cool person, but the whining was taking a toll. Tamara was peeved by her constant wallowing in self-pity. She bet Joel wasn't sitting in a dark Chicago corner agonizing over Zarah. Most likely, he was having a good time while his wife patiently waited for him, as if he were returning home from war. Zarah needed to hear an honest assessment of her marriage, but Tamara knew she was too fragile or naive. She wasn't sure which, and it wouldn't have mattered under normal conditions. However, this was far from normal. Zarah had to be stable. With Tamara running from her past, from her mother, and from the clutches of those who wished to dictate her life, the only path to freedom ran directly through Harmonious Energy and Zarah's ownership of the former DMI West Coast division. That path to freedom kept her on the phone, committed to Zarah.

"Maybe you have too much free time. Have you considered my suggestion about assuming leadership of your father's company?"

"I have not had much energy for business," Zarah replied.

She'd better make energy. If Joel was her priority, lying around in mourning wasn't getting his behind on the highway to Detroit. Zarah had better wake up and stop letting Joel run her life remotely from three hundred miles away. "If I were you, I'd find energy. If you want Joel to become interested in you, I suggest you make yourself more appealing."

"You don't think I look appealing?"

"No, no, I don't mean your physical appearance. I meant you have to become attractive to Joel by letting him see that you have what he wants."

"What's that?"

"Power."

"I don't understand."

Was it the language barrier or the euphoria of an imaginary love affair that caused Zarah to appear childlike? Tamara wanted to bury her head in a pillow and fall asleep, forgetting about everybody with the last name Mitchell. But she couldn't. Her future was at stake. She had to get Zarah to understand the urgency of taking over the Bengali family business. It was Tamara's best shot at being able to buy the West Coast division. If the Harmonious Energy advisory board had a say, they'd probably sell the division to Don and DMI since there was a partnership already established. She couldn't let such a deal happen, because then she'd probably have to succumb to the Mitchell machine and be forced to take a job at DMI. She couldn't entertain that possibility. Zarah was her only answer.

"You have tremendous power at your fingertips. You own the West Coast division. You have part ownership in your father's company. Trust me. Don and DMI don't want to keep the other half. Since the companies' religious philosophies are so conflicting, the DMI board of directors will sell it off the first chance they get. You might as well buy it outright and own the entire thing. If you're controlling a major company and having Joel's baby too, he's bound to come home." Tamara hesitated, struggling to continue with her recommendation. Telling another woman to chase after a man with a baby and bucks latched to both hips was deplorable. She shook her head in disgust. It wasn't Tamara's way of securing a mate, but Zarah was the one who wanted Joel by any means. Therefore, Tamara reasoned, she was helping a friend get what she clearly wanted. "Why wait for Joel to make your decision? Get on with your goals in the meantime. Let him see you as a strong woman."

"Maybe you are correct. I have not thought about it this way."

"What's the worst that could happen? You become CEO of a multimillion-dollar company, you have a beautiful baby, and you wake up happy every day. It doesn't sound like a bad consolation prize to me."

"Yes, your story sounds very nice," Zarah said.

"And maybe you could sell the West Coast division to me, because I can't work at DMI. It's too stressful for me there. I have to start my own company," Tamara added.

"Perhaps we can both have companies to run," Zarah replied.

Zarah's reaction was precisely what Tamara needed to hear. Finally, there was a sign of hope. Tamara was relieved. She would continue encouraging Zarah to take hold of the company. *Let Joel stay in Chicago for the rest of his life, if he wanted,* she thought. Tamara wanted no one to care for him, especially Zarah. He didn't deserve his wife's loyalty or love. He surely didn't deserve a stake in her company. Hopefully, Zarah would reserve those perks for her faithful supporters, a short list which Tamara planned to stay in the number one spot.

She ended the call and plopped onto her bed, giddy. The West Coast division was a tiny bit closer. With a tad more prodding, balanced out with healthy doses of encouragement, Zarah could cross the finish line of independence, with Tamara poised on the sideline, ready to catch the West Coast division. Tamara rolled over and grabbed the TV remote. The day had been intense, like a bulldozer, but it had ended on an upbeat note. She was pleased and was eager to sail into a productive weekend. There was work to do.

Chapter 11

Chicago had been the ideal haven for Joel several weeks ago, before he got the awful news about the pregnancy. He was fighting to keep a healthy outlook on life and stay motivated. Joel wanted to bury his head in the sand lining the Chicago beachfront, but who was he kidding? The millions, maybe billions, of grains of sand weren't sufficient to bury his predicament. His last hope was getting one of his financial propositions to materialize. Then he'd have a greater purpose, beyond answering his wife's cries of desperation.

Joel leaned against the wall in the penthouse foyer, holding his mobile phone.

"Mr. Mitchell, I can't," said the male voice on the other end of the line.

"Please, call me Joel."

"All right, Joel. As I was saying, I can't fund your proposal. It's too risky."

Joel lifted his chin toward the ceiling, searching for a string of convincing words. "Come on. You're a venture capitalist. That's exactly what you do, loan money for risky start-up projects."

"I am, but this is too risky," the venture capitalist stated. "You want fifty million to start a religious consulting firm."

The guy's description wasn't completely accurate. Joel wasn't starting a religious firm. He was planning to provide leadership training to churches. That's what he did at DMI. It was in his DNA. He'd run DMI for several years with unprecedented success. If he was given the financial backing to get started, he could build a profitable clientele again. Joel needed a break, and he was counting on this investor to give him one. Joel couldn't give up without a fight.

"You don't understand. I know this sector of the market," Joel told the guy.

"Look, Joel, I've done my homework. There's already a dominant player in this space, as you know, DMI."

Joel shoved his hand into his pocket. He teetered between being mad and being proud. "Then you also know DMI was my father's company, and I was the CEO for several years, during its most successful era. We had unprecedented sales during my tenure. I lived and breathed DMI. As I said, I know this market better than anyone in the business," he said, raising his voice. Sheba came around the corner with a troubled expression on her face. He nodded and waved her off, mouthing that he was okay. She gave him a friendly smile and retreated.

"Joel, I'm sorry, but the U.S. audience is saturated by DMI. What's left is too small for you to make the kind of profits you're projecting."

Joel pressed his fist against the wall. "Are you kidding me?" His voice was definitely elevated this time. "Do you know how many churches there are in the United States, let alone in the world, that could use leadership and financial management training? As established as DMI is, they could never service the entire country," Joel said, squatting, with his back braced against the wall.

His excitement must have gotten Sheba worried again, because she poked her head around the corner. He waved her off, sealing his affirmation with a wink. Joel stared toward the window and gulped.

"I really need this money." His words were razor sharp, and his head was heavy. His fist was pressed hard into the center of his forehead. "Please, I need your help."

There was an abbreviated silence. Joel read it as a shift in his favor, until he heard, "The answer is no. I just can't help you with this venture. I wish you the best, Mr. Mitchell."

"Joel. It's Joel, man. Call me Joel."

"I'm sorry, Joel. Maybe next time."

"Yeah, maybe," he said as the phone conversation came to a close, smashing his hopes in the process. Joel didn't move right away. Eventually, he sat down completely on the floor with his back against the wall and legs stretched out as thoughts bombarded him.

Sheba came around the corner again. His defeat was consuming him. In the presence of anyone else, he'd have mustered up a facade and pretended everything was fine. Thank goodness for Sheba. He didn't have to present a certain image or coddle her. He grabbed her hand as she plopped down on the floor next to him.

"That bad, huh?"

He nodded yes.

"Can I help?"

He shook his head no.

She laid her head on his shoulder. "It's not as dire as you think. You're a smart man who's successful at anything you set your mind to do."

Her words blanketed him like a warm covering on a cold winter's night. "Have I told you lately how much you mean to me?"

"You have, and the feeling is mutual."

"No, listen. I'm serious," he said, turning to face her. "You have been a rock for me during the craziest time in my life. And not for one second have you judged me or beaten me down for the really dumb decisions I've made."

Sheba patted his hand. "Why would I beat you down? I believe in you. I always have, and you know this."

"I do, and your faith has been with me through hell."

"You'd do the same for me," she told him. They embraced briefly. "Now that we've had our mushy session, how can I help? I guess your appeal to the venture capitalist didn't end as you'd hoped."

"Sure didn't," he said. "This is crazy. I'm too tainted. Even the venture capitalist claimed I am too much of a risk. Can you believe it? I'm damaged goods, Sheba," he said, smirking.

"No, you're not, Mr. Joel Mitchell." She braced her hands on the floor to get up.

"Where are you going?"

"To get my checkbook."

"No, you're not," he said, getting up and helping her up too.

"Yes, I am, and you can't stop me. How much were you asking from the investor?"

"I'm not telling you."

"Fine. Then I'll write a check for twenty-five million or have it wired to your account. I can give you another ten if you need more."

Joel grabbed Sheba around the waist. "Seriously, thank you from the bottom of my heart, but no." His voice was firm as his dignity kicked in. "Your friendship is the only gift I'm going to receive from you. No money, please. Let me do this my way."

He could tell she was determined to help. He greatly appreciated her support, but dragging her into his pit of financial chaos wasn't an option. He valued and respected Sheba far too much to put her in a risky situation. He'd rather go without the seed money than to take it from his confidant. He'd accepted money from her once before, and the deal had gone badly. He had vowed never to do it again, regardless of how anemic his finances were. He aimed to keep his vow. Fortunately, his pride had rescued him from accepting the funds. Now reality was setting in. He had limited money and no plan on how to make more.

"What are you going to do?" Sheba asked as they strolled toward the living room, holding hands.

He'd pursued one idea after another in recent weeks, each leading to the same dead end. "I'm not sure, but I can't stay here." He felt the tightening of her hand in his. "It's time to go home and face the music."

"I'll hate to see you go, but I understand." This generated a smile from him.

She always understood. "Do you remember when we met?" he said, letting affection season the conversation.

"How can I forget? We talked for hours."

"Long before I got married." Sorrow was hovering over him, but he clung to the positive. "I have to admit, you were this spicy entrepreneur who kept me laughing. I'd never met a woman like you, and to this day, I haven't met another one."

She had generated a spark in him that was not easily quenched. He couldn't say it was romantic, although there was an undeniable chemistry between them. He accepted that there wasn't a clear way to define his connection with Sheba. Words seemed too limited. He preferred leaving the definition open, precisely as their relationship was. As far as Joel was concerned, she had a spot in his heart that no one would ever touch.

"Those happy days seem so long ago. So much has happened since then," he mused.

"Many good things have happened," Sheba said, sitting on the couch and gently pulling Joel's hand. He followed suit.

He drew in a long breath and let out the air. "This is it. I'm hitting the road tomorrow." He had no idea what was in store for him, but whatever was waiting, he believed it was in Detroit.

"I'm sure your wife will be glad to see you. The two of you have some big decisions to make."

"She's another story. Honestly, I'm not sure what's going to happen with us." He leaned into Sheba. "I am smart enough to finally realize that I need God to give me some direction."

"About the marriage?"

"That too, but I was really thinking about my business venture. God put me in charge of DMI once, and I can't go back to doing nothing."

Sheba laid her head on him. "Don't worry. You'll find your way. Go home and do what you must. My place will be here for you whenever you need a place to rest, and so will I."

She grabbed the remote and cued the music system. The evening had glided in, so Sheba dimmed the lights. The two gazed out at Lake Michigan, nestled on the couch. Tomorrow was certain to have challenges, but tonight was theirs.

Chapter 12

On Friday morning Joel crept down I-94, the gateway to Detroit. Before leaving Chicago, he'd contacted Zarah. Countless times before his Lamborghini had sped down the road, cutting the five-hour ride down to four. Anticipation generally forced him to press down hard on the gas pedal. The trepidation he was feeling now wasn't to be confused with anticipation. Instead of pressing hard on the gas pedal for this trip, Joel had actually driven in the slower lane most of the way, stopping at each rest station. His sense of urgency didn't propel him. Finally, after nearly eight hours on the road, Joel turned onto his street. He slowed the car too abruptly, nearly forcing it to stall. He eased to the side and put on his hazard lights. Joel rested his head on the steering wheel. This was it. Within fifteen minutes he'd be facing Zarah and possibly the repercussions of his choices.

Time clicked by, with Joel showing no signs of movement. He went back and forth in his mind about what to say, how to feel, how to act once he was in the house. Nothing made sense. His thoughts were just jumbled. Tired of fretting, he did what he should have done the entire ride home. He clutched the steering wheel and cried out.

"God, I'm . . ." he mumbled. "I mean, I need help. I messed up, but I'm asking for your mercy and grace in getting this fixed. Help me, Lord," he shouted aloud. "Please help me," he said, easing the car into gear and up his driveway.

Joel sat in the car awhile before eventually going inside. He left his suitcase in the car in case an overnight stay at a hotel or at his mother's was warranted.

Zarah must have been listening for the door to open. Like flies swarming a corpse, she homed in on him, refusing to give him much space. "I'm very pleased to have you home. We have so much to discuss," she said, grabbing his hand and leading him toward the library. She didn't attempt to hug him, which wasn't surprising to Joel, given that the act wasn't a natural expression or greeting in her family. Gentle nods were more commonplace.

Joel was relieved. They sat down simultaneously. She sat close to him. He didn't resist. Ironically, he recalled being in a similar scene several months ago with Zarah. His lack of resistance that lone evening had the two of them facing an unexpected pregnancy now. Joel chuckled inside and casually slid over.

"I'm very happy about our baby," she said, clearly excited. The same level of enthusiasm didn't spill over to him. He was stuck in reflection, while Zarah was in "We're married and having a baby" gear. The more he thought about the baby, the more his head hurt. He rubbed his temples as Zarah chatted uncontrollably. He'd never seen her quite so animated. He didn't dare take away her elation. He only wished she wasn't asking him to join her.

"We have to make plans for the nursery. We have to schedule painters and order the furniture. This will be very nice for us to do together."

"No, you go ahead," he said, unclasping Zarah's hand from his and setting it on her thigh.

"Yes, I'm so sorry. You are too busy for the nursery. It's no worry. I have plenty of help here for the nursery. But we must speak about making arrangements for the baby to be blessed in the temple. We must travel to India as soon after the birth as possible. We want the gods to bless our child with health, happiness, and prosperity."

Joel had to pause, having never thought about how their children would be raised given that he was Christian and Zarah paid homage to many gods, drawing on her internal energy as the source of her faith. She had her gods, and he had his God. Not until this moment had he fully weighed the gravity of his decision to marry Zarah. While he'd gained by marrying her and having access to her father's business, he'd clearly compromised much more—his dignity, his beliefs, and most importantly, his relationship with God. Although he was rusty spiritually, Joel's common sense was intact enough for him to know he wasn't willing to sideline his faith for Zarah's. The magnitude of his decision to stay in or leave the marriage was increasing.

"I'd rather have the baby dedicated in a Christian church. Besides, why would you want to fly so far with a newborn baby when there are plenty of churches right here that I trust?"

He saw her excitement cool down in her expression. "Blessings are most important in my culture and in my family. My child would not be accepted if I didn't go for the blessings," she said as her eyes watered. "I don't want our child to be treated as rubbish. My family would not accept either of us, me or our baby." A tear fell from her eye.

"Calm down and don't upset yourself. We'll work this out."

He had to take her seriously, but what was he to do? If he chose to stay in the marriage, it would be for the child. If he was going to raise a child, it had to be baptized in the church with the Father, the Son, and the Holy Spirit. There was no way he could let his child be blessed by another god or dedicated through any other religion. Joel couldn't fathom the concept. No amount of liberal juice or well-spoken reasons or tears was going to change his mind on this one. They were at an impasse, and she was totally unaware of it. To get into a heated argument with her was pointless. There was a minimum of six months before such a decision had to be made. By then, they might be divorced, anyway.

Too much to think about, Joel thought. The more he reflected on their differences and the conditions by which they were married, the more his inclination to stay married lost traction. Joel had to be honest. He couldn't give Zarah what she wanted. Leading her on would be cruel.

"I'm going to grab a few more clothes."

"And then we can sit down together for dinner. I had the cook make a nice meal before she left. You will be pleased," Zarah told him.

Joel wanted to curl up in the corner and wash away his dread. Zarah was dogging him emotionally at every turn. Her sweet, gentle voice wasn't going to let up, and it made him feel like he was the monster. If he told her he needed time to figure things out, she might feel badly at first, but being honest with her was for the best.

Turning to face her, he saw the radiance in her eyes. She really was happy; making him feel even worse, if that was possible. But then he stopped worrying about her reaction and spit out his words. "Zarah," he said, taking her hand, "I will have dinner with you and then I'll get a room at the Westin until I can figure out what's next."

"No, you must stay here. You've been gone for two weeks. We have had very little time together."

Huh? They'd spent plenty of time together. Her pregnancy was the proof. Joel cringed. "Please, don't fight me on this. I need the space, and you do too."

"I don't ever need space from my husband," she said as several tears fell. "Please stay with me. I don't want to be here without you." She clung to him.

Joel buried his head in his hands and slowly massaged his temples. The bulk of the damaging storm was over, but there was more to come. He'd camp out at the Westin until his plans crystallized. He'd concentrate on his professional recovery and let the marriage sit on the sidelines, out of the way. In the meantime, he had plenty to worry about.

Chapter 13

Zarah couldn't move. She'd sat in the exact same spot for hours, clinging to the desire of his return. When her husband walked out, he'd crushed her spirit. Her tears had dried up after she'd cried off and on for close to two hours. The ache was too deep for her to touch. There was too much to process. How would she face her family? Getting divorced was grounds for being shunned. Being pregnant and divorced was worse than death. At least with death there was peace and a positive flow of energy that would usher her soul to a place of goodness and contentment. She wanted to get up and go somewhere or do something, but her strength faded.

Panic set in. The estate felt too big, empty, and dark. Zarah struggled to settle down. The sharp memory of depression crept in. She'd lost her will to live months ago, when Joel had abandoned her the first time, before he asked for a divorce. She hadn't wanted to live without him. That hadn't changed, but the baby didn't give her the option of giving up. She couldn't lie on her bed until death claimed her sad soul. She had to get better for the sake of her child. Nothing else took precedence, not even Joel.

Zarah wallowed in her sorrow for another twenty minutes. *Enough,* she thought, placing the palm of her hand gently across her abdomen. She needed help, and there was only one person who came to mind. She rushed to the phone and dialed Tamara frantically. The phone rang and rang, and her call finally went to voice mail. She redialed two more times, until Tamara answered.

"You're there!" Zarah shouted. "I rang you twice before."

"I'm sorry I missed your calls. I was picking up my carryout order and didn't hear the phone inside the restaurant."

Zarah sighed loudly.

"What's going on? Are you all right?" Tamara asked.

"No, I'm not good."

"Do I need to ask what's wrong, or do I already know?"

"Joel has left our home for a stay at the hotel."

"When did he get back?"

"This evening he came home. We spoke, and he moved to the hotel. I don't want to live in this house alone. I want my husband."

Zarah had anticipated Tamara's reaction. She'd heard her comments repeatedly, but Tamara didn't understand the stigma that would come from a divorce. Zarah didn't care about the arrangement surrounding her marriage to Joel. He was her husband. She had pledged her heart and her virginity to him and would be committed to him for her whole life. There was no other man, marriage, or relationship for her. Joel Mitchell was the only one. She had to get him home.

"It kills me to see you so caught up in a man who doesn't value you. How long are you going to play this game with him? When are you going to take over your father's business and forget about Joel?"

Zarah was grateful for Tamara's friendship. At least she wasn't in this big country completely alone, but she didn't think Tamara would ever support her desire to be reconciled with Joel. Discussing her marriage further was not good. "I don't want to fight with you. I'm too exhausted." Grief swallowed the room, along with her heart.

"I'm not trying to upset you, but chasing after an uninterested man is the fastest way to run him off. I keep telling you to take charge. Run Harmonious Energy. Let Joel see you're in charge and not paying attention to him. You can do this."

The words stung. Zarah had heard her sister-in-law's appeal repeatedly but hadn't intended to follow her advice. This evening Tamara's words took on new meaning. She'd tried getting Joel to come home by expressing her commitment to him. It hadn't worked. The pregnancy hadn't, either. Zarah knew there weren't many ways left to win Joel's affection. She had to listen to Tamara. Maybe she would give some consideration to running her father's business, at least some portion of it. According to Tamara, this would save her marriage. She had to try.

"I'll look into getting the company, but I won't stop going for my husband. I hope you will honor my wishes."

"What can I do?" Tamara asked in a gentle voice.

Zarah was pleased her sister-in-law wasn't shouting. "I don't believe you can do anything for me."

"How about I come over? We can chat or watch TV, or we can sit and cry over Joel if you'd like."

"I would very much like for you to come here. I feel very alone."

"Say no more. I'm on my way. Give me about forty-five minutes and I'll be there."

Zarah was relieved. The memories of her depression faded. Tamara wasn't Joel, but she was a Mitchell. Staying connected with his family pleased her.

Chapter 14

The weekend had sailed by, and the Monday morning sun ushered in a new week, but Joel didn't feel refreshed. He'd drifted in and out of sleep most of the night. He wanted to jump up and run toward something. Yet he was frozen as he lay across the bed, allowing his anxiety to mount. Finally, after an hour of doing nothing, Joel got dressed and got out of the hotel. His personal existence was in flux. At least if he had a reason to crawl out of bed and get motivated each morning, Joel was confident the other chaos would settle down. He had to get a job or make one. Either way, he had to try every possibility. He smacked down his pride and headed toward the only quasi-refuge he had in Detroit, DMI.

Joel pulled into the parking lot and stopped along the executive row. For nearly three years, he'd parked in the CEO stall. Don was the one parking in the CEO spot now, next to Madeline's convertible Bentley. Intently cruising along the executive row, Joel saw that there wasn't a spot for him. He eased the car into gear and crept to the next row. He found an empty space next to the one reserved for his mother. Joel headed toward the building and a flood of sentiment met him at the door. Positive and negative memories were mixed together, though they were mostly positive. He basked in a sense of comfort as he walked through the lobby. He couldn't resist reflecting on his tenure at DMI and concluded that those years were, undoubtedly, the most successful, challenging, and satisfying ones of his life. Being at the helm of a company was like an insatiable drug, one that drove him to make rash decisions and back alley deals which had clouded his vision. To say he regretted those times would be a lie. He lived to have the sensation of being in charge again.

"Hi, Mr. Mitchell," one of the security guards said.

He returned the greeting. Others approached Joel before he reached the elevators. So far the visit had been good. His troubles were already growing lighter to bear. Hopefully, the rest of his visit would go equally as well, although he didn't have high expectations. The last time he walked out of this building, many whom he'd hurt had stayed. He knew there would be some tension, but he had to try. He was too desperate to let pride force him back to the parking lot without talking with Abigail. No false pretenses. Joel planned to be completely honest.

He reached her office. Peeking inside, he saw her typing on her laptop. She didn't see him in the doorway. He drew in a quiet but long breath, preparing for the hailstorm that might be coming his way. He knocked. Abigail looked up, stared at him, as if she were seeing a stranger. She didn't speak and went back to typing on her laptop.

The warmth he'd felt as he walked through the lobby had already cooled off, and there was no way to deny the truth. He was in a hostile environment. The war might be over, but the fallout was still palpable. He should have walked away after Abigail's subtle display of rejection. The old Joel would have. This one had too great a need to let rejection drive him away. He was poised for a battle.

"Can I come in?" he asked Abigail and entered her office before she could respond. "It's good to see you too," he said, taking a seat in front of her desk. He folded his hands and grinned. In the past, his smile had melted her, along with a long list of other women. Right now, there was only one woman of importance, his loyal friend and former chief advisor. Joel braced his elbows on the chair and kept grinning at Abigail, who looked up at him sporadically. He remained undeterred. It would take a lot more than a disgruntled friend to get him out of that office before he had his say. He pulled the chair closer to her desk. "Are you really going to ignore me?" he asked.

She let out an irritating juvenile scream. "What do you want, Joel?" she said, slamming the laptop shut.

"My, my, I wasn't prepared for such a warm welcome. I was expecting much worse."

"What do you want? Can't you see that I'm very busy?"

Joel reached over to touch her laptop, easing the top open. "Let me see what you're working on," he said, intentionally being slightly annoying in an effort to get Abigail out of her tightly wound mood.

She snatched the laptop away and slammed it shut again. "Stop, Joel. You know this is proprietary."

To a stranger, Abigail would seem agitated to the point of wanting him to leave. Joel knew better. Joking around was a core piece of their relationship. The countless days and evenings they'd spent working together had generated a boatload of silliness between them. He relished those days. *No sense pining,* he thought. That phase of their relationship ended when he decided to marry Zarah instead of Abigail. The close friendship they had shared was no more. His heart wouldn't allow him to believe every aspect of their relationship was over. There had to be a small fragment of it left. Somewhere in her soul, she had to have some compassion for him. That was what Joel was hoping to find this morning.

He stayed close to the desk, causing Abigail to push her chair back on the other side. "So are you still resigning, or did Don convince you to stay?"

"You better believe I'm resigning," she answered very quickly.

Joel pulled back. "Wow. Did I hit a nerve?"

She reopened the laptop. "I told you, I'm very busy. What do you want?" she said while banging on a few keys. "When you were here three or four weeks ago, you told me you were getting divorced and going to Chicago."

"I spent a few weeks in Chicago, just like I said."

She gave him a harsh stare. "How is Sheba?"

The freeze in her tone didn't have to be explained. Abigail had never been comfortable with him and Sheba. Joel had never addressed the issue. Insecurity wasn't addressable as far as he was concerned. Besides, Sheba was the only confidant who hadn't abandoned him after his failure. Nobody on earth was going to cut him off from Sheba, nobody. So he steered the conversation to a more desirable place, talking about business. As angry as Abigail was, she loved a good business venture. There were times when she seemed more driven toward success than he was. That was where they'd connected before, and he believed they would connect there again.

"Abigail," he said, reaching for her hand. She tried pulling it away, but he caught her fingertips. "You don't hate me." He grabbed more of her hand. "We were good here together, and you can't deny it. You can't tell me you don't miss the rush of adrenaline every time we closed another deal. We were unstoppable," he said, gazing at her.

"Those days are gone," she snapped at him.

"But they don't have to be."

She withdrew her hand from his, but not in an angry or anxious way. Those reactions required too much passion, more emotion than she could muster for Joel. As he sat an arm's length away, she felt nothing. There were no sparks flying or harps playing. He'd made sure she shut down her unbridled love for him months ago. His cunning grin didn't excite her as it once had. Didn't mean he was a leper. She genuinely cared about him, the same as she did any homeless guy on the street. Maybe a little more, but it didn't seem like a lot more. She was done with his antics and lack of concern about her well-being.

He raised his arms in the air. "You have another month or so here. Do you have another job lined up?" Joel asked.

"Not yet," she said without looking up.

"See? There you go. Our partnership was meant to be. I'm already out of work, and soon you will be too. What better opportunity for us to start a company together?"

"You must be kidding," Abigail hurled at him.

He drew close to the desk again. "I'm serious. We ran this place like a well-oiled machine together. DMI realized record growth when I was CEO and you were my executive vice president. We ran this place like no one ever has, not even my father."

Abigail shook her head. She'd made the painful climb out of the pit of despair and longing for Joel. Actually, Abigail had Tamara to thank for shoving her into the face of reality. Joel wasn't going to put anyone above his own needs. After Tamara abrasively pointed out what she should have detected several years ago, Abigail broke off her ties with Joel, and now she wasn't going backwards. His presence could be tempting, but not this time. She was going to put Abigail first. She was in complete control. She was confident Joel would be able to relate.

"Come on, Abigail," Joel said. "I need you. I really do."

"I don't think so," she said, almost singing the words. She noticed a charge coming from within. Her love for him had been trampled. She really was free. It was hard even for her to believe it, but it was a fact. His suave presence and convincing lines were an irritation, not a tool of persuasion, not anymore.

"Give me one good reason why we shouldn't start a company together."

She flashed him a look and responded, "You want only one. Wow, that's too easy." She gently closed her laptop again and rested her folded hands on top. Calmly and with as much control as she could muster, Abigail said, "You had your opportunity with me, and you blew it. Go home to your wife or back to Chicago, to your friend Sheba, or whoever it is that happens to be your lady this week."

"Okay, I get it. I hurt you. I've apologized over and over."

"No, you never really apologized, but don't worry. It's not important." She smiled and titled her head slightly. Abigail was certain Joel didn't know how to take the new woman sitting in her office. "Honestly, I'm glad I saw the man you truly are before it was too late. I pity your wife."

"I didn't realize that you're still this upset about me getting married."

"I'm not," she barked at him.

He smirked. "Will you please let me apologize and put the past behind us?"

"Do whatever you'd like. The days of me waiting for table scraps from you or anyone else with the last name of Mitchell are over. I've gotten off this circus ride."

"Okay, but, Abigail, if you're truly being honest, you have to admit that I never misled you. Never." He pushed away from the desk.

Maybe he was right. Maybe he wasn't. She didn't want to think about their history any longer. Chips of anxiety were fluttering around, and she didn't want them to land on her.

He went on. "I told you repeatedly that I wasn't interested in a serious relationship. I made it clear when we began working together that DMI and God were my only priorities."

"Humph, and you don't have much interaction with either after all your professions of faith, do you?" Abigail asked.

"We all make mistakes. There's no doubt I've made plenty, and I want to apologize for what happened between us. I didn't marry Zarah to hurt you. It was purely business, but I am sorry for hurting you."

She pulled out her notepad. His apology was no more than a scrap of paper blowing in the wind. They were done. She went back to drafting her report, willing to let Joel sit there until doomsday, staring at the woman who used to love him with her whole heart. Now she pitied him with the same fervor.

Chapter 15

Joel sat in the seat a while longer. He thought maybe Abigail would soften. After a couple of minutes, she hadn't. He found himself in unfamiliar territory. He was armed for her anger and outrage but hadn't contemplated simply being ignored. He stood with the intent of apologizing once again, as the depth of her hurt had been exposed. Upon further consideration, he kept quiet. He wasn't going to push her. He approached the doorway and turned to face her. Abigail wouldn't look up. He exited her office, not sure if their friendship was completely dead or in a coma. He'd have to wait and see.

What couldn't wait was getting a job. He had to find a gig and fast. It was the only thread enabling him to maintain his grip on sanity. Abigail was a bust, but there was another executive at DMI who had the power to help him.

Joel squared his shoulders and put some pep in his steps. Don's office was several doors down the hallway. He walked every inch of the short distance with confidence. He'd volleyed back and forth between Abigail's office and his old office too many times to count. They'd logged many miles together. Beyond DMI, he missed her friendship, especially now. She was the one he would have discussed the pregnancy with and would have relied on for input. He knew better than to broach the subject. Their relationship was too fractured for him to mention the pregnancy to her. It was clear that she wasn't interested in him, let alone his problems with Zarah. He had to believe she'd allow forgiveness to carve a small place in her heart for him to enter sometime soon. For now, though, he had to focus on his most urgent matter.

He stepped up to the desk of Don's assistant, with whom Joel hadn't worked previously. She greeted him. Although he'd been out of the office for a short period, the group appeared to be much the same. People on the executive floor knew him. He didn't waste time on small talk.

"Is my brother in?"

"He is, and I think he just ended a call. So he's available. Would you like for me to let him know you're here?"

"No," he said, tapping the counter attached to the workstation. Joel took a few steps and knocked on Don's office door and walked in. He found Don at his conference table, across the room from his desk.

"How's it going, big brother?" he asked.

"Good, good." Don stood to shake Joel's hand. "I thought you'd left town."

"I did, and I've returned." They sat.

"I was under the impression you were gone for good. What brings you home so soon?"

"Business . . ." Joel could tell him about the baby, but the timing didn't feel right. He'd keep his personal business off the table and limit the scope of their conversation to DMI, where he had better odds of success.

"What kind of business?" Don asked, fumbling with his pen on the table.

Joel was apprehensive. He didn't have a good sense of where Don was with forgiveness. A lot had happened by Joel's doing, much of it not good for Don or DMI. He understood there were fences to be mended. Don had been the peacemaker in their family over the past year. Joel prayed he was still wearing the cloak of restoration. This was Joel's last option. Don had to give him a break.

"I'm looking for a job. I figured I might as well come here first."

Don peered at his brother without revealing any reaction, causing Joel to grow tense.

"Really? Hmm," Don uttered. He flipped his pen onto the table, latched his hands behind his head, and reared back in his seat. "I certainly didn't anticipate this visit."

"I didn't, either."

Silence hovered over them. Joel couldn't tell if Don was contemplating an answer or recovering from the shock of his request. Silence remained as Don stared into the openness and played with his pen. Joel couldn't take it anymore.

"What do you think?" he asked. Joel watched Don pinch the tip of his nose slowly and let his gaze fall. Joel wasn't sensing positive vibes. He had to convince Don to say yes before his brother said no. "Don't you have to replace Abigail?"

"Maybe."

"What does that mean?" Joel asked.

"I haven't given up on getting her to stay. We both know how valuable she is to DMI. Dad hired her, and I see why. As long as I'm CEO, she has a job."

This time Joel leaned back in his seat. "Good luck with getting her to stay. I just left her office, and Abigail didn't give any indication that she's staying with DMI. Actually, I got the impression she is ready to walk out any minute."

"I'm sure you're right, but time can heal wounds and change our minds."

"That's what I'm counting on," Joel said, digesting the message. "So what do you say, big brother? Is there a place for me here?"

"I don't know."

"Come on, you have at least one vacancy. I don't have to be on executive row."

Don snickered. "So you're willing to take a job in the mail room? Is that what you're telling me?"

Joel snickered too. "Maybe not starting at ground level, but I'm willing to take on a senior vice president or even a vice president role."

Don smirked. "Neither is the role for you, and you know it. You wouldn't be satisfied."

"Try me."

"No, it's not a good idea. Get real. You were the CEO," Don pointed out. "How are you going to be reduced to a junior level role? That's like the president of the United States becoming a city councilman after serving two terms. It's unheard of."

Don had a point. Yet the fact remained that Joel needed a job, a purpose. He had to make a new entrance onto the corporate stage. Being sidelined was agony. "I need this, Don," he confessed. "I've run out of options. You're my last hope."

"Don't put this kind of pressure on me. God is your last hope."

"But he can direct you to help me." Joel rubbed his forehead. He rattled off a silent prayer, not sure where God was with his jumbled state of affairs.

"I'll tell you what," Don said, interrupting Joel's prayer. "I can't say yes, but I'm not saying no, either. I have to figure out where we're taking DMI before I fill any vacancies."

Joel saw the lifeline slipping out of his hands. He made one more effort to hold on. "What about your other company, LTI? Don't you have any openings there? I don't mind going to South Africa, if that's what it takes."

"LTI isn't in the picture," Don said, giving him a rapid response.

It wasn't what Don said that made Joel cringe. It was how his brother spoke that made Joel take notice. He swallowed the rejection and didn't pursue the suggestion any further.

"So you can't think of a single job for me at DMI, not one?"

"Nope, not right now, but I'll keep you in mind."

Joel tapped on the table a few times and pushed his chair back to stand. "If you change your mind, you know where to reach me."

He entered the hallway and meandered to the bank of elevators, drawing on each ounce of dignity he had reserved. There wasn't a large dose available, as humiliation was nibbling at him with every step. Joel kept wondering if God was as merciful as he had once believed. If He was, then his savior had to meet him on the ground floor. Otherwise he was finished.

Finally, the elevator door opened. He stepped into the den of doom. The door closed, and he descended into greater despair.

Chapter 16

The stench of desperation hung in the air long after Joel had left. Don attempted to shove his brother's situation to the rear of his priorities. He flipped his pen around in his hand, pondering and dissecting Joel's request. He couldn't let the conversation rest. There was a nagging feeling that wouldn't go away. It was like a wasp stinging him repeatedly in the dark. The random stings seemed endless. His experience told him Joel was going to make a play for Zarah's ownership stake in Harmonious Energy and the West Coast division. There wasn't much else for Joel to do. Don hated the notion of his brother waging a war over the division, but Don understood Joel's dire straits. It didn't make him happy. Actually, he wanted to gasp. Don wondered when he was going to get a real break at DMI. He'd wrestled with challenge after challenge. What else did God want him to do? Peace was elusive, and he was tired. Don attempted to get some work done off and on for nearly an hour, but he accomplished nothing meaningful.

He snatched up the phone receiver and paged his administrative assistant. "Call Zarah Mitchell, Joel's wife, and set up a meeting," Don told her. "See if she can come into the office."

"What time?" she asked.

Don peered at his watch. He had no idea what Joel was capable of doing in his current state. If Don waited too long to make Zarah an offer on the West Coast division, he might lose out to his brother and sister. Time was not to be wasted. "In an hour or two."

"Do you have a number for her?"

"Get Joel's home number from the executive directory."

Don played with a list of possible deals, each offering as much as required to secure the division while simultaneously unloading DMI's ownership position in Harmonious Energy. He couldn't off-load Bengali's family business fast enough. It would be the last item to clean up from Joel's administration. Don had another incentive to wrap up the deal. The sooner DMI was stable, the faster he could get back to his company, LTI, and his girlfriend in South Africa. Soothing memories of her gentle touch, her African mixed with French accent, and her quiet strength settled his anxiety.

A few minutes passed before Don's assistant rang him on the intercom that went from her desk to his. "Mrs. Mitchell can't meet today. She's not feeling well and can't come into the office. Would you like for me to schedule a meeting later in the week, or should I hold off until next week?"

Don shuddered. Next week would be too late. Joel and Tamara weren't going to wait too long to make their moves. They were on the attack, and if Don was going to be considered a viable contender, he had to get an offer in front of Zarah immediately. He grabbed his coat and went into the hallway.

"Get Zarah on the phone again. She doesn't have to come into the office. I'm going to her house," he told his assistant. She looked puzzled. "Get her on the phone right away and tell her I'll be there in thirty to forty minutes." He didn't wait for an answer. Don left the building and rushed to Joel and Zarah's house as the sun hung high in the noonday sky.

The housekeeper answered the door when he arrived.

"Is Mrs. Mitchell home?" he asked.

"Please come in, Mr. Mitchell."

The housekeeper must have remembered Don from the visit he made to the house with Tamara and Abigail several months ago.

"We've been expecting you."

Then Don remembered his assistant had called ahead too. That was most likely why the housekeeper recognized him. He stepped into the foyer. "Is Joel home?"

"No, he's not home at the moment. Can I please take your coat?"

"Yes, sure. Thank you," Don said, handing it to her.

"Please follow me into the library. I'll have Mrs. Mitchell join you there."

Don followed the housekeeper into the library, which was lined with built-in bookshelves. Eventually, Zarah entered the room to find Don flipping through a book. Aware of her presence, he closed the book and placed it back on the shelf. He greeted his sister-in-law, opting to shake her hand and give her a heavy nod, unsure of the most appropriate gesture. It generated a small smile from her, which helped put Don at ease.

"Please take a seat," she said, sitting too with a shawl across her legs. "What brings you here?"

Don didn't want to jump right in, although sitting around and jabbering wasn't appealing, either. He exchanged common courtesies with Zarah and then got down to business. He wanted to get in and out before Joel got home. Honestly, Don thought DMI had a slim chance of buying the division from Zarah, but he had to try for his mother's sake.

A table and lamp separated Zarah's seat from Don's. He had been in her presence only a few times and hadn't noticed how captivating Zarah was. Her skin was brushed with a richness not easily described. She wasn't light or dark. Zarah was simply attractive. He tried not to stare into her deep-colored eyes, which accentuated the soft hue of her complexion and her dark, silky hair, but found it difficult to refrain. Her brightly colored outfit, particularly the heavy scarf-like material delicately wrapped around her body, held his attention.

He leaned forward. "Zarah, I'm here on business." He gritted his teeth. "I'm not going to beat around the bush. I'd like to return the West Coast division to DMI. So I'm prepared to make you a very generous offer." She didn't respond, forcing Don to elaborate more. "I know there are others who want to buy the company too." Don intentionally didn't mention names. He wasn't sure if Tamara or Joel had made their interest known to Zarah yet. If they hadn't, he wasn't going to do the introductions for them. They'd have to make their own pleas.

"Don, I am pleased about your visit, but I am not ready to sell the division."

"Is it that you don't want to sell the division at all or that you don't want to sell it to me?"

Don noticed she kept rubbing her stomach. "I've decided to keep the division and run my father's company. It is in honor of my family."

Don had to sit up in the chair and shift his weight. Where was this coming from? "I didn't realize you were interested in running a company."

"I have always worked with my father. Many people don't know that about me. Yes, he did have a team of people working with him. You are correct. There was not much interest from me until I spoke with Tamara and received her good advice. She has helped me see the importance of keeping my company."

Don couldn't fully process what Zarah was saying. When did Tamara become a counselor?

"I would like to make you an offer to purchase DMI's fifty-one percent of Harmonious Energy so I can take full charge of the company," Zarah stated.

Don leaned forward again. "Please forgive me, but you've caught me off guard. I wasn't prepared for this. I'll have to think about this and get back to you. For some reason I was under the impression that you wanted to be a housewife. I didn't think you planned to work."

Her mood lightened as a smile consumed her face. She stopped rubbing her stomach and said, "Yes, it is true. Taking care of my home and family is very important to me, especially now that I'm having a baby..."

Don coughed, more like choked. "Excuse me, but what did you say?"

"I'm having a baby."

"Congratulations," Don uttered, not sure if this was good or bad news. He figured it depended on who he asked. Don had met with Joel earlier, and the pregnancy wasn't mentioned. "And you want to run your father's company with a baby on the way?"

"Yes, it is in my father's honor."

Don was through with the conversation. He couldn't handle another heart-stopping revelation. He had to get out of the house.

"Zarah," Don heard Joel yelling from the hallway.

Don frowned. He wasn't looking for an argument, but the fact that he was at Joel's house with the intention of buying Zarah's company wasn't going to be well received. Don stood and prepared to face the fire.

Joel entered the library. Zarah stood immediately but didn't rush to Joel. Don could tell Zarah wanted to, and he wasn't sure why she hadn't. Don didn't attempt to psychoanalyze their relationship. He was bent on getting out of the house with no more than a strong glare from Joel.

"Hey, Joel. I was just leaving," Don blurted out.

"The housekeeper told me you were here. Were you looking for me? Did you change your mind?" Joel asked Don.

The day couldn't slide downhill any faster if it was on an engine-powered bobsled. Don just wanted to leave. "No, I was here on DMI business, but don't worry. I have to go." Don rushed out of the library and zipped to the front door, not allowing Joel to ask any more questions. He hustled outside and sped off in his car.

Chapter 17

A gentle sensation engulfed Zarah. She was pleased that Don had stopped by, even if it was for business. Having a visitor from the Mitchell family, for any reason, was favorable.

"What did he mean by being here on DMI business?" Joel asked.

Having her husband stand there while she sat made Zarah nervous. "He wants to buy the West Coast division."

"Jeez, not that again. I hope you didn't say yes," Joel said in a way that scared her. She remembered how mad Joel was several months back, when he found out Madeline and Don had approached her about selling the West Coast division to them without his knowledge. He was most angry, and she didn't want to see him so upset again.

"I did not agree to his request."

"Good," her husband said, sounding much calmer. She was pleased but didn't tell him. "Because I want to talk to you about buying the West Coast division myself."

"All three of you?" she blurted out.

"Which three?"

"You, Don, and Tamara."

"Oh, come on. What does Tamara want with the division?" he asked.

"She wants to start a new company. It's best for her not to work at DMI." Zarah could hear Tamara's words ringing in her ears. She had to show strength with Joel.

He had to see that she could be in charge of professional matters. "Why do you want the division?" she asked Joel.

Joel looked away, and she waited for his gaze to return to her. After roaming around the room, his gaze did return, exactly as she'd hoped. Patience was her kind companion. She'd cling to it tightly with each step.

"I need a job, simple as that," he said, walking near to her but not close enough to touch.

This was her chance to help her beloved husband, and she was disappointed knowing she couldn't if she was to follow Tamara's advice. "But you must remember, I can't sell the business to you."

"Of course I remember" Joel replied. "How can I forget your father's will and his ridiculous clause that requires us to be married three years before you can transfer the DMI division to me. Yes, I definitely remember," he said and moved farther away from her. "It was his so-called way of making sure I wasn't marrying you with the intent of stealing your company and leaving you destitute." The sound of his hand clap made her nervous again. Then he turned to her with a softer look. "Please don't sell anything without talking to me first."

Zarah's heart leapt and she was ready to say yes, but there was Tamara again. Her advice spoke louder than Joel's. Zarah was afraid to upset him, but she had to win his affection. "I have not decided whose offer to accept."

Joel rushed over to her, erasing the distance between them. "You're not seriously considering selling my division, are you?"

"But my father gave it to me," she responded.

"Only after my father entrusted me with the division and I lost it."

Zarah could see how troubled Joel was. She was sad for him, but she did not waver. She remained quiet for a moment, and then said, "It is my division, and I have not decided what to do."

"Wow. You are seriously considering selling the West Coast division to Don or Tamara? "I can't believe you're doing this to us. We might not be living as a married couple should, but we share the same house."

"There is more than this house that I must share with my husband to be married."

Joel grunted.

She wasn't ready to make direct eye contact with him, but Zarah wanted to speak her mind. "Are you ready to live in this house as husband and wife again? It is my desire. Is it yours?"

Joel grunted again.

She let her gaze travel slowly upward, nudged by her courage. Zarah's boldness rose too, and when her gaze met his, the words flew out. "I am ready to be your wife today, right now," she said, pointing her index finger repeatedly at the floor. "Are you ready?"

"You know I'm not prepared to give you an answer. I've told you so for the past week. I need time to make sense of our situation."

"Situation," she said, uncrossing her legs and gently placing her feet flat on the floor. Zarah stood and flung the smaller scarf she was wearing over her shoulder. "Since I have no husband living here with me, I must learn to make my decisions alone," she said. "Excuse me please, but I must rest."

Zarah wasn't sure how Joel was going to react. She'd never spoken to him in such a way. She prayed Tamara's advice was good and Joel would like her strength. She'd keep working at it until Joel showed interest. She had many months to go before giving birth. There was no rush, and she had a plan.

Joel remained silent. "Good afternoon," Zarah said and walked out of the room. Her sense of satisfaction wiped away her doubts. Normally, Joel walked out of the room first. It was nice to leave before he did. Her steps grew lighter as she reflected on what had just taken place. *Tamara is a very smart lady,* Zarah thought as she hurried up the stairs, eager to go to sleep and dream about her future with the baby and Joel. Joy lined her path.

Her sense of satisfaction was like a drug. Zarah was euphoric. She closed the master bedroom door and locked it. She was pretty sure Joel had left the house, but she didn't want to take a chance. There was a phone on the small table in the sitting room of their bedroom suite, along with a couple of oversized chairs. She claimed one of the chairs and dialed Tamara's number.

Of everyone she knew in the United States, Zarah was closest to Tamara, unless she counted her former assistant, Ann. There was much to do when running a company, and she was going to need help. Perhaps she'd call Ann later.

Tamara answered the phone after a few rings.

"I am very pleased with this evening," Zarah told her.

"Why? What happened?"

"Joel was here. We spoke very deeply about marriage and my plans to run the company."

"Really?" Tamara said. "How did he react? Was he surprised, angry, or what?"

"I believe angry. He was most concerned about me selling the West Coast division."

"Oh, boy. Did you tell him I'm the one who wants to buy the division?"

"I did, and he was not pleased."

"Good. That means you're in charge, not him. Trust me on this one. He doesn't know what to do with you now. He's so used to you doing what he wants. He won't know how to respond to you making decisions without him," Tamara replied. "Yeah, I know he's mad. That's why you can never let him know my involvement. It's better if he doesn't know how much I'm supporting you."

"I agree," Zarah said loudly.

"Well, congratulations on standing up to the big bad bully."

"Sorry, but what did you say?" Zarah asked, not sure how to translate Tamara's words.

"Ah, it's nothing. Just ignore my comments. Anyway, what's next?" Tamara asked.

Zarah didn't know exactly but figured she'd start with Kumar. Her father had relied on him for years to provide advice. She'd do the same. "I'm going to speak with my family attorney and get his help."

"When are you going to call him? We have to get moving on your takeover," Tamara said and laughed.

"Tonight is good." The wall clock showed that it was almost three o'clock in the afternoon, which meant that it was one thirty in the morning in southern India. "I'm going to rest and then call later this evening. Eleven tonight will be nine thirty tomorrow morning for Kumar. That's the right time to call."

"That's late for you. Do you want me to stop by?"

Zarah normally welcomed a visit, but she was really tired. "No. I'm going to rest. I will phone you tomorrow."

"You sure you don't want me to stop by or give you a wake-up call tonight?"

"I am sure," Zarah said. She felt alive, as if her life mattered. She wanted to be a wife, a mother, but most importantly, she wanted to matter. If the plan worked as Tamara had explained, then soon Zarah would be in the master bedroom suite with Joel. He'd be sitting in the chair situated on the other side of the small table, across from her. She closed her eyes and let fulfilling images of her family fill her mind.

Chapter 18

The alarm didn't have to go off. Zarah was awake at 11:00 p.m. She'd actually been up and ready to make the call since seven. She dialed the series of sixteen numbers to reach Kumar. His assistant answered and got him on the line.

"Zarah, are you well?" Kumar asked.

"Yes, I am very well."

"When I got your message about not returning to India, I was most worried. Since you are to be divorced, you must come here and let us set a new plan for you. It is my duty to look after you," he told her.

"There's no need for worry. I'm staying here with my husband."

"You have reconciled?" Kumar asked. Zarah could hear the concern in his voice.

"Soon, very soon."

"I'm not sure what you're saying. Are you married?"

Zarah didn't call to get into a debate with Kumar about Joel. He was her husband, and she was growing tired of so many questions from so many people. "I'm staying here. This is my home. Joel and I will be a family. The gods are with me and my husband too."

"I must speak with Joel to understand his intentions."

"No, you don't and you won't," she said. "I am going to make decisions without my husband until he returns home, which is the reason I'm calling. I'd like to run Harmonious Energy."

"You mean Joel wants to run Harmonious Energy?" the attorney asked.

"No, I want to run the company."

"Zarah, you're frightening me with this rubbish. Are you sure you're well? If not, don't worry. We'll get you the proper treatment. I can come to the States and make the proper arrangements."

"No," she said. "You mustn't come here unless it is to bring the documents allowing me to run Harmonious Energy."

"Zarah, your father would not be pleased."

If asking to run the company was a shock, then wait until Kumar heard the rest, she thought. "I will also need funds to buy the other fifty-one percent of Harmonious Energy from DMI."

"Why would we want to buy it back when your father sold the company to settle your marriage?"

"In order for me to be in charge, it is best for me to own the entire company." Kumar was quiet. "What do you think?" She respected his advice and his important role in the family. Hopefully, he'd agree, and she could get on with it.

"This is not good for any of us. Let me ring up Joel and see what he says."

Zarah was becoming agitated. Kumar didn't need to speak with Joel. Hadn't she already told him her plan to go forward? "This is not for Joel. This is my decision, and you must give me the same respect you gave my father."

"Zarah, I don't think this is wise, but as you wish. I will treat you with the same respect given to your father. Let me know if you need help."

"I do need your help. I must first understand the present state of the business. Do you have materials I can read?"

"We will prepare documents and have a package sent overnight to you."

Zarah thanked Kumar. She was about to say good-bye when he said, "Please don't sell or buy any company without my knowledge, please."

"I promise to ring you up first."

There was a change happening. Zarah couldn't explain why she was so happy. Joel wasn't home with her yet, but she was full of hope wrapped in confidence. She had Tamara to thank. Glancing at the clock, she saw that it was nearly midnight. She laid her palm across her abdomen. Zarah had to get some sleep. Tomorrow was going to be a busy day. She'd share the good news with Tamara in the morning.

Zarah attempted to settle down as the pillow cradled her head, but the excitement she felt within was overpowering. She had taken a big step tonight and was bubbling with satisfaction. If she didn't share the news right now, she was going to erupt. Delaying no longer, she grabbed the phone and dialed franticly. Tamara's phone rang and rang. Zarah was about to give up when she heard Tamara's voice.

"My apologies for ringing you this late, but I couldn't wait until morning."

"Zarah, is everything all right?" Tamara asked in a raspy voice.

"Yes, yes, better than all right. I am very pleased," she said, resting against the headboard. "I rang up Kumar. He has agreed to help me with my father's company."

"You mean as in running it?"

"Yes, I would run the company." Her excitement hadn't cooled. Having something important that Joel wanted was a great source of joy.

"Wow. I'm surprised you actually made the call," Tamara said. Zarah was kind of surprised too but didn't tell Tamara that. "When do you start?"

"I must first prepare. Kumar will send documents for me to review."

"Cool. Let me know if you need any help."

"I will."

"I really can't believe you did it. This is huge. Does Joel know?" Tamara asked.

"He does not."

"Humph. He's definitely going to be stunned and maybe a little mad."

"What do you mean?" Zarah asked, her excitement cooling rapidly. Her actions were intended to make him happy.

"Ah, don't worry. I mean, he might be mad initially because you're taking such a major step without his involvement." Zarah's hope sank. "But as soon as he sees you're doing so well, I'm sure he's going to become very intrigued with you." Zarah's happiness was percolating again. "You know," Tamara said, "you should have a press conference and let the world know you're going to run Harmonious Energy. What a great way to kick off your new role."

Zarah was instantly troubled. "I'm not sure I should do a press conference. It is too much for me," she said, thinking about the baby.

"But you have to get the word out. A press conference is the fastest way. It will shock the socks off Mr. Joel."

Zarah wasn't willing to take on too much stress and risk the baby's health. She wanted to win Joel's love, but her baby couldn't be sacrificed. "I cannot do a press conference."

"Why not? What's the big deal?"

"It is not my choice. I am not ready, and it would be quite stressful for me. I cannot do a conference."

"Fine. What about an article in the paper or a magazine? You can do the interview at home and talk only about what you choose."

Zarah considered the suggestion.

"Come on, you have to do some type of announcement. It's a basic corporate requirement," Tamara added.

Zarah considered the article some more. If she was going to take a big job at Harmonious Energy, fear couldn't rule her actions. She had to be brave and bold in order to do her father proud and to show Joel she was the woman he desired.

"I will do the article. We can speak about it tomorrow," she said. She said good-bye and sank into the pillow, eager to experience what was coming next.

Chapter 19

A week in town and Joel was no closer to getting a job than he was to figuring out if Detroit was for him. He finally stopped by his mother's house after avoiding her for several days.

Joel found her sitting in the kitchen. Sherry had on loungewear as she sipped a cup of coffee. Joel got a bottled drink from the refrigerator.

"Look what the wind has blown in," his mother said, tracing the rim of her half-empty cup.

Joel plopped into a seat at the table and twisted the cap off his cold bottle of ginger ale. He took several gulps.

"My goodness, somebody's pretty thirsty. Don't you have cold drinks at home?" Sherry asked playfully. Joel grinned. "How exciting for our family. I'm thrilled to be a grandmother," she said, gripping the handle of the cup. She sipped her coffee. "How's Zarah doing with her morning sickness?"

"I don't know," he said, taking a few more gulps and hoping his mother would move on to another less complicated topic.

"Why don't you know? The two of you are talking, right?" she asked with a distinct tone of concern.

The flurry of questions was the precise reason he'd avoided visiting his mother for most of the week. She had questions he couldn't answer, which was bound to make her worry. He would work to calm her fears to the best of his ability without lying or overcommitting.

"We're talking, but . . ." he said and paused.

"But what?" Sherry asked, taking her hand off the cup and putting it on Joel's shoulder.

"But we're not living in the same house, at least not for a while," he said, trusting the last part of his statement would soften the revelation.

"Where are you staying?"

"At the Westin for now."

"Joel, for goodness' sake, she's pregnant. She needs you now more than ever." She slapped his shoulder. "How can you be anywhere else except home with her?"

Joel gulped the last of his beverage and left the bottle tilted toward his mouth for a few extra seconds, using the time to shape his response. No answer was going to satisfy his mother, but he wasn't going to lie and create false expectations.

"We needed space."

"You can't tell me Zarah wants space from you. The woman adores you. If anything, it's you who needs space," she said. Sherry slapped his shoulder again and inadvertently knocked over her cup. A small amount of coffee spilled onto the table. "Oops. Look what you've made me do."

"Here, let me help." Joel jumped up and grabbed paper towels, using the accident as an opportunity to avoid further discussion of his marriage. Any distraction was gladly welcomed. He wiped the table, praying his mother was tired of talking about Zarah. He'd nudge her toward another subject. "I was in the office a few days ago to see Don. I'm hoping he will give me a job at DMI," Joel said as he and Sherry finished cleaning up the spill. The tension choked the humor that normally found its way into their conversation. He was dismayed.

His mother was silent for what seemed like hours, but was merely a few seconds. Breaking her silence, she said,

"Joel, I don't understand how you can abandon your wife while she's carrying your child. Who does that?"

"Mom, I'm sorry," he said, grabbing her hand and forcing her to look at him. "I'm not abandoning her."

"Then what do you call it?" she asked, snatching her hand from his grip.

"We . . . Okay, I'll admit that it's me. I need time to sort out my feelings for Zarah and the marriage."

"There's nothing to sort out. You married her," Sherry said spewing each word at him. He could see the tears swelling on her eyelids. "The baby needs both parents to love and protect him or her from the harshness of this world."

Joel attempted to console her, but Sherry refused to accept his gesture. She flicked a tear away. He wasn't a hundred percent sure why she was becoming overly emotional, but he had an inkling. "Mom, don't cry. I will take care of my child."

Watching her cry broke him down, and Joel struggled to maintain his composure. As he sat close to his wounded mother, he was reminded that the pain of their past was only a few words away.

"I can't imagine another generation of Mitchells going through what we did."

"Mom, don't cry," Joel said, handing her a napkin to wipe her face.

"I'm sorry to be sitting here bawling, but I can't help it. I don't want my grandchild growing up without a father."

"Mom, I keep telling you not to worry. I will always take care of my child, whether I live in the same house or not. It won't matter."

"It does matter," she yelled, causing his neck to stiffen. "Why should my grandchild suffer from the same isolation, rejection, and feelings of inferiority as you had to face because his or her father isn't around full-time?"

"Mom, nothing that I say, other than 'I'm staying with Zarah,' will be acceptable to you. So I might as well keep quiet."

"We have to break this cycle of abandonment in our family with this child. Do what you must to make this right and stay with your family."

"I'm not sure why this upsets you so much. Dad lived with us from the day I was born." Joel and his father had a solid relationship.

"But he was never completely committed to us," Sherry said.

"But he was here," Joel stated.

"Then take a good look at Madeline's children and use them as your example."

"Don didn't spend his entire childhood living with Dad, but he hasn't turned out any better or worse than I have. He survived pretty well, if you ask me."

"Really? What about the other three children, the murder-suicide and the rape victim who is mad at the world? Do you want this baby to suffer the same way your father's older children did because he wasn't in the home with them? Huh, do you?"

"No, of course I don't want my child to suffer," Joel said, stroking his chin. "But I don't plan to stay in a dead end-marriage for the sake of my baby, either." His mother and father had enjoyed a measure of success in their marriage. Yet his mother had never liked Madeline being around all the time as the very visible ex-wife. Joel wouldn't dare approach a subject by mentioning his mother, his father, and Madeline in the same sentence. He'd learned that hard lesson long ago. "I have to find a job and then worry about my marriage."

She calmed down and rested her hand on his and gave it a slight squeeze. "Please reconsider what you're doing. This is a repeat of the same mistakes your father and I made. I'm begging you to go home to your wife and show her the kind of love she deserves. I'm pleading with you to put your family above your ambition. Make her your priority and end our cycle of dysfunction."

"Mom, I appreciate what you're saying. I really do, and I'm being honest with you. I am torn."

"About what?"

"Zarah and I don't have much in common. You know I married her with the intent of merging Harmonious Energy and DMI. At the time I was focused on enlarging DMI, taking it into international territory."

"Don't remind me," she mumbled.

"But I wasn't the only one out to get something from this arrangement. Zarah's father wanted a husband for his only daughter. So we both agreed to the marriage for mutual benefit. The reality is that there has never been any genuine love or affection between us."

"You have some type of connection. She's pregnant."

Joel didn't have to get into the specifics. Zarah's pregnancy was an accident, but his mother didn't have to know. He'd stick to reasons she could appreciate, even if she didn't grant him the acceptance he sought. "I just don't see how this is going to work with Zarah. We have different religions, which is an unavoidable problem."

"You act like it's a new piece of information. You knew about her beliefs when you got married. What right do you have to change the rules this late in the process?"

"I'm sorry you don't agree with me, but I have to do what's right for me and my family."

"I am your family too," she reminded him. "And I need you to be a father to my grandchild. I'm asking you to make the sacrifice and go home."

Joel let his gaze slip down. "It's not that easy. I'll have to figure out what to do. Some decisions you just can't make on your own, no matter how hard you try. This is one of those decisions. So I'll have to depend on God to give me direction." he said, feeling powerless. He let his finger and thumb massage his temples as a headache crept up. Until he got out of this state of limbo he found himself in, he suspected there would be many headaches to follow.

Chapter 20

Zarah had arranged to meet Tamara at a café downtown in about an hour. They hadn't spoken since Tamara scheduled the magazine interview for her last week. Once she decided to lead the company, Zarah's schedule had suddenly become very busy. She'd stayed up late the past four nights, reading through important papers related to Harmonious Energy. She had a list of questions and hoped that Tamara might be able to help her figure out the answers to them. Besides doing the work, Zarah was eager to get out of the house and enjoy the cool fall days. She was gathering a tall stack of papers together when the doorbell rang. Immediately afterward the housekeeper came into the kitchen, followed by Ann.

"I'm pleased to see you," Zarah told Ann, offering her a seat at the table.

"I was very shocked to get your call. I thought you'd be in India by now," Ann said.

"I may go for a holiday, but this is my home." A month ago Zarah wouldn't have dared speak with such certainty. But ever since she received the news of her pregnancy and then decided to run Harmonious Energy, her confidence had soared. "I must tell you, I'm having a baby," she said, bursting with pride.

Ann was beaming. "Congratulations. I am most happy for you. This is what you wanted."

Ecstatic, Zarah responded, "Yes, it is."

"Now I see why you didn't go to India," Ann said.

"Yes, now that I am having a baby, I don't want to travel. I will go for a visit after the baby is born." Zarah didn't share her entire plan with Ann or anyone else. The only way she would go to India was with a baby and a husband, nothing less. The baby was secure. The Joel portion of the plan needed more work.

"This is very good news. You're having a child."

"Joel is too," Zarah stated.

"Of course. How is your husband? The last time we spoke, he was ending my job with you."

"Ah, he's very troubled, but we don't want to talk about him now," Zarah said, flailing her hands softly in the air.

"Very well," Ann said, taking off her jacket.

"No, no, you may want to keep it on," Zarah said.

"Why?"

"Because I'm meeting Joel's sister downtown. She's going to help me go through these documents. I'd very much like for you to come with me."

Ann appeared unsure. "I can't come today. I have a doctor's appointment and then a job interview this afternoon."

Zarah peered at her and said, "Cancel your interview."

"Why would I do that? I need a job since your husband let me go."

"And I'm rehiring you."

"What? Why? What will your husband say? No, this is not a good idea."

"It is the best idea. I'm going to buy my father's company and run it myself." Ann appeared confused. "This is a very big job, and I will need your help. You are very smart, and I need smart people to help me." Zarah leaned close to the table. "You must say yes."

"I don't know," Ann said, frowning. "If you're sure it will be okay with Joel."

"I'm giving you the job this time, not Joel. You are my assistant, and I can give you the job if I'd like. He has no say."

"Then, yes, absolutely, I'll take the job."

Zarah felt good. She was beginning to make her own decisions without depending on Joel or Kumar. There was much to learn, but she wasn't afraid.

"Wonderful. Can you start tomorrow?"

"I will be here tomorrow. I guess you want me to come here? Is this where we're going to work?"

"We can use Joel's office down the hall for now, but we have to get a temporary office at DMI or a permanent one somewhere else."

"Then finding office space will be my first task for us," Ann stated.

"That's why I'm so very pleased to have you working with me again, but I must hurry. I'm late."

Ann departed. Zarah pulled a long scarf from the coat closet and grabbed the phone.

"This is Zarah Mitchell. Please send a car to my house. I'd like to go downtown," she told the car service. The driver would be there in twenty minutes. It gave her time to finish dressing and stuffing her bag. She was bubbling with energy for the first time in a long while. Her queasiness was minimal this morning. She got ready quickly and waited at the front door for the car.

When the car arrived, she handed an address to the driver; the one Tamara had given her earlier. After a thirty-minute ride, she was standing in front of the café. She tossed the tail end of her scarf across her shoulder and entered the café. She panned the room without seeing Tamara. When she was about to approach the counter, she saw Tamara standing in the corner and waving her over.

"You made it," Tamara said, sitting down once Zarah reached the table.

"Yes. I am sorry for being late. I was delayed by a meeting with my assistant." Zarah took a seat.

Tamara sipped from a cup. "I haven't heard you talk about her much lately. I didn't think she was working for you any longer."

"She wasn't. I hired her today, and I'm very pleased."

"Really? You hired her back? Wow, that's great." Tamara took another sip. "You're really serious about taking charge of your life. I'm impressed," she said.

Zarah was delighted to get the support and the praise. She hadn't heard such words from Joel, not yet. But the day was coming. She was sure of it.

Tamara set her cup down and slapped a magazine on the table. "Have you seen this?" she asked, opening the magazine and sliding it across to Zarah. "They did a fantastic job."

Zarah stared at the picture of herself on one page and an article on the other. She was in her favorite royal blue sari trimmed in gold. "I have not seen this."

"It's good, really good. You interview very well." When Tamara suggested the article to Zarah, it had seemed like a solid idea. Tamara was even more convinced after reading the flattering comments about Zarah throughout the article. Tamara had to admit, one of the best parts was that Joel's name was not mentioned at all. She was elated about the omission. Her brother was going to be boiling mad. *Great,* Tamara thought.

Zarah blushed. "I'll read it now and return this to you."

"No, you keep this copy. I'll get another one." Tamara signaled for the waitress. "Do you want something to drink? Coffee or tea?"

The waitress came to the table, and Tamara ordered a refill.

"I'll have tea and milk," Zarah told the waitress, who jotted down their orders and then left the table.

"Milk, huh?"

"It's the Indian way to drink tea," Zarah said, feeling stronger than she had in months. Good fortune and blessings were coming her way. She silently thanked her gods. "I must thank you for encouraging me to do this article." She nodded at Tamara as an expression of appreciation. "I wonder if Joel has read the article."

"Who cares?" Tamara responded instantly.

"I do. Maybe I should call him."

"No, you're not," Tamara said. Zarah wasn't convinced. "You're in a good place, for a change. You're finally taking charge. Don't digress now. You've been there for him. Now it's your time to let him chase you. Sit back and wait for him to step up."

Tamara was slightly on edge watching Zarah's resolve weaken. She was prepared to help Zarah maintain her momentum by any means required. Zarah was too close to owning Harmonious Energy outright, and Tamara was too close to getting the West Coast division. There was no room for Joel in the equation. He wanted to be outside of Zarah's world, and Tamara was more than willing to help him remain there until she got her slice of the company. With so much at stake, Tamara had to press hard.

"Don't give into his childish whims. Be strong and make your family proud," she told Zarah.

It was obvious to Tamara that Zarah was reluctant to follow her advice, but her friend eventually agreed. Tamara felt guilty for pushing her, but not enough to back off. She didn't dare, otherwise Joel would swoop in like a vulture over wounded prey and gobble up both her and Zarah's future. He had to be stopped. As far as Tamara was concerned, they were merely getting started with teaching Joel the many lessons he had earned.

Chapter 21

Joel was grateful to have stumbled upon a small park in the western suburbs of Detroit. He rested on a bench, soaking in the filtered sunlight, not needing his sunglasses. The chilly air was a reminder that the sunny days were fleeting and winter wasn't far off.

It didn't take long for him to realize the gravity of his situation as he sat in that remote park. Confusion and craziness abounded and seemed to be hunting Joel down daily. He stared at the captivating woman gracing the article in the center of the Detroit magazine and wondered what other shocking revelation was waiting to trip him up. He was accustomed to seeing Zarah dressed in Indian garb, but her clothes seemed fancier than normal. He wondered if it was the photographer's lighting or if maybe she'd been touched up. There was plenty to speculate about, and Joel wondered if what he was glimpsing in Zarah had always existed. Perhaps seeing Zarah in their home every day had clouded her radiance. The glow in her eyes slapped him in the face. He found it difficult to stare at the picture and acknowledge that this was his wife, the woman from whom he was estranged. He couldn't take his eyes off her.

Fifteen minutes passed as he devoured the article, which was entitled "SPICING UP THE MOTOR CITY." Joel savored each word, particularly the paragraphs about her goals. She wanted to grow the company so that it had a place of dominance in its market sector. Where did that come from he wondered. The reporter had asked what qualified her to run a multimillion-dollar company. Joel was intrigued as he read her answer. He'd never seen her express any interest in business. As a matter of fact, she seemed to avoid business-related topics as much as possible. He was learning several new and intriguing tidbits about her. The article was interesting, and he wanted to keep reading.

He was disappointed that this side of Zarah hadn't surfaced when they were living together. She'd elected to show him the demure, maternal side, which didn't make him feel exhilarated. But this woman in the article was a different person, someone he wanted to know. She was someone he could do business with. She wasn't the Zarah Mitchell he'd married. He returned his focus to the article, determined to learn more about this version of her.

"We understand that you own a division of DMI, a well-known Detroit-based company. What are your plans for the division?" the article read. *"I do own the division, but I have not come to a final decision about the future. There are many options for me with the division. The success of this company is most important to me. This is my father's company, and as his only child, it is my duty to do good work and have his blessings. I must take time to put together a very good plan."*

Joel laid the magazine down on the bench and scratched his head. Where was this coming from? When they were living together, she didn't engage in any business conversations with him. He had figured she was just a shy, pretty girl whose primary goal was to be a wife and mother. Both jobs were important, but at his age, he yearned for more in a mate. He rapped his knuckles on the magazine but didn't open it again. In a million years he wouldn't have guessed she had this in her.

He sat quietly reflecting on the article and his marriage. An equal blend of doubt, about the West Coast division mixed with his interest in the woman featured in the article created an indescribable anxiety. Unable to suppress his curiosity, Joel leapt to his feet. He would pay Zarah a visit, hoping to get the West Coast division from her and to use it as a pawn to get back into DMI. He'd check on the pregnancy too. Zarah deserved his support, and he aimed to give it freely for the baby.

Joel walked briskly to the car, feeling quite motivated. His future could be taking a turn for the better. He yearned to return to DMI, and Zarah might be the ticket. He'd soon see.

Chapter 22

Joel called the house and learned that Zarah was out. Determined to make contact with her, he called her on the cell phone, and she picked up.

"Zarah, are you available to meet with me?" he said without asking her where she was.

"Yes, I am," she said.

He was glad Zarah had answered right away. He wasn't able to tell from the tone of her voice how she was feeling about their last encounter, but maybe the fact that she had picked up the phone was a positive sign. "I know you're not at the house, but I can meet you somewhere else if it's easier."

"I am at a café downtown," she replied.

Venturing out to quaint spots in the city wasn't something the Zarah he knew would do. She was acting more and more like a person he didn't know but wanted to.

"It will take me about forty minutes to get there. Can you wait for me?" He heard voices in the background. There was a series of thumps, and he wondered if she'd dropped or fumbled the phone. "Zarah, are you there?"

"Yes, I am here. I will wait for you."

She gave him the address, and Joel punched the gas pedal. His sudden burst of curiosity was undeniable. He was actually excited to see Zarah, the new one. His anticipation made him press the gas pedal harder, and the forty-minute drive flew by. Joel double-checked the address and peered up and down the street until the café sign was in sight. He found a parking garage with an attendant a half block away and left his Range Rover, the vehicle he drove mostly around town. As he hurried to the café, he paused to straighten his shirt.

Joel entered the café and placed his sunglasses on top of his head as he searched the room for Zarah. She was dressed in her Indian outfit, so it didn't take him long to spot her. He shuffled to the corner and stopped in his tracks. There was Tamara, someone he was not prepared to see. The enthusiasm that had propelled him to the café waned suddenly.

He went to Zarah. She was more radiant than ever. Her long dark hair cascaded along her shoulders, accentuating her olive-colored skin and captivating dark-colored eyes. There was an energy about her that he couldn't deny. She stood, and they embraced briefly. He wanted to ignore Tamara and focus purely on Zarah.

"Hello, little brother," Tamara said, causing him to shriek inside, but he kept his cool.

He slid into the booth, next to Zarah, and placed his sunglasses on the table.

"Hello, ladies," he said, searching for words that wouldn't get Zarah or Tamara riled up. His last encounter with both of them had gone very poorly. He didn't want a repeat, but Tamara's mouth was usually an automatic spark for trouble. He'd try to avoid any conflict for Zarah's sake. She was the reason he was there.

"So what have you been up to, Mr. Joel?" Tamara asked.

"Keeping busy doing a little of this and a little of that." He grinned to hide his irritation with her presence at the table. She'd already crossed the line of respect by calling him in Chicago to discuss his marriage. Maybe she'd leave and then he could talk freely to Zarah.

Tamara wasn't easily fooled by Joel, but she knew Zarah was. His calling and showing up once a week had to be demoralizing. One flattering word and Zarah would succumb to Joel's whims. Tamara didn't want Joel sniffing around and possibly realizing how vulnerable his wife was. As a devoted friend, Tamara believed it was her job to make sure Zarah was impervious to Joel's tricks. Her defense mechanisms were in high gear. Every word crawling out of his mouth was going to be scrutinized. Zarah had come too far out of her shell to let a hug from a so-called husband derail her progress. Tamara had too much invested and too much to lose to let them reunite. Joel had to be stopped, and Tamara decided she was the perfect person to do it. She stirred her latte, ready to jump into battle.

"Why did you want to see Zarah?" she asked.

Joel chuckled and fumbled with his sunglasses before answering. He leaned back in the booth, put his arm around Zarah, and stared Tamara down. "I can see my wife whenever I want to," he said with a smug tone.

Tamara wanted to reach across the table and stuff a scone down his throat. She didn't necessarily want to hurt Joel, just shut him up.

"What's it to you?" he asked when Tamara was silent.

"She's my friend, and I look out for her."

"Wonderful. I'm glad she has a friend," he said, wrapping his arm tighter around Zarah. "But she has a husband too."

The waitress approached the table. "Can I get anyone anything?"

"No," Tamara said, so harshly that she had to apologize.

"I'll take a double espresso," Joel said, then turned to Zarah. "Would you like something else?" he asked.

She told him no, but the question alone infuriated Tamara. His soft words and icy heart weren't fooling her. "Zarah, did you want to walk through the company's staffing plan later this evening or tomorrow?" Tamara asked, wishing Joel would get bored and exit.

He turned to Zarah again. "I was wondering if we could go to dinner later."

Tamara saw the delight in Zarah's reaction. She smiled, drew herself closer to Joel, and had a giddy look on her face. Tamara had to work fast to save the fawn from the poacher's trap. "Didn't you want to meet with Don and the board of directors as soon as possible with your purchase offer?"

Zarah nodded. "Yes."

"Then you'll want to keep plowing through these documents," Tamara advised. "I can stay as long as you'd like, because there's a lot of work ahead of us."

"If you need help, I'm here," Joel offered.

"Thank you," Zarah said, sounding as if she was going to melt in Joel's presence.

Tamara cringed.

Zarah excused herself from the group and went to the restroom, which gave Tamara the ideal opportunity to get Joel out of there.

"She doesn't need your help," Tamara snapped.

"I don't get it. What's with you?"

"That's a loaded question," she stated.

"I don't think so. It's very simple, if you ask me. You're the friend, or whatever," he said, pointing at her, "and I'm the husband."

The waitress eased Joel's cup onto the table without disrupting the conversation. With the way it was heating up, Tamara figured someone should break up the sparing match. Mitchell against Mitchell was most likely going to be a fight to the death. In their family, backing down wasn't plausible if one wanted to survive among the wolves.

"How funny is this? You're *boasting* about being her husband?" Tamara was agitated beyond reason. "You, the same man who shows up once in a while to see how your pregnant wife is doing? Pu-lease! Why don't you crawl back under a rock and leave Zarah alone? She's finally getting a life, without you," she told him.

"Listen up. News flash," Joel snarled. "She's still my wife, and she's carrying my baby. Like it or not, I will always have a connection with Zarah. Can you say the same thing, *friend?*"

Zarah returned to the table as the flames of agitation resonated. Joel rose and let his wife slide into the booth next to him.

"Zarah, can I speak with you privately?" he said, not looking in Tamara's direction.

"Don't fall for his games, Zarah. Stand up for yourself. You don't need him." Tamara noticed a few stares coming from around the café. She consciously lowered her voice, wanting to get her point across without making a public scene. She was mad but not crazy.

"Tamara, it's okay," Zarah interjected. "I want to speak with Joel."

"You don't have to give in to his whims. You can say no and let him walk away," Tamara told her.

"You heard my wife. We're going to talk," he said. "Without you." Joel waved to her. "See you around, Ms. Mitchell."

His glibness threatened to send Tamara over the edge, but she refused to have a shouting match in the café. She had to give him this round, confident more would follow. Tamara gathered her belongings in haste. She couldn't wait to get outside and scream to vent her frustration. Being around Joel and enduring his infantile tactics was too much. But before walking out, she'd give him one final jab.

Tamara leaned in so close to his ear, she was absolutely certain Zarah wouldn't hear her. "I'm watching you, my brother. Know that I'm not Zarah. You can't fool me with this lovey-dovey talk all of a sudden. You're a snake, and it's just a matter of time before my foot crushes your head." She pulled back and grinned.

Joel reciprocated with a grin. "Good-bye. Have a nice afternoon" he said pausing and then added, "alone."

She dug deep to avoid lashing out in retaliation. "I'll call you later," she told Zarah.

"Yes, we will speak soon. Thank you for helping me."

"You're welcome," Tamara said and reluctantly left the café as her fear that her efforts would be erased rapidly escalated.

Chapter 23

Joel relaxed as he watched Tamara walk out the door. Finally, he could talk with Zarah without fighting with his sister. His newfound interest in Zarah had diminished slightly due to Tamara's involvement in Zarah's affairs, but it was nothing major. What had been lost could be rekindled if she kept intriguing him as she'd done thus far. He slid to the edge of the seat in order to absorb her presence. Her beauty shouldn't be a surprise to him, yet it was.

"I'm glad you agreed to meet with me alone."

She nodded, and that was the extent of her reply. This was the point where she would normally become giddy. She didn't, and that caught him off guard and forced him to steer the conversation.

"I guess you and Tamara were working on Harmonious Energy business."

"We were doing quite a lot for a meeting I must have next Thursday with Don and the DMI directors."

He was uneasy talking about DMI. When Joel had stepped down a few months ago, he'd also resigned from his spot on the board of directors. At the time, his decision had seemed right. In hindsight it was a mistake. Being on the fringes of DMI action was equivalent to having a knife stuck in his chest. Every time he heard what was happening at the company without his involvement, it was as if the knife was given a sharp twist. The pain was brutal, and Joel wasn't sure how much longer he could stay away.

Zarah had to let him take over the West Coast division. It was the only leverage he could use to get a foot in the door at DMI. His desperation began turning into despair. He'd have to be careful. Mistakes and poor choices were often made under duress. He knew that too well. He'd move on to a less volatile subject until his composure was intact and business matters didn't cause him angst.

"How are you doing with the pregnancy?"

Her cheeks glowed, and her countenance softened. He'd made the right decision in changing the subject.

"The doctor says I'm doing well," she said, patting her stomach. "I want to be a good mother."

"And you will be." He had no doubt. "But how are you going to run a company and take care of a new baby?"

"I'm not sure, but I will. I must," she said, not sounding as sure.

This was the break he needed to offer his services. "I'm here if you need help with the company. You can take care of the baby, and I can take care of the company. We could be a great team."

She didn't answer.

The silence was discouraging, and he felt forced to break it. "What do you think?" he asked.

"I can't let you run the company," she told him.

"Why not?"

"It is my destiny to run my father's company. I must prove to you and to my father's memory that I'm able to do well with the company. I must do this."

Joel actually understood, and he respected her position, but hated that she had to grow a professional backbone at the precise time when he needed her to lose interest. Oddly, his passion was ignited when he heard her take a stand and set goals. She was fueling his passion to a level that he could not readily overlook. He scooted closer to her. Usually, marriage wasn't in his thoughts.

Zarah was changing that scenario. He scooted even closer. There wasn't much distance between them until she pulled away.

He refused to let her get too far away. He was on the verge of thinking about coming home, but then his dignity kicked in. He was desperate for a job and drawn to her intimately, but he wasn't going to use the baby as a pawn. If he returned to Zarah and the marriage, it would be based on his feelings and a commitment to the relationship. The baby didn't need to bear the brunt of a trying and complex relationship, the way he'd had to do as a child. Zarah was supposed to be the solution to his problems, but it seemed as though this door was closed to him. He'd have to find another way to get his hands on the West Coast division, one that wouldn't carry the stench of guilt for taking advantage of a woman who loved him. He'd find another way. He had to.

Joel and Zarah chatted for over an hour. Other than her frequent trips to the restroom, nothing interrupted them. They'd never talked as freely, as engagingly. Who was this woman sitting next to him? She wasn't the meek person whose father had presented her for marriage.

"Have you been sticking with Indian food, or do you venture out?" he asked. When Zarah came to the States, she had difficulty eating American dishes. For several months he took her to the same group of Indian restaurants. She tried to be accommodating by eating basic American dishes, but it didn't work.

"I have found many new foods I like. There are thousands of places to eat. I'm sure there will be many more foods to my liking."

When they were together, she'd go out to eat infrequently. He hadn't been gone this long for her to make this many changes. Yet he had to admit they'd been separated for most of the marriage. He was either at the office or in Chicago, while she stayed at home and hibernated. Her willingness to get out of the house and enjoy the area heightened her appeal. An edgy, risk-taking woman who appreciated fun was his kind of person. He'd never before viewed her in terms of liking and loving. Peering at her as they sat in the most remote corner of the quaint café, he decided that he should rethink his position.

"I meant what I said about taking you to dinner tonight."

"I'm not sure," she said, looking away.

He followed her gaze, not wanting to lose the connection that was igniting his soul.

"Excuse me, but I am feeling tired. I should go home and rest before dinner," Zarah said.

"Sure, of course," Joel said.

"I have to call the car service."

"Oh no," he said. "Please let me take you home."

"I don't want to be any trouble."

"I want to take you," he said, lightly tapping his chest. Joel wanted to prolong their interaction any way he could.

The ride home was uneventful, a definite improvement from the drama and trauma he'd experienced over the past three weeks. Simple was refreshing, soothing. He dropped her off, giving her a peck on the cheek, and eased out of the driveway, more confused about their relationship than he had been before seeing Zarah. A feeling of emptiness fell over him. The ride to the hotel was arduous, as the tranquility he'd experienced at the café was a mirage, disappearing with each mile he traveled. Despair took hold when he acknowledged that the chances of his business venture getting off the ground were fading. What he was going to do next still had to be determined.

Joel continued reflecting. Finally, at the end of the road, he had no other choice but to pray for guidance. He had toyed with seeking God again. He'd specifically prayed about his marriage and a business opportunity nearly a month ago, when he first got news Zarah was pregnant. God wasn't moving too quickly. Instead of waiting, Joel had opted to take another route. Unfortunately, he'd run into one dead end after another.

He pulled the SUV up to the curb and killed the purring engine a few blocks from the hotel. Joel gripped the leather steering wheel tightly. The words didn't flow as they once had when he addressed God. He was rusty but desperate. "God, I need your help. I can't seem to pull it together. I need you to tell me what to do." He stayed in the vehicle, expecting an answer in return, but in his heart, Joel knew God didn't work that way. Early in his career at DMI, he'd learned to conform his will to God's leading. That was when he'd realized unimaginable success. Somehow his perspective had turned in the complete opposite direction. Somewhere along the way his impatience had taken control and forced him to take action in those instances when God wasn't speaking quickly enough. His results hadn't been good, but he was too far down the path to change overnight.

Waiting and listening weren't feats he performed well. He sat in the car a while longer, hearing and sensing nothing from God, experiencing no rush of peace or flood of wisdom. He'd prayed, and there wasn't a change. The lingering tidbits of hope he'd retained enabled him to cling to the notion that God was giving him a second chance no matter how badly his situation appeared. He couldn't wait indefinitely, though. While God's plan was materializing, Joel decided to keep busy in the interim. He was going to create his own opportunity and forget about the West Coast division, which Zarah was controlling. He was going after the Southern division, the slice of DMI he'd sold to a group of shady investors during his downhill slide.

Joel pulled out his phone to dial his uncle Frank to set up a meeting. His father's brother was in the business of orchestrating unconventional loans and deals. *Heaven help me,* Joel thought. Dealing with Frank Mitchell was truly the last resort and a low point in his route to restoration. He stomped out the negative thoughts, choosing to stay upbeat, although it was an oxymoron when used in the same sentence as "Uncle Frank." Briefly, he reconsidered initiating contact with his uncle but decided to proceed. No one else was giving him a chance, not the long list of investors in Chicago, not Don at DMI, not Abigail, not his wife, and not even God. He winced. He'd tried the right way to get on track, but failure had lined his path. Now it was time to get results the only other way he knew how—by any means necessary. He made the call, feeling charged up and ready to go.

Chapter 24

Wednesday was steamrolling toward quitting time. Madeline was in her office, having resumed her executive marketing role to help Don stabilize the company. There was more work to do, but she was going to pack up early tonight and call it quits around four. Late nights at DMI used to be the norm, but that changed after returning from her recent sabbatical. The persistent need to stay late to conduct DMI business had faded. Her drive and tenacity just weren't there. Perhaps the months away from the company had changed her in a way she couldn't readily identify, or maybe the fact that her children didn't want to run the company together had drained her zeal. Whatever the reason, she was going home early tonight, tomorrow night, definitely on Friday, and certainly until she could rekindle the fire within her.

She flipped to the next page of the Detroit monthly magazine. Her curiosity was piqued when she stumbled across a large photo labeled ZARAH BENGALI MITCHELL, followed by an article titled "SPICING UP THE MOTOR CITY." Madeline adjusted her reading glasses. She dived into the article, devouring each morsel.

Don poked his head in her office about fifteen minutes later. "Good. You're not in a meeting," he said and came in with papers in his hand.

"No meetings for me until ten tomorrow morning," she said, glancing up at him as the reading glasses rested near the tip of her nose.

"I wish I could say the same," he said.

Madeline read a few more lines. She had read three-quarters of the article and was eager to finish. Don took a seat.

"I have a few questions about the marketing budget you submitted," he announced.

She peeled her eyes away from the article. "Sure. No problem." She turned the magazine around and slid it toward the desk's edge. "Have you seen this?"

Don leaned closer to the desk. "What is it?"

"Joel's wife is featured in the business section." Madeline retrieved the magazine. "I didn't realize she was the professional type."

"I know. She shocked me last week, when I went to see her about the West Coast division. I expected her to be hands off and to get rid of the division as fast as she could."

Madeline flipped another page. "Apparently, it's not her plan. The article says she's up for the CEO position at Harmonious Energy."

"Precisely the impression I got," Don said.

"What are you going to do with Harmonious Energy, anyway?" Madeline said, taking off her glasses.

"I'm willing to sell her DMI's ownership stake."

"Really? You're willing to unload it?"

"Absolutely. I have to distance DMI from Harmonious Energy. We can have only one God directing our vision, the one of Abraham, Isaac, and Jacob."

"Oh, that's right. Zarah and her father practice a very different religion." She fumbled with her glasses, which were now folded on the desk. "I still can't get my arms around their religion. It was something about having energy in your soul that could be used in your next life. Shoot, as rough as this life has been, especially those crazy years with your father, one round of living is plenty for me. I'm not going through this life, only to end up as a rock or an ant or something worse. Nope, 'once and done' is my motto," she said, laughing.

Don laughed too. "I'm not sure Joel stopped and considered the ramifications of marrying Zarah and attempting to merge the companies."

"Oil and vinegar do not mix," Madeline said with her arms folded.

"Who's the vinegar?" Don asked.

"Doesn't matter. Those two never had a chance at merging two companies and two religions, let alone staying married."

"Oh, I didn't tell you. Zarah is pregnant."

"No way! Get out of here!" Madeline exclaimed. "When did that happen?"

"I don't know the details, and I'm not looking to find out. She just happened to tell me during my short meeting last week."

"Does this mean they're staying married?"

"I have no idea. I can say Joel has created a royal problem for himself."

"The poor boy. He can't seem to win for losing. One of these days he might get his act together, but by the sound of what you're saying, it's not going to be this week." She put her reading glasses on again. "This is odd, when you think about it. The Zarah I met several months ago was very timid. She had one goal, which was chasing after Joel Mitchell. He was her single priority. She didn't express the slightest interest in the company. What changed, and where does this leave us with regaining ownership of the West Coast division?"

"I'm not sure," Don answered.

Madeline was disheartened as she thought about how hard they were going to have to work in order to regain the West Coast division. "Do you think Joel is behind this?" she asked.

"I don't think so. When he came home last week, Joel seemed surprised to see me there. Zarah and Joel gave off an odd vibe together, so I left."

"This is getting weirder by the minute," Madeline stated.

"As far as the West Coast goes, Zarah shot me down when I made the offer. However, she definitely wants controlling interest in Harmonious Energy and we want our division," Don said.

"Sounds like a deal in the making to me," she said.

"I sure hope you're right," Don uttered. "Mother, back to what you were saying about Zarah. This is weird to see her step up in such a public way. If we're fortunate, Zarah will get tired of the businesswoman venture and eagerly sell the West Coast division to us at a fair market price. The sooner we close out this chapter of DMI, the better."

Madeline nodded in agreement.

"There's another twist I forgot to tell you about."

"What else could there possibly be?" she asked, peering over her glasses.

"Joel asked me for a job."

Madeline snapped the magazine closed. "At your company, LTI?"

"Well, maybe, but his preference is here at DMI."

She snatched her glasses off. "No way! I hope you told him to go jump in the river and swim upstream since he likes going against the current so much. Joel can work for any company stupid enough to hire him, as long as he leaves us alone. He can't come back here," she said, stretching out her arms. It had taken years to get him out so her children could assume their rightful places. She wasn't going backward. "I hope you told him to get lost."

"I didn't use those words, obviously, but the answer was no, at least until we figure out where we're headed."

"What do you mean?" Madeline asked, patting her hair flat on both sides. Don was frightening her. She'd worked too hard to let Joel slither back into DMI. Don had such a kind and forgiving heart. A schemer like Joel would take full advantage of him. She would have to diligently run interference to avoid complications with her plan. "We have to keep an executive position open for Tamara," Madeline said. When she saw his expression, she added, "I already know what you're going to say. Tamara doesn't want the position, not yet, but she'll see the light." Miracles were real. Madeline had become a believer after witnessing Tamara return home and show a willingness to at least be in the same room with her mother. Baby steps were bound to turn into a permanent reconciliation. "Trust me; she'll be here sooner or later."

"I'm glad you have faith, but this is ludicrous," Don replied. "Tamara has made it very clear she's not working here. She's starting her own business, Mother. Face it. She's not going to be able to help me. On top of that, Abigail is leaving, and I have LTI to run in addition to DMI."

"What am I? Chopped liver?" Madeline had encouraged Don to take over DMI from the instant Dave appointed Joel CEO of the company. She was growing tired but couldn't walk out on Don when he sorely needed her.

"No disrespect, Mother, but you're getting older. I doubt you're planning to work into your seventies."

He was correct. She was ready to hang up the corporate mantle and travel the world. With the free time, she might enroll in an art or cooking class, or take an adventure. The possibilities were endless. As long as she had her health and money, her retirement years would be fabulous. Now, if only she could get Don and DMI in order. The events of late told her that was a big "if."

Chapter 25

Joel didn't drive his Lamborghini. The car was too distinctive for his errand. He decelerated as he approached the airport exit and crawled along the frontage road, carefully looking for the Kings Buffet a few minutes before five p.m. He spotted the restaurant on the other side of the road. Joel whipped his SUV across two lanes, generating a series of horn blasts behind him. He sped through the intersection, where the light was yellow, catapulted by a sudden rush of adrenaline. Taking risks wasn't a drug he intentionally sought, but he welcomed risky propositions whenever they arose. Meeting in a clandestine location under the veil of impending darkness might have generated humiliation, doubt, or shame in someone else, but not in Joel. He was riding a wave of exhilaration. As soon as he maneuvered into a parking spot, Joel saw his uncle's two-seater Mercedes roll up next to him.

Over the years, the Mitchell name had taken a beating, thanks to Uncle Frank and his creative approach to financing. Joel had engaged in several deals with his uncle, and each had failed miserably. If placing blame would resolve his current dire dilemma, Joel would have plenty of justification for pointing his finger at his uncle. But clinging to mistakes of the past wasn't going to help him. He knew it and didn't expend the energy dwelling on it.

Without any prompting, Uncle Frank slid out of his Mercedes and into the passenger seat of Joel's vehicle.

"What's going on, nephew? I wasn't expecting a call from you last week. Word on the street is you flew the coop, packed up and left Detroit."

"Can't always believe what you hear," Joel told Uncle Frank. "Are we going inside?"

"Nah, no need," Uncle Frank said. "We can converse here. It's as good a place as any."

Joel pressed his back against the driver's side door to get a better view of his uncle.

"I know you didn't come out here to chitchat. What do you want?" Uncle Frank said.

Not much had changed. Joel wasn't put off by his uncle's brashness. Actually, he appreciated his uncle's candor. Frank wasn't known for being the most law-abiding citizen in town, having embezzled money from DMI and others, but he was direct.

"I'm interested in making a deal," Joel revealed.

"Exactly what kind of deal are we talking about?"

"The Southern division, I want it back."

Uncle Frank slapped his thigh and let out a guttural chuckle, which made Joel uneasy. This might truly be his last chance to slide onto the big corporate stage. He was serious, but he was afraid Uncle Frank didn't think so.

"We've had this conversation before, and it didn't go anywhere." Uncle Frank reached for the door handle. "I agreed to this rendezvous because you're my nephew, but I don't let anybody waste my time. You know that much about me. Shoot, your nonsense is going to make me late for dinner. I'm out of here."

Before he could open the door, Joel yelled out, "Wait. I'm serious this time." When he'd met with his uncle many months ago, Joel wouldn't pay the ridiculously inflated price the new owner wanted for the division. It was worth three hundred million when Joel originally lost it to Uncle Frank's investors. The division was collateral on a deal gone bad. The very next day, the price nearly doubled. At the time Joel was the CEO of DMI, and they'd just purchased a stake in Harmonious Energy. Their cash reserves were depleted, and there were no funds available to make the purchase. That was nearly six months ago. Time had softened his anger toward Uncle Frank and his private investors. Add in desperation, and there he sat, in a parking lot with the man who possibly held the key to his comeback.

"Are you telling me you have the kind of cash these guys are looking to collect for the division? Because you couldn't come up with any real money a few months ago. What's changed?"

Joel didn't have the money then and he didn't have it now, but he wasn't going to let his chance at redemption waltz out of the car without a monstrous plea. There had to be a way to make this deal work. Joel hadn't completely vetted his plan, so he'd resort to his best option for now—a lie.

"Come on, Uncle. I know you as well as anybody." He chuckled to relieve his anxiety and to camouflage his fear. His uncle was an alligator who thrived on fear and could detect it a mile away. Joel did the best acting of his life. His future was riding on his performance. "Would I show up here without having the funds to orchestrate a deal with your people?" His palms were moistening. He gripped the steering wheel with one hand to continue masking his anxiety.

Uncle Frank stared at Joel, making him more uneasy. Finally, his uncle said, "You better be for real, because you know the people who own the division don't play games. You know this." Uncle Frank was pointing his index finger at him. Oh, Joel knew too well. "And while you're coughing up dollars for this venture, don't forget my consulting fee."

"How could I ever forget?"

What were they doing? It was crazy, Joel thought. He was sitting with the former chief financial officer of DMI, the man he had to fire due to his shady dealings. Joel found it difficult to calculate how far they had both fallen. He recalled how fondly his father had spoken about Uncle Frank, about his loyalty and his hard-hitting success during the start-up years. His father had told Joel that the relationship with Uncle Frank was broken after he divorced Madeline and married Sherry. For some reason, Uncle Frank never got over his brother's personal failure. Fast-forward and here Joel was, with Uncle Frank, on the outskirts of town and the Mitchell Empire. Joel drew in a breath. As much as he'd like to blame someone or something for his predicament, Joel didn't. This was on him, his doing. But he had a deep-seated desire to fix his string of bad luck one way or another.

Joel was pleased about his appeal until Uncle Frank continued.

"Look here, nephew. Believe it or not, I like you. So don't take this personal, but I can't take an IOU from you. Word on the street is that you're broke. I need cash up front."

"I can handle my business."

"So you can put your hands on about seven hundred million for the sale, plus another couple million for my fee?"

"Seven hundred? This is higher than the number you gave me six months ago. This is crazy. I sold them the division for three hundred. How can they expect me to pay twice the original price?"

"It's called business, young brother."

Joel wasn't as successful in hanging on to his wishful thinking as he'd been with Uncle Frank. Hope packed up and jumped out the window, running from the car so fast that Joel had no way of catching a break. "I don't have seven hundred."

"How much do you have?" Uncle Frank muttered.

"Maybe three hundred and fifty million." In order to actually come up with that sum, he'd have to liquidate his remaining assets, about three hundred million, and get another twenty-five from both his mother and Sheba.

"I thought you were serious. You're wasting my time, and you know I don't like that." Grasping for an opportunity, Joel begged his uncle to present the offer.

"I'm not going in there with a few dollars, so get real," his uncle stated.

"I'm begging you," Joel said, gripping his uncle's arm.

Uncle Frank jerked his arm away. "You have issues, son, but I like you. Consider this your once-in-a-lifetime favor. It's a ridiculous move, but I'll put a feeler out to see if there are any takers."

"Thank you," Joel said, calming down. The venture had a slim chance of coming to fruition, but he didn't have anything else to hold on to. Hope was way down the road, and pity was banging on the door, trying to get in. He would hold off pity as long as he could, but the barricade was weakening.

Chapter 26

Joel stayed in the right lane on I-94 as he headed to Detroit. A string of cars shot around him, prompting him to at least get his speed up to fifty. He was consumed by his meeting with Uncle Frank. The tranquility he'd soaked up with Zarah earlier at the café had faded. Joel had driven miles and couldn't recall a single sign, car, or face of a passerby. He was at a crossroads both literally and figuratively, with I-94 splitting into multiple routes. He could go to the Westin, to DMI, or to his house with Zarah. None called out to him with certainty. Although he had planned on having dinner with Zarah later, he would stop by his mother's first. It was a place where he was always welcomed. Belief in him was what he craved, a kind word of support without judgment or demands. Fired up, he pressed the accelerator.

The locks hadn't been changed at the estate. He used the same key his father and Madeline had used when they built the house forty-plus years ago. It was the one constant in the Mitchell family. The occupants of the house had changed over the years—his mother trading places with Madeline, and he with his four siblings—but not the locks. It wasn't much, but the fact that one tiny detail of his existence had remained constant was settling. An eerie calm fell over Joel.

"Mom, are you here?" he called out, walking through the main level of the house.

His mother descended the stairs partway. “I’m here. What are you doing here? This is twice in one week. What’s going on?”

He ran up the stairs and gave her a gigantic embrace. She was the other constant in a world spinning out of control. Through the rough spots, she had remained by his side, and he was appreciative. He squeezed her tighter.

“Put me down, mister. Thank you very much,” Sherry said. “Why are you so happy?”

The words startled him. He hadn’t truly been happy in months, maybe closer to a year. Maybe he was on the verge of a new beginning, and happy was fine with him. “I’m happy to see you.”

“Sure,” Sherry said, walking the rest of the way down the stairs. “Are you hungry?”

“No, not really.”

“Well, I am,” Sherry said. “Walk with me to the kitchen. The cook made chicken masala and a nice salad before she left. Why don’t you join me for dinner?”

“I’ll have to pass. I’m meeting Zarah later for dinner.”

“That’s wonderful.”

“Don’t get your hopes up. We’re just having dinner.”

“At least it’s a start,” Sherry said. When they reached the kitchen, his mother took a plate from the cabinet. “I guess its more food for me.”

“I’m not going to let you eat alone. I’ll grab a bite,” he said. “Let me fix the plates. You have a seat,” he said, gently tugging at the plates. She handed them over and sat at the table.

“I hope you’re going to be this attentive to Zarah. Pregnancy is a beautiful experience, but wives need their husband’s support.”

Without warning Joel felt the air being sucked out of the room. He slid down the bunny hole to his den of despair and impending failure. “Can we use this visit to talk about us for a change?” Joel said, trying to soften the edge in his voice.

“You sound a little testy. I’m glad you’re working out your differences with Zarah. She needs you. There is nothing more important than you being a supportive husband to your wife and a good father to your child, nothing.”

Regret filled him. If he’d passed on the stupid plate of chicken masala and hit the road ten minutes ago, this lashing would have been avoided. Joel spooned a very light serving of food onto his plate, wanting his mother to stop needling him. He wasn’t going to be disrespectful, but he had no intention of engaging in a tense discussion about his marriage. He wasn’t going to do it, not tonight. Uncle Frank had already put plenty on Joel’s mind, and miraculously, he’d been able to keep standing. A conversation about Zarah might be the knockout punch, and so it had to be avoided.

“Can we change the subject and enjoy our visit? What do you say?” Joel set one of the plates in front of his mother and the other opposite her and took a seat.

His mother picked at the plate with her fork.

“Joel, I’m not trying to pester you about Zarah.”

Sure seemed like she was, he thought.

She lifted her napkin to the corner of her eye and dabbed it. “But you have to understand where I’m coming from. I used to be Zarah, a young, impressionable woman who fell in love with an outgoing, well-known, and highly successful man. You are your father. You’re suave and very captivating, just like he was. Before I realized what was happening, I was in love with your father. I revolved around him. I gobbled up every minute with him like he was my oxygen. I couldn’t function without him in those early years together.” She dabbed the corner of her eye again, and Joel suddenly felt more compassion for her.

She went on. "Don't get me wrong. Your father was an incredible man, but none of us had one hundred percent of him." Joel guessed she was referring to the fact that his father's loyalty had been split between her and Madeline, his wife and God, his wife and DMI, and his wife and two sets of children. He let her continue talking without interrupting. "I don't want my grandchild reliving the trauma I watched you endure. And don't forget about what happened to Madeline's children. When Dave moved out, the children didn't have a father in the house, and they suffered."

"Mom, you told me this a few weeks ago. Do we really have to talk about this again?"

"I do, because Madeline is wrong about me stealing her husband. They had been divorced for over a year when he asked me to marry him. I know he didn't want a divorce. She was the one who ended the marriage. Doesn't matter now. She acts crazy most of the time, but there's some truth in her accusations. After the divorce, those children didn't have a father in the house. Look what happened. Andre raped Tamara. Sam killed him in retaliation and then committed suicide."

"You can't blame Dad for what happened."

"I'm not blaming anyone, only pointing out the facts. Dave and Madeline divorced, and the children paid the price." She touched his hand. "I don't want heartache for you and your family. Please, fix this with Zarah," she said, no longer dabbing her eyes but wiping them.

Joel was touched. "Mom, don't let this get you worked up. I hear what you're saying, and I'm listening. I will figure this out, trust me," he said.

Her story was compelling. He wanted to address his marriage woes, but Joel had to focus on reestablishing a business presence. Letting his wife carry the financial load wasn't the way. But his mother's plea did seep in. He had an obligation to his child.

He gave his mother a hug and a peck on the forehead. "You have me thinking. I have somewhere to be. I'll call you later," he said, setting his plate in the sink. He stopped in the doorway. "Thank you," he said and blew her a kiss.

It was his duty to check on Zarah and the baby. When he got outside, Joel pulled out his phone and called Zarah to follow through on the dinner plans. Not feeling well, she declined his invitation. Joel didn't settle for no. He wanted to see her and asked if it was okay to come for a visit. She sounded pleased and agreed. He was pleased too.

Excitement propelled him back to his house in the northwestern suburb of Detroit. There was a sweet and tantalizing flavor on his lips from the simple kiss he'd deposited on his wife's cheek that afternoon. Joel had a key to his house, but he chose to knock. He didn't want to startle Zarah. He raised his fist to knock, and then lowered it. He couldn't explain his hesitation. This was his house, his wife. Yet his emotions were those of a sixteen-year-old boy going on a date. The uncertainty was real. A few more seconds passed, and he was able to shake off the butterflies fluttering in the pit of his stomach.

Zarah came to the door. She had taken off her sari and appeared relaxed in a pair of loose-fitting pants and a blouse.

"Thanks for letting me drop by." He entered the house and peered around the room. "Are you here alone?" he asked, concerned that Tamara might be there. He did not want to go another round with her. The constant bickering was too exhausting. He was wishing for a nice quiet evening with Zarah, hoping they'd laugh and talk as they'd done at the café earlier. More calm and less stress was the recipe for this visit.

"Yes, I am alone."

Thank goodness, he thought. He gave a major sigh of relief. His plans hadn't been foiled by mini-Madeline. "Are we going into the library?" he asked, knowing it was her favorite room.

"I prefer the kitchen."

"Sure," he said, following her in close pursuit.

She had a bunch of papers spread across the kitchen table. "What's this?" he asked as they both sat down at the table. He moved his chair closer to her, eager to continue the dialogue they'd begun that afternoon. It was odd being in his house given that he didn't consider the place home.

"Do you remember I was telling you about my meeting with the DMI directors?" Zarah said.

"I do." He couldn't forget, thanks to Tamara. She'd thrown the meeting in his face. He'd managed to dodge her antics. He snickered silently, because Tamara was on the outside. He was the person sitting within arm's reach of Zarah. His sister had better understand marriage if she was going to beat him at this game. It seemed outlandish that she would even try. Erasing Tamara from the picture, Joel struggled with seeing Zarah in a professional capacity. He had read the article and chatted with her extensively earlier. Belief in her monumental change was slow kicking in.

"There are many papers to prepare for the meeting."

She sounded stressed, which couldn't be good for the baby. "Do you need help with the presentation?" He genuinely wanted to help.

"I would like your help very much," she said, letting her gaze meet his.

"Are you nervous?"

"Yes and excited," she said, her voice tapering off. He wasn't sure why. "I very much want to do a pleasing job for my father and for you."

"Why me?" Joel asked, stunned by the comment.

"You are a businessman who has done very well. You don't see me as a woman who can do this job."

Zarah continued startling him with her candor. Previously, she'd allowed him to see only the reserved, needy side of her personality. He had no idea there was a self-sufficient, savvy woman hiding under her sari and scarves. He was continuously drawn to this Zarah. He was drunk in her presence. But every time he let his thoughts drift to their religious differences, Joel sobered instantly. He couldn't be fooled by the air of courtship. They had significant problems. That was certain, but there wasn't any need to dwell on those tonight.

He planned to help Zarah draft a presentation for the directors. He could have said his visit was purely for her sake and out of the kindness of his heart, but that would have been a fib. He was there for his sake as much as hers, and maybe more. He was so mixed up. Sleeping alone night after night at the Westin had grown old, but he wasn't quite ready to make a move. A few more visits or a miraculous move by God would have him out of that temporary space and into the place where he would thrive. He was anxiously waiting for a sign.

In the meantime, he'd see if God was willing to give him direct advice. Instead of praying and waiting, he decided that going to the source might prove faster. He hadn't been to church in a while, but it was sounding better by the second.

Chapter 27

Don was exhausted. Friday had taken too long to arrive. He read the abbreviated status report repeatedly. This was his fourth attempt to digest its content. It wasn't difficult to follow, not usually, but this morning he couldn't muster his concentration. Feuding, scheming, and perpetually recovering from one disaster after the next were bound to take a toll. He yearned for a break. Don flung the report onto the desk and tapped his fingertips together in midair, deep in thought.

He jumped up and went to the snack room to grab a cup of coffee. Halfway down the hall, he changed his mind and veered toward Abigail's office. He poked his head inside and saw that she was alone. *Perfect,* he thought. He could use her listening ear, someone who could be more objective than his mother. Abigail used to be that person for him. Joel, time, and the DMI battleground had eroded the power of their bond. Don and Abigail were cordial, actually friendly, but their working relationship did not have the same intensity they shared when his father was alive. They used to be inseparable in the office, both having been handpicked to work alongside Dave Mitchell. Back then Don had thought the gesture was a way to prepare him for taking over the business. But he was proven wrong when his father gave the leadership of DMI to Joel, who was barely twenty-one at the time.

Don got it together in Abigail's office and took a seat. He had no intentions of rehashing nearly three decades of ill will. Madeline and Joel could swap stories of woe until they were blue in the face. God had delivered Don from rejection and anger. He wasn't sure where Abigail was in the healing process. He'd soon find out.

"Well, if it isn't Mr. Don Mitchell." Abigail pecked a few keys on her laptop, peering at him intermittently.

"Are you busy?" he asked since she didn't appear to be paying him any attention.

"A little," she said, continuing to type.

"Do you have a few minutes for me?"

"Of course," she said, closing the laptop and letting her glance meet his.

He had her attention. Now what was he going to say?

"You look tired," she told him.

"Ah, somewhat," he replied. If she only knew the extent, Don thought.

He didn't bother elaborating. After all, she was a short timer with a handful of weeks remaining before she walked out of DMI for good. He figured Abigail didn't care, which was the very reason Don wanted her opinion about Joel. He could lean on her solid management acumen without Abigail fearing that she was taking sides. There had been a time not so long ago when Abigail would have gladly sacrificed her career to support Joel in his series of poor decisions and selfishness. Apparently, she'd learned guys like Joel didn't understand the concept of loyalty. Too bad her lesson had come at a steep price.

"Your boyfriend asked me for a job," he revealed.

"Who? Joel?"

Don nodded and smirked.

"He's your brother, not my boyfriend. Don't play."

"We're brothers in name only. We don't have much else in common except Dad. You know we used to have the Lord in common too, but I'm not sure where he is with religion these days."

"Especially since he married Zarah, who practices an Eastern religion."

"Tell me about it. You know that's why I have to offload Harmonious Energy. Our long-standing clients are making too much noise to ignore."

"Have you identified any buyers?" she asked, seeming to perk up. Perhaps she did perk up, but most likely, Don was imagining it, in some subconscious attempt to cling to fragments of the past. He missed working with her and had forgotten how refreshing it was to speak with a colleague who knew DMI and him too.

"Zarah wants to buy the DMI majority ownership position."

"Wow. What did you tell her?"

"I told her I'd think about it, but the offer doesn't require any debate. It's simple. I want to sell. She wants to buy. End of story. It doesn't get any better than this."

"Then why don't you sound thrilled?"

"I am. Can't you tell?" Don hadn't expected her to psychoanalyze his mood. She was forcing him to drop the facade, but then, that was why he came to her. She knew him, without him having to point out every problem. He relaxed in the seat, willing to let their friendship lift him out of the sea of confusion he was treading in.

"What's bothering you? And don't tell me, 'Nothing.' You can say you don't want me to know, but please don't act like everything is okay. I can tell it's not," she implored.

He wasn't going to lie. "I'm confused about what to do with DMI."

"I don't know why. You're doing a great job. I saw the quarterly numbers. Looks like you've reversed the losses that we realized for most of Joel's last year in charge. You're on the right track. You should be pretty pleased."

But he wasn't. "I'm content with the numbers, but what about my family?"

"What about them? Madeline has returned to the office. Who knows what your sister is up to? And Joel is out. What's there to worry about?"

Don had to be candid if he wanted honest feedback. "Remember when I went to South Africa?"

"More like abandoned DMI and me."

"Okay, whatever, but you remember how mad I was at Dad and God for letting Joel take over?"

"How could I forget?"

"I didn't want to leave Africa once I got there. But I came back to help my family."

"They haven't made the path easy for you," she said.

"You got that right. They are a handful, but I love them."

"Including Joel?"

"Yes. This is why I have to think about letting him come back to DMI. The problem is I don't trust Joel. He constantly has an angle."

"Joel would be a tremendous asset for you. It's unfortunate you can't trust him, but maybe he does deserve another chance. I don't know."

"That's the real Abigail . . . always jumping to Joel's rescue."

"Don't go there. Those days are long past."

Don wasn't so sure. She'd loved Joel until he broke her heart and married Zarah. "You're telling me Joel is finally out of your system?"

"There is nothing between us, not anymore. He's married and that's it."

"We both know their marriage was doomed from the beginning."

She nodded slowly, twiddling a paper clip. "He has certainly complicated things."

Don's secretary interrupted the meeting by ducking in and informing Don that he had a call from Naledi in the South Africa office.

Abigail giggled. "I guess Joel isn't the only Mitchell who dumped me for someone else."

Don grinned and left to take the call.

Chapter 28

Joel was a gnat constantly biting at Abigail's heels. The pesky critter wasn't visible, but the subtle pricks were a reminder of its presence. Joel wouldn't go away. Pretending not to care about him didn't make her feel better, but it did help her survive the breakup. Actually, *breakup* wasn't the right word for it. In order to break up, they had to be in a relationship. According to Joel, that wasn't the label he'd put on their union. Abigail recalled the relationship differently. She fondly remembered the countless hours they'd worked together. For a year, they'd eaten most dinners in the office as they diligently built his career and the clientele at DMI. Joel sacrificed his personal life during those early days for the good of the company and for what he had deemed was the leading of God. She had never questioned his motivation and had given one hundred percent, working tirelessly by his side in the trenches to fulfill his goals and Dave's vision for the company.

At Joel's request, she had even managed the construction of his new house, the one she thought he was building for them to share. Every inch of every room had been approved by her. She smirked again and snatched her pen off the desk to doodle on the pad of paper lying before her. She'd put her best effort into completing that project on time, under budget, and with as much dedication and love as her heart could muster. The thanks she got was a news flash one night on the local TV network, which showed Joel and his bride arriving from India after their secret wedding. She was devastated and was in denial for months. She set the pen down and stopped doodling. The shroud of pining over a man who didn't reciprocate her affection had lifted once she acknowledged that Joel, her perceived soul mate, was too self-absorbed to care about anyone other than himself.

In their recent past, reflecting on the old days might have caused her to shed a tear. But now she simply smirked, having grown in wisdom. She wanted to weep only for the naive young woman who stood passionately by her man with unwavering faith. She had refused to accept the shortcomings of the relationship, despite seeing the obvious, hearing the rumors, and being told the truth directly.

Her reminiscing was cut short when Don knocked on the door. "Can I come in?" he asked.

"Sure," she said, ripping the doodled sheet of paper from the pad, balling it up, and tossing it in the trash can underneath her desk. "Come right on in and have a seat, Mr. Mitchell."

"Mister, huh? Why so formal, Ms. Gerard?"

She giggled. "Ah, just messing with you."

Don took the seat she offered. "What has you acting silly?"

Suddenly the past disappeared in her rearview mirror, at least for today. "You don't want to know," she said, glancing away from Don.

"Uh-huh. I know what that look means." She was certain he did, and they didn't have to go any further with the conversation. Squandering ten minutes a day on Joel was her limit. She'd already exceeded it, and her soul was keeping a tight grip on the rest of the day.

"Anyway, what's going on with you today?" she asked.

"Funny you should ask. I've come to pick your brain about my plans."

"Oh, boy, are you getting engaged to Naledi?" she asked delicately, not wanting to appear jealous.

"Nothing like that . . . not yet, anyway."

Abigail squirmed in her seat, but it wasn't noticeable. Joel had maliciously broken her heart, but she'd crushed Don's. However, she hadn't assumed total responsibility. She and Don had been close friends for five years, working hand in hand under Dave's leadership. She was young and didn't recognize the signs of a man's interest. How was she supposed to know Don was in love with her if he never said anything? She didn't find out until Don quit DMI and asked her to come with him. Afterward, he was angry at her for staying at DMI to assist Joel. Don interpreted her action as a betrayal of her friendship and loyalty.

He fled Detroit, and the rest was history. Their friendship was strained for most of the two years he'd lived abroad. It wasn't until she'd suffered heartache in her relationship with Joel that Abigail began examining her feelings for Don. By the time she acknowledged him as the right Mitchell man for her, it was seemingly too late. He'd gone to South Africa, fallen in love with Naledi, and disposed of his attachment to Abigail. Admittedly, his rejection hurt, but what could she do except move on? Joel had, Don had, and she had to do the same.

"So, if you're not here to talk about Naledi, what's on your mind?"

"Well, I'm thinking about taking a break."

"You're kidding!" she exclaimed. Don had worked his behind off, just as she and Madeline had, to get DMI back on track after the company found itself in dire financial straits under Joel's leadership. They were rolling again. The company's reputation was on an upswing. "DMI needs you now more than ever."

"Nah, we're doing all right," he responded.

"I know, but it's because of you," she said emphatically.

"I think this is an ideal opportunity for me to step down. My family is finally showing signs of reconciliation."

"Really, you think so? Exactly who do you think has reconciled? Madeline and Joel don't get along. Tamara and Joel don't either. Sherry and Madeline will never be friends. So who exactly are you saying has reconciled?"

"Good point, but we're at least in the same city. There's hope yet for my crazy family, but I'm not going to sit around and wait for perfection. I'm going to take where we are as a win and start the next chapter of my life."

Abigail spun the pen on her desk and stared at it. "You're referring to building a life with Ms. Naledi, I guess, the woman who shoved me out of your heart."

"You don't want to go there," he said in a lighthearted tone. "She wasn't in the picture until you dumped me for my little brother."

"Ah, ah, ah," she chimed, shaking her finger at him. "We've been down this road too. I didn't dump you. I simply didn't know you had feelings for me when I chose to stay at DMI with Joel. Technically, this is your fault, not mine."

Don tapped his fingertips together, his elbows resting on the arms of his seat. "Touché. So here we sit, still civil, I hope."

"Definitely," she said, suppressing her disappointment about them not being able to start over. Yet she understood how they'd gotten to this place, and had to accept the outcome. She resumed twiddling the pen. "We can't change the past. So I guess we weren't meant to be."

"Guess not," he agreed.

There was a lull in the conversation, until Don jumpstarted it. "Let's talk about DMI, which was my primary purpose for popping into your office. I'd like you to reconsider your resignation."

Staying wasn't up for debate. In order to breathe fresh air, escape the Mitchell drama, she had to go. That was final. "We've had this talk several times, and I keep giving you the same answer."

"Can't blame me for trying to keep my valued employee. We need you here. *I* need you," Don said pressing his thumbs backward against his chest.

"What? So you can leave the country and go court Naledi? You must be delusional, asking me to reconsider my plans."

"I see it as an honor. I need a leader who can be trusted and who's capable of running DMI in my absence."

"What about Joel and Tamara?"

Don shook his head. "They both have too many issues for me to even remotely consider letting either of my siblings run this place."

"What about Madeline?"

"My mother is ready to retire. She has zero interest in running DMI. Look, I've given this a lot of thought, and you win the candidate race, hands down."

"I should be flattered, and maybe I am, but the answer is no." She had her reasons, but she wasn't sharing them with Don. There wasn't any joy in hurting him. She had no desire to continue to pour her time and dedication into DMI while being unappreciated. The bunch of them wanted her to give all the time she could to the company, while they continued their perpetual squabble. She was tired of their dysfunction. Better possibilities awaited her on the open market. The Mitchell family had taken advantage of her for the last time.

"Is there anything I can say or do to change your mind?"

"No. I'm committed to starting a consulting firm. I have to step out." They stared at one another, and then she broke the silence that had come between them. "Unless you're making me CEO?"

He hesitated, which was the answer she had anticipated.

"That's what I thought," she said.

"Until I can get my mother to season her dream with a giant dose of reality, Tamara is on the short list of candidates."

"And Joel would be the next contender, as a Mitchell," she mused. She wasn't surprised at Don's answer, which was why he shouldn't be shocked about hers. Abigail couldn't wait to get out of there and let the Mitchells self-destruct without being around to help clean up the carnage.

"I can't give you the top spot, but you can have the next highest-ranking position as president. Since I'm going to be in South Africa, running LTI, you will have total control. It would be just like you were in the CEO position." Don leaned close to the desk. "Come on now. I've seen your corporate drive and how much you love the challenge associated with working here."

"You're right, and that's what I'm counting on with my new firm." She leaned in close. "Thank you, but no thanks. I'm heading out on my own, and I wish you and DMI's team the very best."

She exhaled, feeling finally in control of her destiny without the DMI noose tightening around her neck. Tamara, Joel, Madeline, Sherry, and Don could fight until the earth exploded, and she wouldn't care. Freedom was satisfying and, she hoped, long lasting. She'd soon see.

Chapter 29

Something nagged at Don with each step he took away from Abigail's office, which was troubling. He'd come to learn that when God was in the midst of a situation, there was only peace. None of this anguish, confusion, and fighting. Three years of strife had ensued after his father appointed Joel CEO of DMI and nudged the family toward an all-out war. Don longed for some rest, the kind he'd found in Cape Town, South Africa. He kept walking toward his office, but much more slowly now. He was smart enough to know it hadn't solely been his physical location in South Africa that had led to him finding peace. Although, hearing the story about Nelson Mandela's unbelievable ability to forgive those who had wrongfully imprisoned him for twenty-seven years had inspired Don to release the anger he held against his father and brother. But even the gravity of Mandela's testimony wasn't what made the difference. He knew in the core of his being that the Lord had orchestrated the solitude he found outside of Detroit, away from DMI and beyond the Mitchells' reach.

God had restored him and drawn him home to get the family reconciled. It wasn't an easy job, not with the people he was working with. They were incorrigible, insensitive, pigheaded, but, most importantly, they were family. When Don reached the doorway to his office, he stopped and pressed his hand against the frame. His family was a pack of wild animals, inciting fear in those they encountered. *Yet they weren't hopeless,* he thought. Don pressed both hands into the door frame and let his mind settle.

Calm ushered in wisdom. Then it hit him. He'd been going about this the wrong way. He was naively acting as if the feud in the family was completely over. The Mitchell fight had ended no more than a month ago. Maybe the word *ended* was too optimistic. The cease-fire was more a result of everyone laying down their weapons of corporate destruction and retreating to their corners. He had no idea how long the cease-fire would last between his mother and his sister, between Joel and his mother, and between Joel and Abigail. There was no telling with this bunch.

"Is everything okay?" his assistant inquired.

Don had lost track of who was nearby. "Oh, I'm sorry," he said, taking both hands off the door frame and turning to face his assistant. "Yes, everything is fine. I just have a few things on my mind. Nothing new," he added, chuckling, with the intent of convincing her to move on and let him reflect openly without being questioned. His tactic must have worked, since she returned to her work and didn't ask any other questions. Don stepped into his office.

He said a quick prayer for guidance. He refused to believe that God would have him return to DMI, restore the company to financial solvency, rescue Tamara from an abusive boyfriend in Europe, and soften his heart toward Sherry, with the objective of letting the family resume their bickering and fall apart again. He knew God had better plans in store for the Mitchell family, but Don questioned his role in the journey they had to take if reconciliation was truly going to come. He milled around his office. What was God saying? He'd prayed, but the answer wasn't falling upon him. A wise man didn't get into a pit of snakes unless he had the proper protection, especially with the group Don was dealing with. His family seemed to thrive on chaos and contention. He'd have to wait until there was a clear direction.

He meditated a little while longer. Then he darted out the door and down the hallway to Abigail. She was still in her office. He burst in.

"What are you doing Sunday?"

"I don't know," she said. "Why?"

"Because I want you to come to church with me, like we used to do. I need to clear my head and get a spiritual tune-up so I can hear God clearly. I have to go to church on Sunday."

"All right. I'll go with you. Where?"

"Where else? Greater Faith Chapel. I hope Mother Walker is there, because she knows how to fire you up. She's no joke when it comes to the Lord and understanding purpose."

"I agree. She'll have you running from the church, begging God to use you for some grand calling. On second thought, maybe I don't want to go," Abigail said.

"I don't have a choice, and as my dear friend, you don't, either." He cackled. "I'll pick you up on Sunday." As he turned to leave, he added, "Thanks."

"For what?"

"For always being there for me. No matter what has or hasn't happened between us, our relationship is very special to me." Abigail wasn't the wife for him, but he hoped there would be some way to maintain their friendship long after they were both married and raising families. Perhaps his dream was unrealistic, but Abigail meant that much. Letting her go completely was unimaginable, and he'd continue working on a way to keep her close.

Chapter 30

Saturday came and went. Early Sunday morning, Don and Abigail found themselves in the Greater Faith Chapel parking lot. He had gotten up without an alarm clock, eager to get to church on time. Abigail wasn't upset when he showed up a half hour early. She'd rushed to finish getting dressed without complaining. That was the Abigail he knew, consistently supportive. They might have experienced a few bumpy moments over the past couple of months, but Don didn't believe a bond like theirs could be erased over a few disagreements. He just had to convince Abigail.

"You can tell we're pretty early. There aren't many cars in the parking lot. When we visited before, we couldn't get near the building unless we parked in the visitors' row."

Don agreed. "Since we've been here three or four times, I don't feel right parking in a visitor's space. We have to fend for ourselves and park in the spaces for regular folks."

After parking, the two talked as they walked toward the entrance. Several people had gathered in the vestibule, because the sanctuary doors were closed.

"Is an earlier service going on?" Don asked an usher.

"Oh, no. They're in devotion."

"If you don't mind me asking, what is devotion?" Abigail asked.

"It's the warm-up for our main service." The male usher laughed. "We welcome the Holy Spirit into this church early in the morning and keep Him with us until the afternoon." The usher laughed some more. "I hope you're ready to worship the Lord, because that's what we do here at Greater Faith. We worship the Lord all day long."

Don peered at Abigail. She had to be as humored as he was.

"Well, well, well," Don heard someone say. He turned to find Joel standing behind him.

"What are you doing here?" Don asked.

"Same as you. I've come to get some religion," he said, grinning. Joel directed his attention to Abigail. "I guess we're all trying to get some religion," he said softly. "I didn't realize the two of you were together."

"We're not," Abigail responded quickly.

Don was taken aback by the fact that she had so easily discounted him. He let it go, though, without adding his own commentary. The three lingered a few minutes before the doors leading into the sanctuary finally opened. They took a few steps away from the doors to let people come out.

"Can we go in?" Abigail asked the usher once the sanctuary had emptied.

"Yes, you can. Service will start in about fifteen minutes. I hope you enjoy the fellowship with us today."

"I'm sure we will," Don replied.

"Excuse me," Joel said to a person in the lobby who was wearing a church name tag. "Do you know if Mother Emma Walker is here today?"

"I haven't seen her, but I'm sure she's around here somewhere."

"Could you let her know Joel Mitchell said hello?"

"I sure will," the church member said.

Don was overjoyed when Joel asked about the church mother. He hoped to see Mother Walker but wasn't comfortable asking for her directly. It was too much like hunting down a word from God. He saw those gullible people on the TV ministries, the ones who ran behind evangelists and prophets, begging for a word from God. He definitely wanted a word, but he wasn't going to appear like a fanatic. It wasn't God's way, and Don knew as much. But he wouldn't pass up a word from Mother Walker if she came to him.

"We better go in and get seats," Abigail said.

"What's the hurry? We have time." Don wouldn't dare reveal his true motivation for lingering in the vestibule.

"I'm going in," Joel said.

Don checked his watch. Nine fifty-five. He'd give in and go sit down. Chasing a prophetic word was like ordering from a drive-through menu. It felt ridiculous, and he squashed the notion. "All right. Let's go in," he replied. God knew where to find him.

As soon as the three agreed to enter the sanctuary, a soft voice rose up in the vestibule. "My goodness, if it isn't the Mitchell boys. Ooh, look what the cat done dragged in."

"Mother Walker, it's a pleasure to see you," Don replied. He was excited, as if she was an angel the Lord had sent directly to him.

"It is good to see you, Mother Walker," Joel added.

Mother Walker flung her hands in the air and hugged them. "No need to be so formal. Everybody around here calls me Big Mama. You can too." Don and Joel nodded, acknowledging her request. "It's been, what? The better part of a year since the two of you came to fellowship with us?"

Don attempted to tell her he'd been to the church earlier in the year, but Big Mama was the equivalent of a rock star. She had him tongue-tied. He cleared his throat several times to regain his composure. Joel didn't seem bothered, but he wasn't speaking much, either. Abigail was quiet too.

"Service is going to be starting in a few minutes. Please take your seat in the sanctuary," an usher announced.

Don wasn't going anywhere. Big Mama had his complete attention.

The ushers corralled people inside. "Excuse me, Big Mama, but we're getting ready to start. Did you want me to escort you down front?" an usher asked.

She flung her hands in the air again. "No need. I'm able-bodied. I sho' thank you for offering to help me get to my seat, but I'm not going in yet. I want to visit a little piece longer with our guests."

The usher didn't resist.

Big Mama turned to Joel. "You're still running, huh?"

"What? Excuse me?" Joel replied.

"You've been gone for a long time, but now you need to come home," she told Joel.

"You're right. I was in Chicago, but I returned to Detroit a few weeks ago."

The church mother hesitated and shook her head. "I mean, you need to come back home in the spirit. You've been gone too long. God is waiting on you to return to Him. He's a patient God, but you don't want to keep Him waiting too long." She patted his hand. "Hear me good," she said.

Anxiety was swelling within Don. He was like a kid who was waiting his turn to ride the roller coaster. But Big Mama grabbed Abigail's hand next.

"What's going on with you?" she asked.

"Not much," Abigail said.

"When you've done all you can do, then stand," she said, squeezing Abigail's hand tighter.

"Enjoy the service and come see us anytime. We're glad to have you," Big Mama told them.

Where was the rest? Where was his prophetic word? There had to be something left for Don. Joel and Abigail had gotten theirs. Now it was his turn. Yet Big Mama was walking away. He wanted to throw himself in her path and ask for a confirmation. She was getting farther away, and then he sighed. What was he thinking? His relationship with God had matured over the past three years enough for Don to know that He often spoke in quiet moments. God was the master of heaven and earth, full of power and resources. Each challenge and disappointment had laid a brick in the foundation of Don's faith. He had a personal relationship with God that was rooted in prayer, peace, faith, and thanksgiving. Don was embarrassed to be chasing after a person to give him a word from God. Where was his faith?

"Are you ready to go inside?" Don asked Joel and Abigail.

"I am. But you have to admit, the old lady makes some wild comments. Still, I like her," Joel whispered. "Everything she has told us in the past has come true in one way or another, but you need an interpreter to understand the message."

Abigail agreed, and Don too. They went inside for the service. The differences among them were left at the door, and for a brief season they were fellowshipping.

When the church service ended, Don exchanged pleasantries with his brother. Finally, he asked, "Anyone interested in lunch?"

"I'm going to decline," Abigail told him.

"Why? You can't possibly be working today," Don said.

"No, it's not work," she said, cutting her gaze at Joel.

"Don't worry, big brother. She's telling the truth," Joel observed. "It's not work that's holding her back. It's being around me that's churning her stomach."

Don shook his head. “She doesn’t have a problem with you.”

“You’re wrong, big brother, on this one.” Joel turned to Abigail. Isn’t he?”

“You seem to have all the answers,” Abigail said.

“See? I told you,” Joel told Don. “But it’s okay. I’m going to see Zarah. So I have to take a rain check, anyway.”

Don didn’t attempt to change their minds. It required too much effort. He was going to drop Abigail off and go to lunch alone. Sometimes the only route to peace was sitting alone. Sometimes it was the only way to hear from God and get clarity on the direction he had to go.

Eager to escape, Don was suddenly relieved that both Joel and Abigail had declined his lunch invitation.

Chapter 31

Monday morning presented a fresh start. Joel had survived the series of letdowns from last week. He sat on a park bench as Mother Walker's words circled in his mind. She had told him to call her Big Mama, and he would in person, but Joel had become accustomed to her more formal name. Regardless of which name she used, her messages were like double-sided tape. Once she attached a message to you, there was no way to escape. A person was stuck with trying to understand the implications. Odd as it sounded, he was as glad to see Mother Walker as he had been intimidated. Usually, he didn't have a clue about what she was saying. Yesterday was no exception. He understood the need to rebuild his faith and his reliance on God's plan. He was open to developing his spiritual prowess. The problem was Mother Walker didn't provide definitive instructions for what he needed to do. She might as well have given him a treasure chest without the key. When Joel finally figured out how to open the chest, he might be forty years old, well beyond his prime.

If worrying was effective, he'd gladly partake. Even in the middle of a spiritual drought, he knew worrying wasn't the answer. So he didn't. He stretched his arms out across the bench. The air was chilly, but not so frigid that he wanted to pack up and leave. Minor discomforts he could handle. It was the major ones that threatened to knock him onto the canvas.

Mother Walker wasn't the only visitor consuming his thoughts this morning. Zarah had an equal presence. What was going on with her? He had thoroughly enjoyed the last couple of encounters. He wasn't familiar with the enthusiastic, intelligent, and passionate side of Zarah. His memory was lined with the unflattering remnants of a dull, docile, and dependent girl. He wanted the woman who could challenge him professionally, could stand her ground spiritually, and was able to capture the attention of every onlooker in the room. Any woman who brought less to the relationship wasn't likely to get the best from him. Iron sharpened iron. He was on top of his game when there was an equal exchange. He had an indescribable bond with Sheba, a mutual exchange of support and respect, a natural fit. He patted his chest, thinking about Sheba, until the image of Zarah aggressively cut in. She didn't seem to be fleeing. He sat on the bench and let the sweet memories of both women marinate.

The ringing zapped his period of reflection. He fumbled to get the phone out of his pocket and answered quickly when he saw the number displayed.

"Uncle Frank, just the man I wanted to hear from," he said. "What's the good news?"

"It's a bust, nephew."

The statement sliced into him. "Oh, come on, Uncle Frank. I thought you had clout with these guys."

"My clout isn't the problem. It's your bank account. They want eight hundred million. Based on our last conversation, that number seems too big for your wallet."

Joel was getting riled up. He stood and put his foot on the bench. "How can they justify eight hundred million dollars for one small division? That's ridiculous!" he shouted. "That's highway robbery!"

Uncle Frank chuckled. "What do you expect? These are simple businessmen trying to make a profit on their investment, the investment you handed to them on a silver platter, nephew."

Joel was aware of how these guys had acquired the division. He didn't need Uncle Frank to remind him of his mistake. They needed to dwell on the present and let the past stay buried.

"You told me this deal was coming in at seven hundred million, not eight."

"Do you have seven hundred?" Uncle Frank fired back.

"No," Joel replied quietly. His mother would gladly donate something to his cause, although she had nowhere near seven or eight hundred. He wouldn't dare ask Sheba. Joel was on his own, and he wanted it that way. "I don't have seven, but—"

"But nothing," Uncle Frank interrupted, and then chuckled. His incessant chuckling was driving Joel batty. "You don't get it, do you? These cats are no joke. They're not playing games. If you want the division, show them the money. If you don't have it, shut up and stop wasting my time. Otherwise, I'll have to charge you for these consulting sessions with or without a deal."

Joel considered sharing a few choice words with his uncle, but he couldn't bring himself to do it. As much as he hated what his uncle was saying, Joel acknowledged there was a great deal of underlying truth. Uncle Frank didn't create the original problem. It was a result of Joel's handiwork. He was humbled and had to fully accept the consequences of his decisions.

"Uncle Frank?"

"What?" his uncle replied with resounding agitation in his voice.

"Thank you for reaching out to your investors on my behalf. It didn't work out, but I appreciate your effort."

A reaction he didn't expect to hear followed.

"Hang in there, nephew. You're smart, and you know how to make things happen. You're going to land on your feet. I'm sure of it." Joel wasn't seeking validation, but it was a welcomed surprise from his father's brother. "Take my advice. When you make a deal, always make sure it's an equal exchange. If you're giving up too much to close a deal, then it's probably one you should walk away from." Uncle Frank chuckled. It didn't bother Joel this time. He was in a different place emotionally. And the advice didn't sting. Joel actually found it insightful. "I'm giving you this tidbit for free, no charge on this one."

They said their good-byes and terminated the call, along with Joel's plan.

Chapter 32

Joel should have been devastated that one of his few remaining ventures had been taken off the table. There wasn't a company for him to buy or one for him to run. He was out of luck. Joel rested his elbow on his bent knee, remembering a nugget of wisdom his father had once shared. Joel had to rely either on luck or on God, not both. His weakened spirit cried out for him to continue pursuing a solution through the Lord. He was growing weary and didn't want to continue beating his head for a lost cause, but his determination wouldn't allow him to become sidelined. There had to be more he could do before completely surrendering to faith. He just wasn't ready to make a comprehensive return to God, not yet, not while his plans were in disarray. Admittedly, he had created his problems and had to be the one to fix them. When he was able to put the pieces back together and embark on a path to success, then he could seek restoration from God as a winner.

He attempted to clear the flurry of revelations and the chaos from his mind. There had to be something he was missing. If he could just think clearly, he'd see it. While laboring over the matter, he kept thinking about Zarah. She was it. Somehow acquiring control or ownership of her division really was the way forward. He poked out his chest, feeling much more confident about his success rate with her than with Uncle Frank and his partners.

Shrouded in confidence, Joel went to his car. He would go home and plead his case directly to his wife. Joel was prepared to cash his chips in on the strength of one hand. Right and wrong seemed to be waging a minor struggle within him, but he wasn't going to let doubt overcome necessity. He needed this deal. Zarah had to understand. As concrete as his plan appeared to be, honestly, he couldn't forget the church mother's comments. She'd given him crucial advice in the past, several times, mostly warnings about his decisions. He hadn't heeded her wisdom then, and his whole world had crumbled.

He tried at each turn to forget her words from Sunday morning, but he was unsuccessful in shaking himself free from that encounter with her. He zipped down the highway, reaching his exit in about thirty minutes. A whole host of scenarios played out in his head. He had to develop a cohesive strategy before approaching Zarah. In the past, he could roll in with a grin and a lullaby. Since she'd taken on a new persona, he didn't want to underestimate her. He'd give her the same professional courtesy others got.

He whipped into a coffee shop situated off the highway. Inside, Joel ordered an espresso and grabbed a stack of napkins.

The waitress gave him a wide smile. "I haven't seen you in here before," the young lady said.

Joel guessed she was around seventeen or eighteen, certainly not in his twenty-six year old league. She was flattering him, and there was a time when he would have played along. Today his priority was business. She set the espresso on the counter.

"Thanks," he told her.

"Anytime," she replied, leaning against the counter and maintaining the wide smile.

"Can I ask you a favor?"

"Sure," she said immediately. "What can I do for you?"

Reacting was enticing, but he would pass. He had more important matters to handle. "Do you have a pen I could use?" he said, sealing the request with his signature grin.

She blushed and quickly fumbled for a pen underneath the counter. She surfaced with the writing utensil, appearing proud about her accomplishment. Joel winked as he took the pen, and his hand touched hers. She giggled.

"Joel Mitchell," he heard someone call out. He turned to find an old acquaintance, Samantha Tate, standing nearby. "I saw the canary-yellow Lamborghini in the parking lot and wondered if it could possibly be your car. And what do you know? It is. Well, well, well, how long has it been?" she asked.

Joel turned toward the counter to get his espresso. The waitress's smile had converted to a bitter-looking snarl, and she stomped off. "I think it's been about a year. What's been going on with you?"

"Still working at the TV station."

He'd met the reporter during a local talk show interview several years ago. They had connected before he got married, and had spent a considerable amount of time together. She was tall, thin, and quite pleasing in the looks department. Her milk chocolate–colored skin, with a generous portion of cream, blended well with her brown hair.

"Let's grab a seat. Do you want anything?" he asked, spilling a few drops of coffee onto the counter.

"I'll have what you're having," she said, letting her dimples punctuate the statement.

Joel tried getting the waitress's attention. She wasn't eager to respond. "Excuse me, miss. Can I place another order?" he called out.

The waitress schlepped over to him without exhibiting any of the courtesies she had extended earlier. He understood and chuckled. Her interest was fleeting. He hoped Zarah's interest in his offer wouldn't suffer the same death.

"Can I please get another espresso?"

"Yeah, sure," the waitress said.

Joel was glad to see the coffee machine in plain view. Otherwise, he might be concerned about Samantha drinking a cup of coffee made by his new admirer. When the order was ready, he grabbed the cup and hurriedly led the way to a table. He didn't need any more disgruntled women on his list.

"So, what brings you to this neck of the woods?" he said, as they found a table and sat. He drank from his cup.

"I had an interview with Zarah Bengali."

Some of Joel's coffee spurted out of his mouth, and then he gave a series of heavy coughs.

"Are you all right?" Samantha asked.

Joel snatched a handful of napkins he'd taken from the counter and began wiping off the table.

"You okay?"

Joel cleared his throat. "I'm good. Thanks for asking." He wiped up the remaining coffee. "Did you say Zarah Bengali?"

"Yes—"

Joel wondered if it was Samantha or Zarah who had chosen to use the last name of Bengali instead of Mitchell. The omission bothered him. "You know she's my wife?"

"I do, and your marriage is intriguing."

"Really?" he said, wiping the table although the coffee was gone. "How so?"

"You have to admit it's not every day when a prominent executive from Detroit takes a wife from India and combines two multimillion-dollar companies. This is big news for us."

Joel didn't want to be in the middle of a media circus because Zarah was venturing into the corporate sector and nosy spectators wanted details. He was nervous as he thought about what kind of information might have been revealed under the guise of getting the scoop. He cringed, thinking about the possibilities.

"What did you talk about?" he asked, afraid of what was coming next.

"She's very intriguing. I didn't realize just how stunning your wife is," Samantha said. "We did a ten-minute segment on women in the corporate sector."

"I'm surprised you picked her. She's new on the scene."

"You'd never know. She was poised and very articulate," Samantha said after sipping her coffee. "Other than her accent, of course."

He was irritated by watching people flock to Zarah in droves, each with their own agenda. They might not be living as husband and wife, but he wasn't going to tolerate people taking advantage of the predicament. Not his family and certainly not members of the press, even if they were as enticing as Ms. Tate had been in the past.

Fifteen minutes evaporated, and Joel was anxious to get moving. He had urgent matters to handle.

"It was nice seeing you," he told her, wrapping up their conversation.

"You too," she responded. Samantha reached into her purse but kept her gaze locked on Joel's. "Here's my card, in case you lost the other one. Perhaps we can do dinner sometime and reminisce with a bottle of wine instead of an espresso."

Joel took the card, and they parted. He pulled off in his car right after balling up the card and stuffing it into his pants pocket. He'd toss the card at the first opportunity, harboring no desire to pursue the invitation. If he didn't know what to do with Zarah, there definitely wasn't room for another woman. Those days were behind him or, at a minimum, on hold. Intrigue, passion, and a boatload of women had each contributed to his demise, as they'd scarfed down his attention. Pursuing prior indiscretions was too much torment. He had to move forward.

During his two-mile ride to the house, God briefly entered his mind. He hadn't forgotten his desire to establish a connection with Him, but he was realizing that fully committing to the Lord's approach for restoring his life wasn't easy. Giving up total control to anyone wasn't his way. Doubt and a mixture of emotions took over, leaving Joel wandering. He needed a breakthrough, just one glimmer of success on the business front, and the rest would work out naturally. He accelerated, eager to see Zarah. She was the key.

Chapter 33

Joel was more relaxed during this visit than he'd been during the one last week, but he couldn't shake the nagging feeling that Tamara was going to be waiting at the door, posing an inconvenience to him, as she typically did. He reached the house, parked, and forgot about Tamara. She was incidental in the grand scheme of what had to be accomplished during this visit. He approached the front door and paused, choosing not to use his key. The house was 100 percent Zarah's for now, until he figured out how to organize each piece of the chaotic puzzle that was his life. He rapped on the door, and the housekeeper opened it.

"It's good to see you, Mr. Mitchell."

Greetings were exchanged, and Joel was directed into the kitchen, where he found Zarah leaning against the counter in her gown and robe.

Zarah fumbled with the cup she was holding and spilled some type of liquid onto the floor and her clothes. "Joel, I didn't realize you were coming for a visit," she sputtered.

Joel was tickled but didn't want to embarrass her. "I was in the area and wanted to stop by to see you. Is this a good time?"

"Yes, of course," she said, rushing to him, beaming with glee.

He had only a few seconds to decide how far to go with the physical contact. Tossing caution out the window, Joel embraced Zarah. An unexpected surge of passion overcame him, and he opted to hold her longer. She offered no resistance. Joel eventually pulled away, took her by the hand, and gently guided her through the foyer, the family room, out the French doors, and onto the patio. Several times he felt her tense up, but he didn't stop. Joel wanted to speak with her privately and in a different setting than they normally chose. This could possibly be a new start for him and them as a couple, and he wasn't going to let up until Zarah understood the sincerity of his appeal.

"I would have prepared for your visit if you'd told me you were coming."

He lifted both her hands and extended his arms. "You look amazing, no matter what you're wearing," he said and twirled her around slowly. She looked like she was going to burst with elation. Joel was glad she was in a good mood. The more positive she felt going into their conversation, the better his chances of getting a favorable outcome. His request had to work; there was nothing else left for him.

"You're doing well with the pregnancy, right?" he asked, taking a seat in one of the patio chairs. She followed his lead.

"I am well," she replied, laying her hand on her stomach.

"I want you to get plenty of rest and not to work too much."

"I am very pleased about your concern. You will be pleased to know I'm getting my rest and taking very good care of our baby. This baby will have the best chance to be born healthy and strong, just like its father," she said and reached over and touched Joel's hand.

More chitchat might be warranted and might be a wiser approach, but Joel didn't have the patience. He was exploding with anxiety and wanted to say the right words.

He would rely on the premise that in a marriage there was mutual support, mutual help, and mutual sacrifice. He was willing to help Zarah and had to believe she was willing to return the favor. He'd soon see.

"How's the presentation coming along for the DMI board of directors meeting?" he asked.

"I am ready, except for a few more questions," she said, rubbing her stomach.

"If you need any more help, just let me know." He paused. "Speaking of DMI, I have been giving more thought to the West Coast division."

"You don't have to worry. I have not spoken to Don about the division since you were here last week," Zarah stated.

"That's good, real good, but this isn't about Don."

She wiggled to the edge of the chair; a distressed look was on her face. He had no intention of letting her stew. He wanted this over and done quickly.

He went on. "I'd like to put in an official offer to buy the division from you." Her distress didn't appear to diminish, but he wasn't going to let that sway him. This had to be done. "Zarah, you have no idea how important this is to me," he said, kneeling in front of her with her hands nestled in his. "I have run out of other ideas. You're my lifeline. The West Coast division would allow me to get reestablished in the corporate sector. Please don't say no. I'm serious. This is the most important priority in my life right now."

He didn't care about the legal technicality blocking his ownership. They could hire a team of lawyers to dissect the clause Zarah's father had included in his will. Worse case, they could sell the division to his mother and she could transfer ownership to him. There were ways around the obstacle. Nothing could dissuade him.

Zarah pulled her hands from his grip with force. Tears filled her eyes. "I am very tired. I must go for a nap."

"Why? Are you ill?" he asked.

She'd been fine a few seconds ago. Unless the baby was in duress, he needed her to stay and finish the discussion. He was absolutely certain his chance to buy the West Coast division was fleeting with sharks like Tamara and Don circling. If he could convince her to stay outside with him, Joel was fairly sure she'd have compassion for his plight and agree to sell the division. He refused to accept any other outcome. Yet he had to confirm that Zarah and the baby were okay.

"Why don't you take a deep breath and rest here?" he said. "There's no hurry to go anywhere or do anything. I'm here. I can take care of you and the baby."

Tears streamed down her cheeks. "I will be fine after a nap. Please excuse me. I must go."

Relieved that there wasn't a problem with the pregnancy, he instantly resumed his appeal. "Before you go, can I get an answer about the division?"

She didn't answer. Instead, she whimpered as her tears flowed freely. He rose to get out of her way. She didn't utter another sound, didn't say "Good-bye" or "See you later," not a word. He stood there, unable to move, as she retreated into the house and slammed the door on his future. Stunned, he gathered up the dignity to walk out of the house without letting the depth of his rejection show. Joel moseyed through the house, and when he opened the front door to leave, there stood the knife in his backside—Tamara. He was a wounded lion seeking a secure place to lick his wounds. He didn't have the heart to go a fresh round with a formidable opponent. He prayed she'd offer him a way to escape.

"I didn't expect to see you here," she said. "It's about time you started checking on your wife and baby, especially since Zarah doesn't have any other family in the United States except for me and your trifling behind."

Joel decided to take a lesson from Zarah and walk away without speaking. Any other day it would have been difficult not to spar with Tamara. Fortunately for Tamara, she'd caught him on a day when he didn't care. He stepped around her and went to his car, speeding off to nowhere in particular, so long as it was away from there.

Chapter 34

Tamara enjoyed toying with Joel and watching him squirm. Once in a while it was therapeutic for him to get a dose of his own hoity-toity medicine. She took satisfaction in knocking him down a peg. She walked inside the house since Joel had left the front door open. She panned the room and didn't see anyone.

"Hello," she called out. She roamed around several rooms until the housekeeper surfaced. "The door was open," she said pointing in the direction of the door. "So I came in. I hope you don't mind."

"You're fine. Is Mrs. Mitchell expecting you?"

"No, not really," Tamara stated. "Is she busy?" She figured Zarah was home since Joel had been there.

"She wasn't well after Mr. Mitchell's visit."

Not surprising, Tamara thought. He had a sickening effect on people. "Where is she?"

"Upstairs, in the master suite."

Tamara ran to the stairs and began ascending them.

"Wait. I'll let Mrs. Mitchell know you're here," the housekeeper said, hustling to the staircase. She was too late to catch Tamara, who was practically at the top of the staircase.

"Don't worry. She won't mind if I pop my head in to check on her. Besides, I'm family," Tamara announced, figuring the added dash of clout would assuage the housekeeper's concern. It must have worked, because she ended the pursuit. Tamara was more relieved than she appeared.

Tamara wandered around upstairs for a few minutes. She hadn't gone upstairs before and didn't have an inkling about which room was the master. After opening the door to five rooms situated on a long hallway, she reached the end. To her left was a massive double-door entryway, which had to be the master. Her legs weren't going fast enough. She was anxious to see Zarah.

As Tamara approached the double doors, she could hear faint whimpering. She walked briskly into the room as the whimpering intensified. From her vantage point, she saw Zarah lying across the bed. Tamara rushed to her side.

"What's wrong? What did Joel do?" she asked. She'd continue asking until she got an answer. Tamara's fury was being aroused, and it wouldn't take long to gather steam.

"Go away please. I don't feel much up to a visit. Please leave me," Zarah wheezed and buried her face in the mound of pillows thrown across the bed.

Tamara was torn between honoring the request and not leaving Zarah in a pitifully distraught state. Compassion won out. She'd stay. "What did Joel say or do to upset you?" Tamara asked, gently resting her hand on Zarah's shoulder.

Her sister-in-law flinched from the contact. Tamara wasn't dismayed. She pressed on, committed to finding out what that *brother* of hers had done.

"You can tell me. Maybe I can help." As if Tamara had inserted the correct key in a lock, Zarah sat up and glided her fingertips beneath her tear-soaked eyes. Tamara moved a bit to give her sister-in-law ample space. "Is this about Joel?"

Zarah nodded in affirmation.

Tamara had figured as much. How much more could he get away with before Zarah shut him down? Getting mad wasn't going to fix the problem. Tamara kept quiet. It was the only way she could avoid saying the wrong thing and having to apologize later. She fidgeted instead.

Zarah stood and journeyed to the sitting area but didn't sit. Tamara followed and took a seat. "My husband came for a visit. I was very pleased to have him come to check on me and the baby." It sounded as if Joel was doing the right thing for a change, Tamara figured. Zarah got choked up. "I was pleased until I discovered he didn't come for me or the baby." Tamara was confused but didn't interrupt. "He came to offer me money for the West Coast division."

"What?" Tamara said, leaping to her feet and reacting without weighing the cost. "You can't sell him the division. I want that division more than anyone, and I'll double whatever price he's offering." She couldn't believe Joel had weaseled his way into the West Coast division conversation. Tamara wasn't going to be blindsided and go down without a fight. Joel had better bring it on with heat if he was going to beat her in this deal.

Zarah was dumbfounded and stood still, like a statue, not responding.

"Did you hear me?" Tamara asked.

"This is too much for me to handle today. No more talk of deals for me. I must rest for the baby," Zarah said, finally taking a seat.

Tamara wasn't comfortable letting the conversation die and potentially losing her slice of the Mitchell Empire, but she couldn't push too hard. Zarah didn't look well. Tamara was forced to stand down and save the battle for another day. "Can I take you to the doctor or the hospital?"

"No," Zarah said, waving her off. "I just need rest, please."

"Are you sure?" Tamara asked, having set aside her "mogul hat" and evincing only the affection of a friend.

"I am sure."

Tamara expressed her support again and then left the room. She would continue the discussion later. She had to find a way to get the West Coast division. She felt justified in her pursuit. After all, she wasn't asking for much. It was DMI's smallest division, representing only a tiny corner of the company, one that Joel had carelessly given away. He didn't deserve the division. She did. Convincing Zarah was the tricky mission.

Chapter 35

Don pulled up to the twelve-foot-tall wrought-iron gates leading into his mother's estate, the home of his youth. He had mixed memories, some harmonious blended with a nearly equal share of tragedy. He was six years old when his parents divorced and he, his mother, and his siblings moved from their real home into this place without Dave. His mother made every effort to make their lives pleasant and filled with love. She did a pretty good job from his perspective, but history told a modified story. The four children who were raised in this house, Don included, had problems. Don briefly nursed accounts of the past and then quickly tossed them aside. He wasn't going to get sucked into a state of doubt, doom, and regrets. He expeditiously pushed the buzzer to open the gates.

His mother answered and buzzed him in. Don zoomed along the quarter-mile driveway, which was more like a road. He cleared his head of the depressing memories. He was homing in on the present and the task of stabilizing DMI's leadership team. Madeline and Don had been talking on and off for several days about what to do. No solid plan had materialized, only bits and pieces. Since Madeline wasn't coming into the office today, she'd asked him to drop by for lunch. Apparently, she had an epiphany to share. He was cautiously curious. His mother's ideas didn't always fall within his boundaries. He came anyway. Putting this issue to rest was his priority, as it would free him from the weighty role of CEO. He exited the car, willing to keep an open mind and listen before countering.

He found her in the kitchen, and they did their usual greeting sealed with a hug. Don had clung to his mother from his early childhood years. She seemed to make his tough situations easier when he was growing up. Interacting with her as an adult brought a different set of dynamics. Madeline was a lot to manage, but nonetheless, she was his hero.

"Jeez, why do you have this much food? Is someone else joining us for lunch?" Don asked, seeing the spread of salad, pasta, sandwiches, fruit, and cookies.

"No one but the two of us," she answered. "That seems to be our story these days, just the two of us against the world."

He detected the softening of her voice and steered her away from a sad moment. "Let's dig in while you tell me what has you so fired up." He grabbed a plate and began loading food onto it. His mother did the same.

They sat at the table.

"I've done nothing but think about how to change Tamara's mind about DMI and get her on board. I have racked my brain and finally have a potential solution," she said, waving her index finger in the air and giving him a controlled grin.

Don was intrigued. "You have the floor. Tell me what you've concocted," he stated and took a bite of his pastrami sandwich.

"Oh, come on," she said, playfully swatting his shoulder. "*Concocted* sounds like a witch brewing up a spell."

"Well, if the broom fits, ride it," he replied, toying with Madeline, glad to see her moving far away from the sadness that had tried to surface a few minutes ago.

"That's no way to talk about your mother," she said, snickering.

"You're tough. I know you can handle it. Now, tell me about this plan of yours, Broom Hilda," he said, laughing into his napkin.

She rolled her eyes at him and smirked. Madeline slid her plate toward the middle of the table. "Here's what I'm thinking. We know none of the DMI divisions were structured to run as stand-alone companies."

Don agreed. "Dad was adamant about keeping the company together."

"You're right. He told Joel, practically on his deathbed, not to let DMI get broken into pieces. And look what Joel did. Exactly what your father told him not to do."

"Selling two out of the four divisions almost drove the company into financial ruin. Apparently, Father knew more than we did about this."

"Of course he did. Your father was a wise man when it came to running DMI. I've never doubted his aptitude. Now, his personal choices were a totally different story."

"And we don't want to go there, do we?"

Madeline poked at the pasta on her plate with her fork. "No, we don't."

"And you were saying," Don said, attempting to steer her clear of the ditch named Dave and Sherry Mitchell.

She instantly perked up and returned to the topic at hand. "I was saying, what if we push Zarah aggressively to sell us the West Coast division? We could fold it back into DMI, where it rightfully belongs."

"Have you forgotten Tamara wants the division?"

"How can I forget? It's kept me awake for the last week. But I'm thinking that if we get the division, it can be used as a bargaining chip with Tamara. What do you think?"

Don's eyebrows arched. He took another bite of his sandwich in order to buy a few more seconds before having to respond. Madeline continually stared at him with each chew. He grabbed the napkin and wiped his mouth, gaining a few additional seconds before being forced to reply.

Surprisingly, he wasn't completely opposed to the idea. There was definitely merit in wanting the division restored to DMI. The part causing him angst was her use of the term *bargaining chip*.

"Well, say something," Madeline demanded.

"My initial reaction is that you have a decent plan, with the exception of trying to bargain with Tamara. You know how much she hates feeling manipulated or pressured into a situation. She'll never go for it."

Madeline let her gaze dip. She played with the uneaten food on her plate for a bit and finally said, "You have a point, but I'm not left with many other choices. We have to get the division from Zarah."

"It may become a bidding war. How much are you prepared to spend?"

"Money is no object when it comes to my children's well-being. I'll spend ten times the market value if necessary," she declared and gripped his forearm briefly. "This has to work."

Don wasn't so sure. He saw the merit in both pursuing the division and walking away to let Zarah have it. He decided to stay neutral unless compelled to take a position. "Where do we go from here?"

"Call Zarah and set up a meeting where we can present the offer."

"Are you sure about this?" he asked, sliding his plate away.

"A thousand percent sure. Make the call," she said, slapping the table with force.

Chapter 36

Madeline's persistence wasn't to be ignored. Don reluctantly placed a call to Zarah from his cell phone, having no idea what to expect. With his mother fixated on him like a laser beam, he attempted to dodge the heat.

"Zarah, this is Don Mitchell," he stated, shifting his glance from Madeline so as not to get distracted. "I hope this is a good time to speak with you."

"Not really, Don. I am not well today. I'm very tired. I would be honored to speak with you in a few days, once I've rested."

Don scooted away from the table. "I'm sorry to hear you're not doing well." He didn't want to push. Even with his back to Madeline, he could sense the heat of her desperation scorching him. Yet he couldn't justify pressuring a pregnant woman into an undesired conversation. Madeline would have to accept that she wasn't getting the division back today and maybe no other day. Time would tell. For now, this conversation was over. "I'm sorry to have bothered you."

"Don't you dare hang up," Madeline mouthed, not speaking loud enough for Zarah to hear.

Don fumbled to mute the phone after asking Zarah to hold for a minute. "What, Mother?" he answered, quite irritated. His mother wasn't known for her decorum when it came to holding back on sensitive issues.

"Put her on the speakerphone," Madeline demanded and reached for Don's phone.

"No, Mother, she's sick. I'm not going to stress a pregnant woman. This can wait."

"No, it can't," she retorted. "Put her on the speakerphone. If you don't want to ask her about the division, I will."

Don shut his eyes and handed her the phone, absolutely certain he was making the wrong decision. He prayed silently, recognizing that when his mother was on a mission, only the Lord in heaven was going to slow her down. Anyone else had better steer clear of Madeline Mitchell, or they'd get run down.

"Zarah, this is Madeline," she said after unmuting the phone, trying to sound gentle. Don didn't know whether to laugh at her boldness or hide under the table due to her bullying and recklessness. "I understand you're not feeling well. So let me keep this very short. We'd like to buy the West Coast division from you." Madeline paused. Don didn't know why. "Price is not the most important factor, which means any serious offer from you will be considered. How does this sound to you?"

Zarah was silent.

Madeline pushed the mute button and flung her hands in the air. "Is she deaf?"

Don saw how anxious his mother was becoming. It hadn't been his choice to make the call, but the deed was done. He had to find a way to salvage his mother's offer, since a bottomless bucket of cash didn't appear to influence Zarah. He had to sweeten the deal. Don unmuted the phone, put Zarah on speakerphone, and tossed in their trump card. "We are willing to consider an even exchange of DMI's majority ownership in Harmonious Energy for the West Coast division."

Don watched as his mother's tension eased. He didn't want to think about what they were forfeiting. An equal exchange was a steal for Zarah, but neither Don nor

Madeline planned to quibble over the offer. The possibility of such a monumental win for the family outweighed the financial loss.

But Zarah remained silent.

"Did you hear him? You can have your father's company. Fifty-one percent is worth about eight hundred million on the sales block. The West Coast division isn't worth more than a hundred million, max, if it's run independently from DMI. Zarah, please be smart about this," Madeline said.

Don could taste freedom and a break in his near future. He wanted this deal to work almost as much as Madeline did, but he contained his enthusiasm.

"I am overwhelmed with so many offers," Zarah said.

Don's and Madeline's stares were frozen. As the number of bidders went up, the cost would too. The revelation wasn't encouraging for DMI. Don figured Madeline was beginning to get antsy about her bottomless offer. She could anticipate overpaying significantly to stay on the bidder list. Maybe Zarah wasn't as docile as she appeared. Don suspected Madeline was going to find out, having practically offered a blank check.

"Exactly how many offers are you talking?"

"There have been three, if you and Don are counted. There's also Tamara and my husband."

"Joel?" Madeline yelled as the oomph drained from her. "You're kidding," she said, barely above a whisper.

Don was numb. Without sufficient preparation, he was engaged in a battle pitting four Mitchells against each other. Would it ever end? He wanted to flee from his mother's house and keep on running until he reached the airport. Quarrelling had taken its toll. He was sitting out this round. Madeline would have to duel alone.

He was about to say good-bye when Zarah's voice rang out. "I must speak with my attorney about your offer. It is a very good deal."

With the snap of a finger, Madeline's zeal was restored. Don could tell by how animated Madeline was becoming as she listened to Zarah.

"Are you saying yes to our offer?" she asked.

"I cannot answer this for you until I meet with my family's attorney."

"That's fair," Don said.

"Why don't you take time to digest the offer and we can call you in a few days? How does this sound?" Madeline asked.

"I must go. I'm not well," Zarah stated.

Madeline rattled off a question before Zarah could escape. "Can you at least agree not to make a decision without letting us know? We'd like to counter any offer submitted to you."

"I can make you aware."

"One more question," Madeline said, but Zarah abruptly ended the call, citing she was going to be sick and had to go.

Madeline stewed a bit. "I wanted to ask how much of a shot we have, but Ms. Zarah hung up."

Don didn't add to his mother's disappointment. He'd sit quietly until she was ready to talk about a plan B, as plan A had most likely run to the restroom with morning sickness that had extended into the afternoon. He'd roll his sleeves up and get busy with drafting a refined strategy, one that didn't depend on Zarah. He got up to grab another sandwich. It was going to be a long afternoon for sure.

Chapter 37

Monday afternoon skipped by. Madeline was pleased with the proposal she and Don had labored over for the past five hours. With the exception of a couple bathroom breaks, she'd stayed planted at the table. She gathered a bunch of loose papers spread across the table and produced a neat stack. She tapped the top page.

"This is it. I'll have my assistant type this up first thing tomorrow," Madeline said, wanting to believe this was going to work.

"Have her run it by legal too. Let's kill two birds with one stone," Don replied.

"Agreed," she said, reaching for a glass of water, intentionally suppressing any inkling of doubt she had. She had to be sure and project confidence too. "Ah, this is warm. I'm going to get some ice. You want anything?"

Don yawned. "Nah, I'm beat. I'm calling it a day and going home. I'll see you tomorrow, that is if you come into the office," he said, chuckling.

"Look, I've paid my dues. I've earned every day off and more. It's your and Tamara's turn to run DMI."

"Not so fast, Mother. You don't look like someone who is ready to be put out to pasture. Cut the drama."

She stood and walked to the refrigerator. "Seriously, I'm not retiring this week, but the day is coming quickly."

Madeline pressed her glass against the ice dispenser on the refrigerator door.

Don approached her. "And you think buying the division from Zarah will be the impetus for Tamara to take a position at DMI?"

"Absolutely. I have to believe it."

Don leaned his hand against the refrigerator. "I'm not nearly as confident as you are."

Madeline swished the glass rapidly, letting the ice hit the sides. She chose her words very carefully. She couldn't lose Don's support. "You know, you're right. I've spent the entire afternoon drafting a deal. What I should have been doing was presenting our case directly to Tamara." Madeline plopped the glass on the island counter. "She has to understand what this is about," she said.

Don placed his hand on hers. "We've put our best offer together. We can't do any more. Let's get it typed, present it to Zarah, and see what happens. I'm praying for God's direction, because we need all the help we can get before dealing with Joel's wife and your daughter." He chuckled. Madeline didn't.

"I'm not waiting for the formal document."

"And what does that mean?" Don asked, his voice quivering.

"I'm going to find Tamara this evening and tell her what's going on," she said, leaning her hip against the counter and folding her arms tightly. She sincerely wanted to be transparent with Tamara. One of the challenges of their relationship in the past was an inability to communicate. Madeline wasn't going to lose ground with her daughter. She preferred putting the facts out in the open and let Tamara handle it like adults did. "It's no secret. We're going after the West Coast division. She has to be told."

"I don't think we should tell her unless Zarah agrees to our deal." Madeline shook her head frantically, her eyes closed, as Don continued. "Why create tension for no reason? If Zarah says no, and there's a fifty to sixty percent chance she will, then you will have stirred your sleeping giant. And you can believe there will be a price to pay from her."

Madeline looked Don straight in the eyes and said, "Tamara doesn't scare me."

"Me, either, but why start a fight with her if we don't have to?"

"Thank you for your input, but I'm going to see Tamara." Madeline glanced at her watch. Five thirty. "She should be home, don't you think?"

"I don't know," Don said. "Since she moved out of my place, we haven't spoken much."

Madeline wasn't sure she should believe him. "Well, give me her new address."

"No way."

"Why not?" she replied indignantly.

"It's not a good idea. The two of you should keep your distance until this business stuff is resolved. I don't have a good feeling about this."

Madeline pressed against the counter again with her arms stretched out, and her neck bent downward, as if she were about to do a push-up. "This isn't about feelings. It's about birthright." She lifted her gaze to pierce his. "If you won't give me her address, that's no problem. As my mother used to say, there's more than one way to skin a cat. My phone works fine. So I'll call her."

"Suit yourself," Don said. Madeline detected a sharp bite in his tone. "You don't need me to run this train off the track. I'm out of here," he said, going to get his keys from the table.

"Wait," she said. "I need your phone."

"Why, Mother?"

"You know Tamara might not answer when she sees my number come up."

"I don't want to be in this."

"Are you telling me no?"

"I am," he replied.

Madeline didn't know whether to be more upset with Don for telling her no or for hindering her effort to contact Tamara. She could have badgered him until he gave in, but she had no desire to do so. Madeline would take her chances and use her own phone.

"I'll see you tomorrow?" Don said.

"Maybe," she said as cordially as she could given her disappointment.

Don laughed briefly. "Oh, Mother, you're something else. You're in my prayers."

"Uh-huh," she uttered. She wasn't asking God for help, and Don shouldn't act like he had to on her behalf. Madeline and God hadn't always maintained stellar communication. As a matter of fact, they didn't have any. During her twenties and possibly her thirties, she could have used His help with Dave and his wavering commitment to the marriage. She could have used His interaction during her single parenting years. Yet there had been nothing. As far as she was concerned, Dave and Don could keep God to themselves. She'd handle her problem solo. Madeline liked her odds better that way.

Chapter 38

Don was gone. Madeline drew on heaps of fortitude and then went to get her phone upstairs. Shockingly, Tamara answered. Madeline wasn't prepared. She hadn't formulated her spiel and wouldn't get the chance now. Madeline realized that if she didn't start talking quickly, Tamara was going to hang up, and who knew when she'd answer her mother's call again.

"Hello, darling," Madeline said to lay the foundation for a sensible discussion.

Tamara returned the greeting. "What do you want, Mother?"

Cranky and irritated was the way Tamara sounded. Madeline wasn't deterred.

"I have to tell you something very important."

"Did something happen to Don?" she asked, sounding overly distressed.

"No, no, nothing like that."

"Oh, you scared me for a second."

"Didn't mean to," Madeline said, stalling. The proposal had to come across perfectly for Tamara to give it any serious consideration. Madeline smirked. She could present a proposal to a board of directors without losing an ounce of rest. But not to her daughter. Tamara was her Kryptonite.

"If it's not Don, what about you? Is there something wrong with you?"

"Nothing a good night's sleep can't cure."

"Then what is it?" Tamara demanded.

There were a million ways to tell Tamara they were going after the division, but none sounded right. Madeline wasn't going to beat around the bush any longer. She decided to blurt out the truth and deal with the fallout. "You need to know that DMI is going after the West Coast division, and we're offering a sizable price, far above market value."

"Really?" Tamara retorted, her tone snide. "When did this happen?" she ranted.

"Today. We're pitching the proposal to Zarah as soon as the paperwork is finished."

"DMI wasn't interested in the division until you found out I wanted it. Why am I surprised?" Tamara said, cackling and then abruptly quieting down.

Madeline didn't want to let Tamara get too angry. "This move is for you."

"For me? You must be kidding." She cackled again. "This is about you, Mother. It always is. I should have known not to let you get too close. You've burned me again."

Madeline had to find the mechanism that would calm Tamara down and allow her to see the big picture, the one where their family was working together. "I am doing this for you and Don. You both mean the world to me."

"Huh, you have a funny way of showing your love, going behind my back to buy a company you knew I wanted."

"I'm sorry you feel this way." One division wasn't a company. If Tamara had the business savvy necessary to build a company, she would understand the flaw in her statement. Yet Madeline would rather eat nails than criticize Tamara, a daughter who was three seconds from ending the call and possibly their relationship. Madeline swallowed her negativity, and her pride slid down her throat too.

"Just so you know, I'm not withdrawing my interest. You might have more money, but I have a friendship with Zarah. It's got to be worth something," Tamara declared.

Friendship was great, but offering Zarah an even exchange for Harmonious Energy wasn't to be matched. Madeline opted not to share that piece of information. The fire was already burning out of control without fuel being added. "Once you think this through, I'm hoping you'll agree this is best for everyone. You can return to DMI and assume your rightful place as president."

"Second in charge, right?"

"I don't think you should see it as second."

"I really don't care what you think, Mother." Under normal circumstances, Madeline wouldn't allow such a flagrant show of disrespect from her child or anybody else's. She'd give Tamara a pass in this case but placed no guarantees on doing the same in future encounters. "Mother, I'm not letting you bully me into changing my mind."

"Is that what you think I'm doing?"

"It's exactly what you're doing, and I'm not letting you get away with this. The past is dead. I'm not a child. If I want to buy my own company, I'll do just that," she said, drilling the message into Madeline's soul. "I will never be controlled or overpowered by anyone again, including you."

Madeline could have fired back but didn't.

"So go ahead and put in your overpriced offer, and I'll put in mine."

"You're seriously going to do this?" Madeline replied, running out of ways to reach Tamara.

"Oh no, not me. *You* did this. May the best Mitchell win."

Madeline was crushed. "Do you think we'll ever be able to fix our relationship?"

"Never know, Mother. I'm willing, but you have to show me some respect. It's the only way I can let you back into my life."

"I guess there's hope."

"Of course, but it will be up to you. Bidding on the West Coast division isn't the ideal step toward fixing our relationship, but you are who you are."

Madeline grinned. "That I am."

"I'm going now," Tamara said.

Madeline reluctantly said good-bye.

Right before Tamara disconnected, she said one more thing. "Mother, you're a trip, but I love you. I have to go." She hung up the phone without letting Madeline reply.

The line went dead. "I love you too," Madeline uttered, with no one on the other end of the call to hear her.

Melancholy poured into her soul. Madeline lay across her bed and allowed herself to recall only positive memories of her only daughter. Tamara's comment about the past being dead lingered in her mind, and perhaps it was true. Madeline didn't care. With her future in flux, clinging to the past was her greatest treasure, and she'd cling to it with all her might.

Chapter 39

Cats were said to have nine lives. If Tamara counted the run-in with her ex-boyfriend, her brother, and the multiple rounds with her mother, she was down to maybe two or three. Running into Madeline today was bound to burn through a couple more lives. She couldn't really take the risk of having to argue her way past her mother. Yet Tamara had no choice but to seek help. Madeline was out of control. Don was the only one who had the slightest chance of talking some sense into the woman they called Mother.

Tamara hustled out of the cab and flew by the security guards at DMI and tackled the stairs in a whirlwind. So far she was in the clear. The fact that she'd seen no sign of Madeline brought her relief, but as long as Tamara was in the building, danger lurked. She'd get into Don's office, plead her case, get support, and get the heck out of DMI before the she lion was roused from her slumber.

After reaching the sixth floor, Tamara straightened her shirt and regained her composure. No one on executive row was going to see her as the tattered Mitchell girl. She had learned that much from her mother, to never let outsiders see her vulnerability. She hadn't mastered the art as well as the Mitchells had, but progress was being made.

Tamara slowed to a saunter. There was a bubbling in the pit of her stomach, and she knew why. Tamara had been so obsessed with getting into the building undetected by

Madeline that she'd forgotten her primary objective. She had to convince Don that their mother needed to back off the West Coast division. She didn't know if he'd be receptive, since Don was a loyal Madeline advocate. Tamara walked idly around the administrative station for a few minutes and then approached Don's door, knocking out her fear. She boldly stepped into the office after waving off the assistant's offer to get Don. Tamara didn't need or want assistance in reaching her brother. She was a Mitchell, and that gave her extensive rights and privileges within DMI's walls. She relished the taste of significance.

"Tamara, I didn't know you were coming by the office this morning. How's it going?" Don asked, peering up from the document on his desk and the folder lying next to it.

"Not well," she replied, aiming to make her request for his support, and get over his possible rejection, as quickly as possible.

"What's the problem?" he asked, tucking the papers into the folder and giving her his undivided attention.

Tamara was on center stage, with the beam of light shining on her. Fear had her catatonic. She couldn't believe how difficult this was. Don was her brother, and a loving one. She didn't have to be afraid of him. Yet, Tamara felt severely uncomfortable about proceeding. Then she focused on her plans, boosting her confidence. She decided in that instance not to leave without an answer, preferably a yes.

"Mother called me last night and told me DMI is going after the West Coast division hard," she said, causing Don to lean forward in his chair. "Regardless of what you guys are doing, I'm not taking my offer off the table for the West Coast division."

Don tossed his pen in the air but didn't speak. She wanted him to yell or challenge her. She knew how to handle those reactions. Silence was a secret weapon Tamara wasn't prepared to handle. She felt compelled to keep talking. She took a seat. Don cradled his head between his thumb and index finger. His glance seemed to slice her into pieces. She ignored his piercing stare and returned to pleading her case. It was the only way to reach her brother.

"You know what I've been through, and by some miracle, I'm still here," she said, tapping the arms of the chair. "I've gotten past the rough times, and now I'm ready to stand on my own. I'm sure you can appreciate where I'm coming from."

Don remained silent. His refusal to speak was becoming annoying. She wasn't invisible. "Can't you say something?"

"Like what?" he asked, twirling the pen that was lying on the desk. "You seem to have the answers. Between you and Mother, there's not much for me to say."

The lack of concern in his tone was troubling. Don was her greatest ally. He'd always tried to help her, even when she didn't want it. She could tell Don was hurt, and Tamara felt awful. She didn't want to lose his support or his love. His reaction tugged at her heart, causing Tamara to be torn between proceeding with her pursuit of independence or ending the discussion and keeping her relationship intact with her brother. Each had merit. Who could say which was right and which was wrong? Should she fight to maintain her sanity or put her brother first? She was reeling with emotions. One fact was true: she loved Don and didn't want him to be mad. She had much to contemplate. For now, she'd treat him with the respect he deserved. His years of unconditional love had earned him as much.

"I might not be going about this the right way, but who's to say Mother is, either? To be honest, she has this whole company," Tamara said, opening her arms wide and tracing the room with a finger in the air. "I'm asking for a tiny division, the smallest one. Why can't she let me have it?"

"We know how Mother can be, but at the core of it all, she loves us." Don's interpretation of their mother's love translated into being controlling for Tamara. "You know she's not trying to hurt you, Tamara," Don said, sounding slightly less agitated, but not at all cheery. She'd continue treading lightly.

"No, I don't know that."

"Oh, please," Don said, shifting his head to lean on the other hand.

"No, seriously," Tamara replied. "When a person willfully commits an act against someone, calling it an accident or a poor decision doesn't make the hurt any less real." Madeline had made her decisions very carefully and was old enough to know when to back off. Tamara wasn't buying Don's sympathy for their mother. "Mother knows what she's doing, and even when it's uncomfortable for us, she does it, anyway." She tapped both heels on the floor. "So, no, I don't agree."

"Too bad. One day, when you're able to see this situation more objectively, you might have a different perspective."

Maybe, but Tamara wasn't worried about *one day*. Her concern was today.

Don stared at Tamara. "Sis, I really don't get you," he said, shaking his head.

"What do you mean?"

He scratched the tiny hairs on his chin and looked away, only to let his gaze return to her with a piercing force. "We grew up in the same house. Mother wasn't perfect. I get that, but what did she do that was so bad that you're bent on making her pay forever?"

Tamara could tell Don was mad, and she felt awful, but she wasn't taking sole responsibility for the issues between her and their mother. "I'm not just mad at her. I'm mad at Dad and Sherry too." Don had asked the question, so she was going to tell him the truth, sparing no one. Her parents hadn't bothered to spare her feelings. "They were all so selfish and so focused on their drama that they forgot about us kids."

"Come on, Tamara. We were kids then. We're adults now, and our father is dead. When are you going to let it go?"

"Why should I?" Why couldn't anyone understand her feelings about the family? Even Don wasn't listening. Just like their mother, he wanted her to shove the past under a rug and walk away like nothing had happened. It was fine with her if they wanted to live in a fairy tale, but she would not. "They created this situation, Mother, Sherry, and Dad."

"So why is your anger directed mostly at Mother?"

Tamara couldn't tell him the real reason, which was simply that she needed someone to blame. Since Dad and Andre were gone, and she didn't care enough about Sherry to make her a viable candidate to hate, only Madeline was left. Tamara wasn't going to tell that to Don. She had a more pleasing answer for him. "We lived with her, not Dad. If she'd spent more time with us while we were growing up, instead of spending all those hours at DMI and chasing behind Dad, then maybe things would have been different for us, different for me," she said, feeling melancholy.

"One day you'll have to acknowledge that your old hurt is constantly stirring up new pain. You need to find a way to let the past go."

"Easy for you to say," she said, hoping to relieve the pressure building up inside her.

"No easier for me than it is for you." She didn't agree. Don continued. "I know what you're thinking, and I would never minimize your trauma. But you have to acknowledge that others suffered in our family too. Like me; I had to learn how to live with my father's rejection. Can you imagine how it felt to have him choose his other son over me?"

"It's not the same thing, not by a longshot," she said, becoming tired of the topic.

"You're right, but look at it this way, Tamara. Andre raped you, but your anger and unwillingness to forgive is preventing you from having a peace of mind." He slid to the edge of the seat, peering at her, and said, "So, I ask you again, when are you going to let the past go and give Mother a break?"

"You're always defending her."

"Funny, because she says I'm always defending you. Maybe I need to stop running interference between the two of you and let you battle it out until one or both of you become exhausted or gain some sense. At this point, I'm okay with both outcomes," he said, playfully tossing the pen into the air.

"Yes, I fight with Mother, but I don't want to with you. I just wish you could see how my getting the West Coast division is best for the family."

"How?"

"Because I can get a fresh start. Remember, I've been home only for a few months. This is still new to me . . . being in the same city with you and Mother. It can be smothering for someone like me." She could feel her emotions rising up, but she refused to cry. "I've been on my own for so long. I'm actually glad to be in the States, but I have much more healing to do on my terms—not Mother's," she said, talking louder to combat the lump of emotions settling in her throat. "I love Madeline, but I need distance from her."

Don's harsh stare softened, and she could see the compassion in his gaze. "I get that, but it doesn't justify you and Mother being at odds."

"Then you need to talk to her, because she's the one who created this tension over the West Coast division."

"She can't fight unless you participate," Don told her.

"Well, I'm not backing down. Mother can throw her money around, but Zarah and I are close friends. I have an excellent shot at this too, and I'm taking it."

Don's hand slid slowly down his face as his hope for a cordial resolution drained from him. "You need to be careful with Zarah. She's pregnant with Joel's child. You can believe he's not going to be far away."

Joel wasn't a problem. He didn't want to be with Zarah, and Tamara was hoping Zarah didn't want him anymore. "They're separated. He's not a factor."

"Believe that if you want to." Don chuckled, reacting more strongly than he had in the past twenty minutes.

"He's staying at the hotel and doesn't want much to do with Zarah," Tamara announced.

"So what? They are still married. Trust me. You don't want to get caught in the middle of their relationship. It could backfire," he said.

"I'm not worried," she fired at him.

"Okay," he said, twirling the pen on his desk again. "Well, good luck, because if you think Mother is a challenge, how about rumbling with her and Joel simultaneously?"

Tamara hadn't given any thought previously to that scenario. Rumbling with both of them wasn't ideal, but that would be up to them. She was moving ahead with her offer on the West Coast division.

"Thanks for listening. I'm going to head out. I love you," she said. Nothing had been resolved with her visit, but the heart-to-heart had been well worth the trip. At least Don knew she loved him and Madeline too. That was important in case the bidding war became very heated and relationships had to be temporarily pushed to the sidelines.

She felt strangely invigorated. Tamara would call Zarah right away and schedule a meeting. She didn't want to play around. If she was going to get the division, she had to make a move before Madeline submitted her gigantic offer. Tamara hustled outside, plucking her cell phone from her pocket en route. Her victory might be closer than expected, and she couldn't wait.

Chapter 40

Zarah had stuck with tea for breakfast, lunch, and dinner. Solid food just wasn't settling well. She'd lain on her bed most of the day, not feeling too good. There was a knock on the master bedroom door. Zarah suspected it was the housekeeper since she's sent the cook home hours ago and Ann was busy with a personal appointment. Unable to get up, Zarah called out, "Come in."

The door opened, and the housekeeper entered. "Mrs. Mitchell, I'm about to leave, unless there's something else you'd like for me to do."

"No, there's nothing," Zarah told her without budging from her spot on the bed.

"Are you sure?" the housekeeper asked, sounding a bit worried.

"I'm sure."

"Would you like for me to call Mr. Mitchell for you?"

"No," Zarah replied curtly. "I'm fine." She mustered the strength to sit up so she'd appear to be okay. "Go on home and don't worry about me. I only need a bit of rest, and I'll be up and about tomorrow."

The housekeeper was about to reply, then paused, acquiescing. She left the room, maintaining her worried look.

After the door closed, Zarah's head was heavy and so was her heart. She wandered from the bed to the chair, seeking comfort without success. She climbed back on the bed and buried her face in the pillow, wanting relief from the stress and the discomfort in her belly. Many thoughts tried to grip her, and they were mostly negative. She didn't dare think about the baby being in trouble. Her baby was blessed. It had to be.

Negativity was winning out. She finally dozed off to sleep, only to be awakened by a rush of anxiety. She practically popped up in the bed like a jack-in-the-box. Being in the house alone became overwhelming. The house staff was gone. Ann was on business. She wanted to reach out to someone. Her initial instinct was to call Joel. Gloom swarmed her as she feared his reaction. What if she called and he didn't answer? Worse, what if he answered but wouldn't come? She eased her head down on the pillow. Her only option was to call Tamara and have her come by. Her sister-in-law had been supportive, but there were times when she caused Zarah to feel badly about her commitment to Joel. Zarah wasn't up for debating with Tamara. She contemplated what to do.

Zarah decided to dial whatever name popped into her mind first. When she picked up the cordless phone lying on the nightstand near her bed, she heard broken beeps, which indicated she had messages. She eased herself against the headboard and retrieved the messages, looking for one from Joel.

"First message," the voice rang out. "Zarah, this is Madeline Mitchell. I'd like to continue our conversation about the West Coast division as soon as possible. DMI has put together a deal that guarantees you ownership of Harmonious Energy. Give me a call as soon as you get this message. We're eager to get this deal done. I look forward to hearing from you today. Thanks." Zarah gripped the phone tighter as her anxiety nudged upward. She listened to the next message in search of Joel's voice.

"Next message," the voice announced. "Zarah, this is Tamara. I need to see you today. I have to work out a deal with you for the West Coast division. My mother might have called you already and offered you a ton of money, but please don't sell her the division without giving me a chance. This is a matter of life and death for me. Please wait until I see you." Zarah moaned.

Initially she'd been intrigued about taking on a leadership role in the company. With Tamara's encouragement, she came to see the job as a way to honor her father's legacy and, more importantly, to gain her husband's heart. Faced with so much hard work, constant fights between Joel and Tamara, and pressure from Don and Madeline, Zarah didn't have the same excitement anymore. Her joy had been further squelched with each phone message.

She should have hung up the phone but let the messages continue playing. "Next message," the voice said. Zarah was expecting it to be Don, asking about the division too. "Zarah, I'm calling to check on you." Her eyes widened when she heard Joel's voice, and she drew her knees to her chest. Some of her stress melted away. "We also have to talk about the West Coast division. We didn't get to talk through my proposal before, but it's critical that we do so."

Not him too. She was deeply saddened. Wasn't anyone calling to see about her and the baby without asking about the division? Did anyone care? Anxiety rushed through her veins uncontrollably. Suddenly she felt a sharp pain in her abdomen. She winced from the pain but refused to panic. She drew in long, slow breaths. Despite her attempts to manage the pain, it intensified. She grasped for positive thoughts, finding none. She didn't know what to do. Instinctively, she wanted to call Joel. Under duress, she decided not to upset him prematurely. Fear and pain meshed, raising an alarm. Another wave of pain hit, and her alarm meter went into overdrive, with bells of panic ringing in her head.

She touched a small patch of moisture on the bed and looked down to find a few spots of blood on the sheet. Terror set in. She sprang from the bed and ran into the bathroom. Once inside, she found a few more spots of blood on her clothing. Doubt, fear, and panic rolled into a giant ball. She was paralyzed, unable to move. Losing her child couldn't happen. It just couldn't. She had to believe her baby was well. Denial seemed less frightening.

Chapter 41

Spinning his wheels at the hotel was driving Joel crazy. Most of the week had been wasted, including the botched visit with Zarah. He had to get moving and make something happen. He drove onto the street without a clear direction. The admonishment from the church mother continuously replayed in his head. *You need to come back home in the spirit. You've been gone too long.* Joel was much more mindful of her advice than he'd been in the past. He wasn't discounting God totally. He couldn't, having experienced the power of God's presence supernaturally on numerous occasions. He definitely knew who God was, but he wasn't ready to give up his personal desires. The allure of being back in the limelight and in charge was a powerful drug, constantly pulling at him and taking precedence.

He revved the engine at the stoplight to bolster his enthusiasm. None was flowing personally or professionally. Zarah had discounted his last appeal. Yet she kept popping into his head. She had a board meeting with DMI coming up in a few days. The meeting was just as important to him as it was to her, although she probably didn't know why. The strength of her presentation could determine whether she got control of Harmonious Energy and then have the heart to let him have the West Coast division. He had made countless presentations to the board of directors and had a feel for what they liked. He could help Zarah tremendously in her preparation for the meeting. She hadn't asked for help, but it didn't mean she wouldn't welcome his input. *What the heck,* he thought, inching his way into the right-hand lane. He would zip onto the highway and go see Zarah. He would go unannounced, hoping she'd let him in. He didn't dwell on the alternative.

He punched the accelerator, intending to cut the drive down to a minimum. With each mile clocked, he grew more eager to see Zarah.

When he got to the house, he jumped out of the car, hurried to the door, and rang the bell. No one answered. It was after eight o'clock. The staff was gone, but normally Zarah was at home in the evening, at least the former Zarah used to be. The new one was hard to gauge. He rang the doorbell again and waited a few minutes. Again nobody answered. He plucked his cell phone from his pocket and dialed the house phone. No answer. He held the phone, not sure what to do. Where could she be, other than off somewhere with Tamara? Joel's zeal was doused. *Too late. You're out of luck,* he thought grimly. He pressed the doorbell once again and began walking to the car, dialing the house phone as he went. This time, Zarah answered.

"Hey, you *are* home," he said, halting.

"Yes. I am resting."

"Are you alone?"

"Yes," she replied.

"Fabulous," he wanted to say, relieved Tamara wasn't on the scene. "Would you like company?"

She didn't answer immediately, but he wasn't leaving without a yes.

"Because I'm at the front door if you do," he added.

She still didn't answer, forcing him to be direct.

"I'd like to come in."

"Do you have the key with you?" she asked.

"Why?" Joel asked before realizing he was being defensive. It was too late to retract the question.

"Because I don't want to come down the stairs. If you have a key, it would be most helpful for me."

Joel had the key in his car. "Okay, I'll let myself in. Where are you? Upstairs?" he asked.

"Yes, I'm in the bedroom."

"Give me a few minutes, and I'll be right up. Is there anything I can get for you?"

"No, thank you," she said in a strange tone.

Zarah didn't seem to have the same eagerness to see him as she had during other recent visits. Joel wasn't certain, but he figured Tamara had something to do with the mood change. He didn't let it bother him. He got the key and went inside Zarah's house, which was his house too, and savored the advantage he had over Tamara. She had a mouth and many unsolicited opinions, but what Tamara didn't have was a key. She was an outsider who had access to his wife only when invited. Joel's steps slowed as he reclaimed his influence on Zarah.

She didn't want him to bring her anything, but Joel stopped by the kitchen and got two bottles of water, one for each of them. He climbed the stairs and headed to the master bedroom. He hadn't been in there in over a month. Before leaving for Chicago, he had shared the room with Zarah on occasion, but his love had been absent. He swallowed the awkwardness, opened the door, and approached Zarah, who was lying on the bed. She didn't move when he entered the room. He found it slightly odd but was not alarmed. He'd maneuver gently through the conversation until Zarah either kicked him out or warmed to his visit.

"You're not feeling well?" he asked, remembering what she'd said earlier.

"I'm fine."

She didn't appear fine, but he didn't harp on her appearance. Joel certainly didn't want to make her self-conscious about the way she looked. He rerouted the conversation away from her health, assuming that she wasn't having a problem. "Are you ready for the board meeting coming up?"

"I don't want to talk about business," she said, cutting him off abruptly. She stood. "I have much pressure from everyone in the family, and it's very stressful for me and the baby." She clutched her stomach. "I can't take the pressure," she said, crying out and clutching her stomach tighter.

Joel rushed to her. "What's going on?" he asked. He could see she was in pain. "Here," he said leading her to the chair. "Sit down and have some water." He handed her one of the bottles he'd gotten from the kitchen. Joel wasn't a medical technician, but he didn't have to be one to see that something was wrong. He feared for her and the baby. "What's wrong?" he asked, determined to get an answer.

A second later Zarah was wincing, with her fists balled tightly and pressed against her abdomen. He tried to get her to tell him what was happening, but nothing coherent reached his ears. Zarah became increasingly hysterical. He was out of his element and didn't know exactly what to do.

Without a better idea, he yelled at her in a loud, commanding voice. "Zarah, you have to calm down and tell me what's going on," he shouted from a squatting position in front of her.

"I can't lose the baby," she repeated over and over.

"You won't," he replied, with the sole purpose of reassuring her.

He had to get her to calm down; otherwise there was no telling what could go wrong. It didn't take long for Joel to realize he was in way over his head and had to get help.

"Let me call the ambulance and get you to the hospital," he said.

He went to stand, and she dug her hand into his arm. "No, no hospital. I don't want to be there."

"But you're in pain," he said, exacerbated by the entire ordeal. Her condition wasn't one to play around with. Indecision could mean the difference between the baby living and dying. Joel was motivated to action. His baby had to live. "I have to get you to the hospital."

"Please, no," she pleaded. "Rest is what I need, not the hospital."

Joel was torn. She continued pleading, which wore him down. Against his better judgment, he caved. "All right, I won't call nine-one-one. I'll let you rest for a while."

She leaned forward and hugged him. "Thank you."

He pushed her back gently in order to make eye contact. "I will not let you stay here alone. I won't call so long as you let me stay here with you." He sensed the stress rising in her as she tightened her grip on his arm. He quickly worked to diffuse her worry. "I will feel much better sleeping close by in the guest room." Before she could reject his appeal, he added, "And this is nonnegotiable. I stay, or I place the call. The choice is yours." He peered straight at her without wavering.

She must have noted the seriousness in his voice, because Zarah agreed without resistance. He figured she was probably as glad to have him there as he was to be there. She let her body relax in the chair.

"I'm glad you're not fighting me on this," he said. "Can you stand?"

"Not very well," she told him.

In a flash, Joel gently scooped Zarah up from the chair and carried her to the bed. He delicately placed her on top of the sheets. She slid underneath. He tucked her in, harboring the same reluctance about not going to the hospital. Joel hoped it wasn't a decision he'd live to regret. He sat on the edge of the bed.

"Remember, I'll be right next door. Call me for anything. Do you hear me? Anything."

She nodded in affirmation.

He tucked the phone next to her. "Don't get up for anything. Call me first."

She agreed.

Joel brushed the hair from her face and leaned in to kiss her cheek. "Don't worry. I'm here."

She sighed, and he could tell Zarah's discomfort hadn't subsided.

"Can I get you an aspirin or a pain pill?"

"No," she blurted out. "I won't hurt the baby. No medicine."

Joel stroked her face again, frustrated that he'd upset her. "Okay, no medicine," he told her. Joel would keep his promise for as long as he could, but he couldn't guarantee he wouldn't change his mind later. "Good night," he told her and turned out the light on his way out of the room.

He went down the hallway and around the corner to the closest guest room. With each step, the distance seemed too far from Zarah. He'd be more at ease sleeping outside her room. Once she fell asleep, he might even take a nap on the chair in her room. He'd decide right after placing a call to his mother. This was a big deal, and he needed his mother's advice.

Chapter 42

Joel took off his watch and laid it on the dresser, then unbuttoned his shirt. He was in for the evening. They weren't going anywhere, unless it was by ambulance to the hospital. Before he settled into his room and called Sherry, he would lock up downstairs and turn off the lights. As he stepped foot on the bottom stair, the doorbell rang. Whoever was dropping by had to return another day. He'd express his apologies and get them off the doorstep in a matter of minutes. He peeked through the stained glass near the front door, and his tolerance withered. He leaned against the doorknob and scratched his head, peering at the floor. He could ignore the bell, but it wouldn't solve his immediate problem. There was only one thing to do—confront the thorn in his side. He gathered his emotions and snatched the door open.

"Tamara, how can I help you?" He forced each word out with such a cutting edge that it figuratively slit his tongue.

Tamara stood there with a bewildered expression. "Well, hello to you too," she retorted. "What are you doing answering Zarah's door?"

Joel wasn't sparring with Tamara tonight. He had to get back upstairs. Fiddling around with Tamara wasn't going to happen. "How can I help you?" he asked again.

"I'm here to see Zarah." Tamara gestured as if she was going to push past Joel to gain entry to the house.

Pests were too difficult to get out once they crawled in. There was no way he could let her in. He had pressing issues upstairs, and her antics weren't going to distract him from completing his mission of getting Zarah settled. He let his stature dominate the doorway, his arms folded and his legs spread a shoulder's length apart.

Brushing up against Joel's stone wall of a physique, she instantly halted. "Can I come in and check on her?"

"No, but I can let her know you dropped by."

"I don't want you to deliver a message. I can talk to her myself." Tamara took an extra step back, almost as if being too close to him repulsed her.

He didn't understand what thoughts were churning in her head, and he wasn't trying to find out. It would be up to her and a therapist to unravel her idiosyncrasies, as long as she got off his doorstep. If she kept dragging out her goodbye, he might have to assist her in vacating the premises.

"Leaving a message is your best bet tonight."

"And who made you king?" she roared. "You're not able to decide who she talks to. She's not a child."

"Why don't you leave?" he suggested. "I don't want any trouble."

She planted her hand on her waist. "You better not have caused her any harm, or you'll see what trouble is," she barked at him.

"Yada, yada, yada,' he replied, not caving in to her threat. "I'm shaking in my shoes about what big bad Tamara is going to do to me. Woo," he said, intentionally fueling her anger. Then he took a serious tone. "Don't you worry about my wife. I'm here now. I'll take good care of her." He sealed the statement with a wink.

What did he do that for? Tamara's temper blazed with "You are pathetic, taking advantage of a woman who had the poor luck of ending up with you for a husband."

Joel discounted her observation. He didn't care what she thought. Zarah was his concern. Still, Tamara's comment was piercing, causing him to reflect. So what if he had professional reasons for pursuing Zarah? Tonight was purely personal. He'd made mistakes previously, too many to count. The last month had been filled with confusion. With the baby in jeopardy, the decision seemed clear. He couldn't and wouldn't leave Zarah. She was the mother of his unborn child. She deserved his respect.

"Tamara, you don't have to worry. I'm not mistreating her. You'll be glad to know that her well-being is my primary concern right now." He leaned against the door and let his glance meet Tamara's. "I'm serious."

"I hope you're telling me the truth," she said, showing signs of relief, or at least Joel saw the reaction in her that he wanted. "Before I leave, can you tell me if she's sick?" Tamara asked with a glimmer of raw concern.

Joel hadn't seen her express concern for anybody. It was a shock, and he didn't quite know how to react.

Tamara went on. "Because I've called her several times today, and she hasn't returned any of my calls. That's unusual. She usually calls me back right away."

Joel buttoned his shirt partially as the night air swept in. "She's been tired, but I'll definitely let her know you are concerned. Give her a day or two and I'm sure she'll be in touch." Hopefully, Tamara would take the suggestion he'd offered and walk away. He wasn't going to share any details about Zarah's health scare, and Joel most certainly wasn't letting her in.

A veil of apprehension covered Tamara's face, but she seemed to accept his explanation. "I'll check on her tomorrow," she said, turning to walk away. Sincerity enveloped her.

As her guard lowered, so did his. In a moment of compassion, kindness rose within him. "Do you need to use the phone to call a ride?"

She eased the long purse strap over her head and let it rest on her shoulder. "No thank you. The cab is parked at the foot of the driveway," she said.

Joel peered down the driveway and saw the cab facing the road. "All right. Then we'll see you later."

Tamara turned her back and schlepped to the cab.

Joel called out, "Tamara."

She stopped and turned around.

"Thanks for checking on Zarah."

She smirked.

"Seriously, you've been a good friend for her. You've been here when she needed you. So I'm saying thank you for looking out for Zarah and my baby," Joel said, truly meaning what he was saying.

She waved at him with a grin. He guessed her reaction meant she was receiving his gratitude. He waited at the door until she was safely in the car and it pulled away.

The cordial encounter he'd just experienced with Tamara was unexpected but refreshing. However, Joel wasn't putting much stock in the truce. He eased the door shut and locked it. He cleared his thoughts and dashed up the stairs to check on his family.

Chapter 43

After ascending the stairs, Joel stood in the doorway of the master bedroom. Zarah appeared to be resting quietly. He wanted to go inside and make sure, but he didn't want to take the chance of waking her while she was sleeping peacefully. He stood in the doorway for a few minutes. When she didn't move, he heaved a sigh of relief and retreated to his room.

He glanced at the clock. Eight thirty wasn't too late. He dialed his mother's number, and she answered.

"I'm glad you're there," he told her. Comfort from his mother was exactly what Joel needed in order to get through this ordeal.

"Why? What's going on?" she asked, unaware of the weighty response coming.

"I'm at the house with Zarah. She was in a lot of pain earlier."

"Did you take her to the hospital?" Sherry blurted out.

"No. She wouldn't let me call the ambulance."

"What do you mean, she wouldn't let you? Just dial the number. She can't stop you."

Joel didn't want to second-guess his decision. He'd come to terms with not getting help. He didn't want his mother to stir up his doubt. Zarah was sleeping. He'd stay positive, although he respected what his mother was saying.

"I guess she didn't want to get alarmed if there wasn't a real problem. Since I didn't want to contribute to her stress, I went along with her request. She seems to be okay now. She's sleeping."

"Well, that's good, but I think she should see her doctor first thing in the morning and get checked out."

"I'm staying here tonight, and I'll make sure she goes to the doctor tomorrow."

"Good. It's better to be safe than sorry with a pregnancy."

"I agree, Mom. Thanks for the support. I needed to hear that."

"If you give me an hour, I can throw on some clothes and come over."

"Oh no, I don't want you worrying. She's going to be fine. We're going to be fine," he said, letting his statement serve as affirmation.

"I don't mind coming over, not one bit," she told him. "I can sit with her and give you a break."

"Thanks, Mom, but why don't you stay put tonight? Trust me, Zarah is in capable hands. If I need you, I'll call." He wasn't about to let his mother get worked up and stressed out too. Then he'd have two women in crisis; one was plenty. He appreciated her sentiments but graciously declined again.

"Okay, son. Please call me in the morning to let me know how she's doing. Please give her my love too."

"I will," he said.

Joel held the phone like it was a comforting blanket. His mother had given him the encouragement he needed, but it wasn't quite sufficient. He had to get a more substantive dose. Joel did something he hadn't done in months: he sincerely prayed for someone other than himself. He knelt on the floor and extended his arm and prayed for Zarah's strength and healing. He tarried on his knees, wanting to get confirmation from God that his prayer had been heard. The presence of God didn't saturate the room, but his inner peace was sufficient. He let the quiet soothe his soul.

Renewed with a touch of grace, he tiptoed into the master bedroom and sat in a chair not far from the bed. He fidgeted to find a relaxing position. After a while, he gave up, realizing that as long as Zarah was in danger, there wasn't a relaxing position for him. As she suffered, so would he.

"Ahhh," Zarah cried out. "Help me. Help me!"

Joel heard the piercing cries, but he was groggy and couldn't instantly process where he was or what was happening. He had dozed off in one chair, his legs outstretched and his feet resting on another. His glance sprinted around the room, searching for familiarity. Finally, the setting was registering. He was in their bedroom at home.

"Help me, please!" Zarah wailed.

Joel sprang into action. He kicked the chair out of his way and ran to the bedside. "I'm here," he said, desperate to calm her down. The room was dark, but he could see Zarah's silhouette. He grabbed her hand while attempting to turn on the light switch.

"The baby," she said, gripping his hand.

He felt wetness on her hand and didn't think much of it until the light came on. Joel stood next to the bed with her hand in his, stunned. Her hand was covered with blood, and the sheet had a large red spot near Zarah. His heart was pounding and his thoughts were racing, but Joel had to remain composed, despite the mounting horror. Zarah had to be put at ease until he could get her to the hospital.

"Lie back," he said and lifted her legs onto the bed. "Stay calm. I'm calling the ambulance."

"Joel, I don't want—"

He placed his index finger across her lips. “Shh. I’m not taking no for an answer. I’m calling the ambulance, and that’s the end of this discussion.” He rushed to the phone and dialed 9-1-1. He rattled off the requested information and set the phone on the nightstand.

Zarah was balled up in the fetal position and moaning. Joel wished there was more he could do. He had to resign himself to waiting for the paramedics. He stroked her hair, believing his touch provided some small bit of relief. Her moans grew louder and more strained. He patted her hands, offering what comfort he could.

“I have to run downstairs and open the door for the paramedics.”

She clung to his hand, squeezing tightly. “Don’t leave me,” she whispered.

He kissed her forehead, willing to use any technique that would help her to calm down. “I’ll run down and be back in less than a minute, but you have to let me go,” he said, peeling each of Zarah’s fingers from his hand. She gripped his arm as though he hadn’t said a word. “I promise to hurry down and be right back,” he said, kissing her forehead again, and pulled away.

In dramatic fashion she reached for him. Joel exited the room and literally ran down the hallway and dashed down the stairs. He got to the door just as flashing lights were circling the foyer through the door’s side glass panels. He unlocked the door and snatched it open.

“Is this the Mitchell residence?” one paramedic asked, entering the house with a medical kit.

“Yes. Come right in,” he said, stepping to the side. “My wife, Zarah, is upstairs, in the master bedroom. It’s down the hall and around the corner.”

Two paramedics traipsed up the stairs. Joel stayed out of their way but wasn’t far behind. When he approached the bedroom, he heard one of the medics asking Zarah questions. She was riled up and not very responsive. Joel poked his head around the corner so she could see him and hopefully settle down. His plan must have worked, because her muttering stopped once she made eye contact with him. Joel didn't want to blink, afraid he'd lose his effect on her. The paramedics worked quickly. One continued checking her vital signs, while the other bolted downstairs and returned with a portable gurney.

"Do you need me to help you get her downstairs?" Joel asked, uncomfortable with strangers carrying his wife.

"We have her secured, Mr. Mitchell. We're ready for transport."

They descended the stairs and carried Zarah outside to the ambulance. They slid the gurney inside.

Joel watched. The scene seemed surreal to him. As the ambulance doors closed, he snapped back to the present. "Hang on!" he shouted. "I'm riding with my wife."

"Okay, but you'd better hurry. We're ready to move."

Joel thanked the paramedics and hopped in. He sat next to Zarah in a cramped space, not caring two hoots about the inconvenience. Being with her negated the discomfort. Zarah was going in and out of consciousness. Despite the trauma she was suffering at the hands of fate, her beauty shone in the tight space.

He traced the rim of her face. "I'm sorry for not coming home sooner," he said, bending close to her ear.

He wasn't certain she could hear him. He clutched her hand and closed his eyes tightly as the ambulance careened down the road. Without prompting or pretense, he uttered a prayer, prepared to beg God for Zarah's and the baby's health. Joel remembered that he didn't have to beg God for favors, blessings, or miracles. What God was going to do was done out of His grace, mercy, and abiding love.

Joel reflected on those gifts from God, cleared his throat, and changed the tone of his prayer. “God, I’m asking you for divine healing for Zarah and the baby, but not because you owe me anything,” he said in a muffled voice. “I’m asking because you are God, and you are the almighty ruler of heaven and earth. Help my wife and baby right now, Lord, in Jesus’s name.” He closed with “Amen,” and a load dropped from his shoulders. A wave of peace flowed into the ambulance. Not only was Zarah going to be all right, but Joel also believed he was going to be too. He didn’t know how, but that wasn’t his concern. He’d let God work out the details. Joel’s hands were already filled with more than he could handle.

Chapter 44

Zarah was put into an examining room with a team of medical professionals. She wasn't completely sedated, but the doctor had given her something to relax her. She was quiet and was resting comfortably while tests were performed. Joel had approved a transfusion since she'd lost a pint of blood. He knew her religious beliefs didn't permit heroic efforts, but what was he supposed to do? He couldn't let Zarah and his baby die without medical intervention. It seemed as if each decision he made was greeted with controversy. Joel was barely hanging on. He'd step into the hallway to contact his mother. She'd want to know.

"Mom," he said, "I'm at the hospital with Zarah."

She cleared her throat. "I'm glad you decided to take her, instead of waiting until the morning. I feel much better," she said, punctuating her speech with a dry cough.

Then it dawned on him. She went to bed rather early most evenings. He'd probably startled her awake by calling after ten, but now it was too late to undo ringing her phone. He'd press ahead and convey the troubling news. "I had no choice. She got worse."

"How much worse?" Sherry asked, sounding worried, which bothered him greatly. He didn't want to worry her. His mother was one of the bright spots in his life, and Joel would fiercely protect her best interests, even against challenges he couldn't control.

"She had some bleeding—"

His mother cut him off to say, "That's not good. Has she lost the baby?"

Joel didn't know for sure. The ER team was working on her, and he didn't want to entertain the notion. So he conveyed the little he knew and the results he desired. "The doctors are doing the best they can, but I'm praying for her to be okay. She has to be," he said, bracing himself against the wall. "My baby has to be okay." He knew God had the power to fix this problem. He'd have to dust off his faith and let it tackle doubt and fear.

"Don't you worry, son. I'm on my way."

"Mom, there's no need for you to come. It's late. Why don't you wait until morning?"

"Joel, in a few more hours it *will* be morning."

He chuckled.

"And you're wasting time trying to stop me from coming to the hospital. I'm on my way. I'll see you soon, and I love you dearly." He soaked in her consoling words. "We'll get through this together."

He thanked his mother and breathed slower. Help was in progress, and comfort was on the way. His moment should have been complete, but there was a nagging omission. Admittedly, Tamara wasn't his favorite person, but she'd been some sort of confidant to his wife. He couldn't discount their bond; neither did Joel feel a need to do so. Zarah was in crisis and could use every extra ounce of encouragement available to her. His wife would want Tamara to know. More importantly, she deserved to know. He searched his contact list and queued up a text message.

Zarah at Providence Park Hospital in Novi.

Over the next hour, Joel grew anxious. Nobody was telling him anything. Zarah was sleeping, but she wasn't out of danger. He had to get answers. He jumped up and hustled into the hallway, nearly slamming into his mother, who was on her way into the room.

"Excuse me, Mom. I didn't see you," he said after practically plowing her down.

"Don't bother about me. How's Zarah? Is there any update on the baby's condition?"

Joel ran his hand over his head and let his gaze sweep the floor. "I haven't heard anything for the past hour. Somebody has to tell me something," he said, raising his voice.

Sherry tapped his shoulder. "Getting worked up isn't going to help. Why don't you find a doctor, get some answers? I'll sit here with Zarah."

Joel took the advice. He harnessed his anxiety and slowed the hustle in his steps. He went to the nurses' station.

"Can someone give me an update on Zarah Mitchell?" he asked the two people sitting behind the counter, not sure if they were nurses or doctors. He really didn't care who they were as long as they provided an update on his wife's health.

"I'll have the doctor meet you in the room. Right now she's upstairs with another fetal emergency."

Joel leaned on the counter. "Is there only one doctor on duty in the ER?"

"Only one ob-gyn."

His anxiety boiled again. "So who's taking care of my wife?"

"Rest assured, Mr. Mitchell, that your wife is receiving quality care."

He bit his tongue in frustration. Debating with the nurse wasn't useful. He terminated the conversation.

"Joel!" he heard someone shout. He turned and saw Tamara barreling toward him. "I got your message.

Where's Zarah? How is she?" Tamara rattled off her questions frantically.

"She's in an examining room," he said, walking away from the counter. Tamara followed.

"I've been worried to death since I got your message. Thanks for letting me know. Is she going to be okay?"

"I don't know," Joel answered curtly.

Tamara grabbed his arm, forcing him to stop. "Why don't you know?"

He wiggled from her grip. "Because they haven't told me yet." Joel wasn't irritated by her line of questioning. He was just angry that he didn't have suitable answers. It wasn't Tamara's fault. It was his.

They continued another ten yards before they reached Zarah's room. He found his mother sitting close to Zarah's bed with trails of tears lining her cheeks. Tamara was on his heels. Shockingly, he wasn't bothered. He actually appreciated her concern. He hadn't known her to express support for anyone. So Zarah had to be special to get Tamara's heart to warm up.

"Mom, what's wrong?" he asked, approaching her and Zarah's bedside.

Sherry wiped her face with the smashed tissue she was holding. "Oh, excuse me. I didn't know Tamara was with you."

"Hi, Sherry."

Joel could tell something had happened, and his mother seemed uneasy about talking with Tamara in the room. "Tamara, do you mind stepping out for a minute?" he asked. "I need to speak privately with my mother."

"Can I at least stay for Zarah?" Tamara asked, with such a look of despair, he was compelled to oblige.

"Sure, but please don't wake her up."

Tamara went around to the other side of the bed and touched Zarah's hand. "It's Tamara. I'm here for you.

Whatever you need, I'm here," she said with her voice cracking. Joel didn't have to ask her to leave again. After her words were spoken, Tamara dashed from the room. Joel was too focused on what his mother had to say to follow Tamara and decipher her emotional state of mind.

"Mom, I can tell you've been crying. What has you upset? Did the doctor come in while I was gone?" Zarah stirred, causing Joel to lower his voice to a whisper.

"No one came in. These tears aren't for Zarah," Sherry replied, generating more confusion. He couldn't understand why she was visibly upset.

"Then what are they for?"

"For my child," he said.

"Who? Me?"

Sherry wiped her eyes with the tattered tissue and reached to get a fresh one from the table. "No. The baby I lost before you were born." She dabbed her eyes again. "Seeing Zarah lying there, so helpless, has opened a wound I thought had long been healed. I guess you never really get over losing a child." She squeezed her eyes and lips tightly, not letting another tear roll or a painful memory seep out. Zarah stirred again, but Joel wasn't going to let up on his mother. She couldn't drop a revelation like that and expect him to ignore her pain.

"Mom, I didn't think about the impact this might have on you. I shouldn't have let you come here."

"You didn't have to let me. This is where I belong. With my family, you, Zarah, and my grandbaby," she said, extending her hand so that it hovered near the bed while clutching a wad of used tissues.

"Mr. Mitchell," the doctor said, sailing into the room. "I'd like to speak with you in the hallway."

Joel wanted to console his mother, but his gesture would have to wait. "Sure," Joel said and hurried out. He and the doctor walked several doors away from Zarah's room. Joel watched Tamara ease back into the room.

"How is she?" Joel asked, not letting the doctor give him a drawn-out spiel. He wanted the facts and fast, otherwise Joel would move her to Henry Ford Hospital, where there was no question about the quality of care Zarah would receive. "Tell me straight."

The doctor dropped the chart to his side. "The baby is in distress, and Zarah has lost quite a bit of blood."

Joel listened intently, but he didn't hear anything he didn't already know. "And . . ."

"She's still in the first trimester, which is a very critical phase of the gestation period. We'll do everything we can to prolong the pregnancy. The good news is that she didn't miscarry. The baby's heartbeat is strong, but we are in the danger zone and have to consider this a high-risk pregnancy."

Thank goodness she hadn't miscarried, Joel thought. He took solace in the news. "What's the probability of our baby living?"

"It's hard to tell," the doctor stated without further explanation.

"Come on. You must have a better answer."

"I understand you want answers, but I won't give you false hope."

"Give me an answer," Joel demanded, drawing stares from the few nurses at the nurses' station.

"Fifty-fifty," the doctor blurted.

He'd demanded an answer, and once it came, Joel wasn't prepared for the implications. He was crushed. He'd finally come to terms with being a father, and now that might be in jeopardy. "Is there another specialist we can get?"

The doctor raised the chart and made a few marks with his pen. "Mr. Mitchell, I understand your concern, but you can rest assured your wife is receiving the best care we can provide."

Joel wasn't convinced. He couldn't be. Joel thanked the doctor and walked away, realizing that neither he nor the hospital could offer any more help.

He trudged to Zarah's room, squashing his feelings. His wife would see only the best of him, the strength that God was going to give him. She needed a hero, and he would be one for her. He entered the room, wearing a borrowed smile and exuding love for her, more than he'd given Zarah since she vowed to be his wife.

When he entered the room, Zarah was awake, with Sherry on one side of the bed and Tamara on the other. Zarah saw him and reached out for him. He didn't hesitate in responding.

"Joel, is our baby well?" she asked, appearing very troubled.

Tamara stepped out of the way to let Joel slide as close to the bed as he could get. He nestled his wife's hand in his. "Don't worry about our baby. Don't worry about anything." He leaned close and kissed her forehead, letting the affection linger. "Let me do the worrying. I want you to rest, Mrs. Mitchell."

"But—"

"Shh," he whispered. "We'll get through this together."

Sherry and Tamara stood quietly on the other side of the bed. He was glad to have the support. Zarah must have believed him. She nestled her face against his hand and closed her eyes. A sense of relief filled Joel when he felt the strength of God stirring inside.

Chapter 45

Shortly after midnight, Zarah was moved from the emergency center to a private room in the maternity ward for overnight observation. Around 2:00 a.m., Joel convinced his mother and Tamara to go home. They put up some resistance but eventually listened to reason and went home. They couldn't help Zarah tonight. Joel preferred that they go home and get prepared to help him when Zarah went home. He insisted on walking them to the parking lot. Tamara accepted a ride from his mother, and they were on their way.

Instead of rushing back inside the hospital, Joel stayed outside to think. He wasn't thrilled with the care Zarah had gotten thus far. He wanted more done sooner. He wasn't sure if another hospital could do any better, but other care would be considered. He wanted Zarah to receive the best treatment. Joel wasn't going to take less for his wife and child. With the way things had played out in slow motion, he definitely wasn't going to be too far from Zarah's side. In the middle of the night, she'd called for him several times. The best he could do was climb slowly onto the bed and gently place her head on his lap. He had attempted to ease her head onto the pillow without waking her but was unsuccessful, and so he had been forced to sleep practically in an upright position. Joel was ready to get back inside and resume his watch over Zarah.

Before Joel knew it, it was six in the morning. He was anxious for more answers but not crazy out of his mind with worry. He sincerely wanted to give faith a try. Throughout his years of wandering, strategizing, and trying to claw his way out of his grave of failures, there was one person who'd consistently popped up in his path at the oddest times, Mother Walker. Today was no different. She was a woman who didn't appear to have much advanced education, but it was evident she had a special relationship with God.

Joel slowly opened the door to Zarah's room and walked out into the hallway, thinking. Mother Walker had given him the most meaningful advice of anyone he'd known with the exception of his dad. Joel was certain she could get a prayer through to God for him. Strangely, Joel had stored her number in his phone two years ago, not realizing he'd need it today. It was early, but he bet she was an early riser. He'd take a chance on reaching her. He dialed, and thank God, she answered. He identified himself, and she knew who it was immediately.

"Mother Walker . . . I'm sorry. . . . I mean Big Mama." She'd reminded him to call her Big Mama on several occasions, but he kept forgetting. He found a quiet refuge near the waiting area. He leaned against the wall for support. "I apologize for calling you this early."

"It's all right. I've been up for several hours, praying and meditating on my scriptures. Can I help you with something?" she asked with such a genuine tone that he was put at ease.

"I have a situation, and I'm hoping you can pray for my wife. She's having challenges with the pregnancy, and I'd like for you to pray for us. I'm afraid my prayers might not be working, and I don't want to take a chance with something so important."

"I will surely pray for you and your family, but you don't need me to reach God for you. You know the Lord for yourself. You have always had an anointing and a calling on your life. He knows you and will hear your prayer."

"I used to think so, but I've had some challenges these past few years."

"The Lord knows who you are and where you've been. We weren't born perfect, son. Jesus died that we might be redeemed from sin and saved from the consequences that come from sin. Yes, you've made your mistakes, but you're alive. You have breath in your body. That means you have time to get back on the path God has created for you."

"I'm sure it's not quite that easy."

"Why isn't it? If the God we serve can create the heavens and the earth and part the Red Sea, then surely He can fix your little stuff. Son, you have to know God is bigger than your problems. He loves you, and He's right in front of you with his arms wide open, waiting for you to fall back into His arms, into His grace. Let your Father love you, son. This is your time to rise up and take authority. God's call on your life didn't change just because you walked away from Him."

"I know, but I'm not worried about my role or future. I'm calling to ask for your prayers regarding my child and Zarah."

"I will gladly pray with you, but the plans God has for you might not be what you've planned for yourself. The way He answers might not solve the problem that you see. Do you understand?"

He did, but he didn't. Joel had learned to believe what she said, although it might take months or years for the revelation to materialize. She'd never told him what he wanted to hear, but Big Mama always told him what he was supposed to hear. He acknowledged this as one of those instances.

***

The sun's rays snuck into Zarah's room around seven thirty that morning, robbing him of privacy. He would have preferred that the room remain dark so Zarah could continue sleeping but didn't have the power to constrain the light of day.

He heard her whimpering but wasn't able to decipher the comment. "Zarah," he whispered, "are you awake?"

"Ohhh," she moaned.

"You are awake," he said, sitting at her bedside. "Good morning, sleepyhead," he said with laughter that wouldn't be silenced. Joel was ecstatic to see her awake. They'd suffered through a long night, and finally it was day. *Thank the Lord,* he thought. Prayer worked.

"Is our baby well?" she asked, popping up.

He touched her shoulder, hoping to soothe her. "Why don't you lay back and rest? The doctor doesn't want you to become overly excited. It's not healthy for you or our baby. He wants you to take it easy," he told her.

She took his advice and lay back, placing her hand snugly on her abdomen. "What about the blood?"

Joel didn't have an explanation, not that she needed to have extra information to think about. However, he didn't like being ignorant about important matters that impacted his life and those he loved. He'd deal with getting a second, third, and fourth opinion later. Right now, Zarah had his undivided attention, which he was freely giving.

He squeezed her hand and stroked her face, pleased at his calming abilities, until she popped up again. "What day is it?" she asked, exhibiting a gush of fear. She caused his heart to beat fast. He wondered what had her so alarmed.

"It's Wednesday."

She tried getting out of bed, and he stopped her.

"What are you doing?" he asked forcefully.

"I have a meeting with the DMI board of directors tomorrow. I can't miss it," she said, appearing frantic.

"Wait a minute," he said, blocking her path from the bed. "You're in no condition to attend a board meeting today or tomorrow. Didn't you hear me say the doctor wants you to take it easy?" he said, working hard to contain his frustration.

"But I must be ready for the meeting. We are discussing Harmonious Energy and the offer they are proposing. I can't miss this opportunity to own my father's company. It is most important to me," she said, pushing against him.

"Is it more important than keeping our baby safe?"

In a split second, her anxiety melted. She stopped pushing against him and slowly eased herself down on the bed. "What can I do?"

"Don't worry. I'll take care of the meeting for you," he said.

"You?" she said, sounding very unsure.

"Yes, me. Remember, I know a thing or two about the board of directors," he said, which was accurate since he'd been a former member. "Once upon a time I was a master at structuring deals." She showed hints of a smile. "And let's face it. Nobody knows more about unraveling DMI and Harmonious Energy than I do, since it was my vision to merge the two companies in the first place."

"You are right," she said, hugging him tightly.

He offered no opposition. Actually, he soaked up her heartfelt appreciation. Joel was glad he had something of value to offer her in the hour of her greatest need. For the first time in a very long while, he was satisfied with his actions. The feeling was like an addictive drug. The more he got, the more he desired.

Chapter 46

The atmosphere in the hospital room unnerved Joel, causing him to feel restless. It was 9:20 a.m. He looked over at his wife and found her sleeping comfortably, which put him at ease. Joel was about to get up and go grab a cup of coffee when there was a tug in his spirit. He hadn't experienced such a sensation since the earlier years of his tenure as CEO of DMI. Those were the days when he and God spoke daily, when he trusted the Lord to confirm each decision he made. He reared back in the seat, tapped his fingertips together and reflected. Those days had passed, but God was still God. And Joel was still alive, which meant there was time to make amends.

The tug in his spirit grew stronger, and he chose not to resist. The church mother's admonishment had stuck to him like premium Velcro. He'd done too much on his own for too long. He gave a deep sigh. He was tired of running and clamoring for solutions to his man-made problems. Only a fool would find himself in a hole and keep digging. Well, Joel resigned himself to the fact that his foolish days were over. As of right now, this instant, he decided this was his day, his time to fix the root of his problem. Marrying Zarah for professional purposes, chopping up DMI for financial gain, and fighting his brother for control of DMI weren't at the core of his struggles. He couldn't even blame Madeline, regardless of the slander and malice she'd mercilessly released over the years. She wasn't his problem. Zarah, Don, and Abigail weren't the source of his anguish. Truthfully, Tamara wasn't, either.

As Joel sat back and meditated on his path to destruction, the road ahead, which had seemed blurred and rocky a few hours ago, was quite clear. If he traced his missteps to the source of his despair, Joel was certain they would lead directly to the feet of Jesus. When he had elected to abandon God's plan for his life and to pursue his own agenda, the anointing and unprecedented favor he'd relished for months had left him. It dawned on Joel that his plan represented his will. God's plan represented God's will. The revelation was like an anvil dropping from the sky and waking him into consciousness. So many decisions flashed before him. He felt spiritually naked.

Zarah stirred and turned from lying on her left side to her right, but she didn't wake up. Joel continued with the spiritual purging exercise in progress. He prayed that she would stay asleep awhile longer, because Joel didn't want to abandon this self-assessment he was undergoing. His spirit was leaping within as his soul cried out for redemption and salvation. They were double-teaming him. He had no choice but to seek God for forgiveness and restoration, confident he didn't have the knowledge, strength, or temperance to manage his life successfully.

In that moment a water main burst in his soul, and he was humbled and fell to his knees. Tears streamed down Joel's cheeks as he prayed silently so as not to wake Zarah. He repented and pleaded with God for forgiveness, even though Joel knew begging wasn't God's way. He had to ask his Father only once and believe by faith that it was done, according to His will. Joel thought about the countless instances when he hadn't been obedient. He'd grown accustom to ignoring God's messages and blowing right through blockades in his path. The results hadn't been pleasant, but that was the Joel of old. This Joel, the one humbled before God, had suffered sufficiently. He was eager to listen, to take instruction.

Joel rose from his knees with a twinkle in his eyes and vigor in his step. He believed his burden had been lifted and his restart button had been pressed. He was alive and couldn't wait to show God how serious he was about making changes and being a faithful steward of his second chance.

He checked on Zarah once again. She was in a tranquil state, and he was grateful to see her resting. He'd use the break to make a few calls. He went into the hallway to call his mother. Joel knew she'd want an update, and he was pleased to give her some good news.

"Mom, Zarah is resting comfortably."

"Good, good," she said. "How long does she have to stay in the hospital?"

"I'm not sure, but the doctor said the baby's heartbeat is strong."

"Well, that's good, but did you find out why she was bleeding?"

Joel's glee dipped. The uncertainty about Zarah's condition was bugging him. He had continuously contemplated moving her to Henry Ford and hadn't ruled out the possibility. "No, not yet."

"Well, then, we'll have to keep a close eye on Ms. Zarah."

"I guess so," he said, wanting to do more.

"I'll let you get back to Zarah. And I'll see you at the hospital in a few hours. Then you can get some relief and let me sit with her this afternoon."

"Mom, I don't want to burden you with my responsibilities."

"Don't insult me, son. You and Zarah are my family, which makes you my responsibility."

He was glad to have her and wouldn't complain. He graciously accepted her support and ended the call.

Next up was Don, who happened to be in his office when Joel called.

"Don, I'm glad I caught you."

"What's up?"

Joel didn't want to mince words. He wanted to be direct, without revealing too much personal information about Zarah's condition. It was a private matter and didn't warrant public attention. He'd safeguard his immediate family's business. "I'm calling about the board meeting Zarah has with the board of directors tomorrow."

"What about it?" Don asked. Joel detected the sharpness in his brother's voice, but he wasn't going to be drawn into a verbal feud.

"Zarah has been ill the past couple of days and can't attend the meeting."

"I'm sorry to hear that she's sick. I hope she gets better soon."

Joel thanked Don for the well wishes.

"As you probably know, we were going to discuss the Harmonious Energy and West Coast division acquisition proposals." Don hesitated before adding, "I guess we'll have to cancel this session, but the DMI board is eager to walk through the proposal details. How soon can we reschedule?"

Joel hated to tell him the truth, but he had no choice. "Zarah's going to be out indefinitely."

"Really? Just how sick is she?"

Joel had already opened the box marked PRIVATE. He might as well pour out the contents for Don. "She's in the hospital due to complications from the pregnancy."

"Oh, I'm sorry to hear this. She'll be in my prayers." Joel welcomed prayers, especially from someone who he knew had a love for the Lord and could get a request beyond the ceiling. "Is there anything I can do to help?" Don asked.

"Not much. Just pray. The rest is on me. The doctor says she's under too much stress. So she'll have to ease up on the DMI and Harmonious Energy front."

"I totally understand," Don said, sincerity ringing out.

Joel was encouraged. "If the baby has any chance, she needs take it easy for quite a while."

"Agreed, so take care of home and let me know what I can do to help. And don't worry about the board meeting. I'll take care of it. When the timing is right, we can reschedule. God will work it out. All right?" Don told him.

"All right," Joel replied.

After the conversation was over, the old Joel wanted to rear his head. A notion popped into his mind. He could go ahead with the meeting and use the situation as an opportunity to assume control of Harmonious Energy while Zarah was out of commission. As quickly as the notion flew into his mind, Joel's spirit kicked it out. He wasn't going to betray Zarah. More importantly, he wasn't going to squander the second chance God had given him. This was his turn to make things right, and that was precisely what Joel intended on doing with God's help.

Chapter 47

Don was stunned. He pondered the news from Joel. He couldn't ignore the adverse implications for DMI and the family. The Harmonious Energy divestiture was officially on hold, and there wasn't a single thing Don could do. He trotted off to his mother's office.

When he plopped into a seat, she asked, "What's that look for?"

"What look?"

"The one that says we have trouble," Madeline said, taking off her reading glasses and setting them on the desk. She clasped her hands together and placed them on top of her notepad. "Come on. Out with it. Tell me what's on your mind. I'm ready."

Don chuckled at how well his mother knew him. "You're right. We have trouble."

Madeline squirmed in her chair but kept glaring at him.

"The Harmonious Energy and West Coast division deals are on hold."

"What?" she shouted, forgoing decorum. "Why?"

"I just received a call from Joel."

"I should have known this has something to do with him." She tossed a bunch of paper clips in the air, and Don watched as they landed on the desk. "What has he screwed up?"

Don leaned in. "Nothing. It's Zarah. She's sick and can't attend the board meeting."

"So move it back a few days."

Don shook his head. "Won't work. She needs to be out longer."

"Fine," Madeline said, flailing her hand in the air. "Push it out a few weeks, a month, whatever. Just get the meeting rescheduled."

"Mother, it's not going to happen."

"Why not?" she snapped.

"Because I'm not willing to participate in this battle for the West Coast division. I'm done. We've been fighting for decades. How long is long enough?" he told her. "I'm tired of this, and you should be too."

"I'm never tired of fighting for what's right," she retorted.

"What's right? How do you know what's right? Did God come down from heaven and tell you to pursue the West Coast division?" he asked boldly, without crossing the line of respect.

Madeline fidgeted and shifted her gaze away.

"Well, did He?" She cut her gaze at him. "I didn't think so."

Madeline opened her desk drawer and appeared to be shuffling through it for something. He realized it was difficult for her to have this conversation, but Don wasn't going to stop until he had conveyed the truth.

"Look, I'm engaging in a fresh round of DMI wars with innocent casualties like Zarah having to pay the price. I'm not doing it," he said forcefully. "I'm done. This is it for me." Clarity overwhelmed him. It was as if God had opened the heavens and poured out the insight he'd been seeking for months. "I'm dropping out of the bidding war over the West Coast division."

"You can't do that."

"I can, and I am." Don refused to contribute any further to Zarah's health challenges. He was certain God had a better plan. "Zarah is sick, and Joel said it has to do with stress."

"I'm sorry to hear that, but she's the one who wanted to tout herself as a businesswoman. This job is not for the fainthearted."

"Regardless of how she got involved, I'm not contributing to the demise of another Mitchell under the guise of restoring our family business." He was well aware of the destructive nature his family exhibited once they locked themselves into the DMI world. They were willing to win at all costs. "There's no wisdom in regaining ownership of the division if it comes at the price of destroying the same family we've spent years hoping to reunite."

"Humph," Madeline responded, which was as close as he was going to get to an affirmation from her. "So you're just going to give up despite the massive work we've put in, that I've put into regaining control of DMI for you and your sister? I guess my efforts don't count."

He was far beyond allowing guilt or pity to sway his judgment. He had compassion for his mother's perspective but a greater desire to honor God's leading. He'd sought the Lord for an answer on how to proceed. Now that he had the answer, nothing or no one was going to prevent him from obeying. "I know you don't want to hear this, but I'm content letting Joel and Tamara battle it out without me."

"You bet I don't want to hear that. I think you're being overdramatic. Zarah is sick and needs a few days of rest. That's it. She'll feel better in a week, and we can continue as planned with the board meeting."

Don saw that his mother wasn't going to be reasonable without having all the information to consider. So he obliged. "Zarah isn't going to be better in a few days. Not according to Joel. She's in the hospital, dealing with complications related to her pregnancy. When I spoke to him, he sounded worried and was very concerned about Zarah avoiding stressful situations," he said, squinting one eye. Stress might as well be the Mitchell family's nickname. No one could be a bona fide Mitchell and live without a healthy dose of it. Unfortunately, Zarah was no exception.

Madeline fumbled in her desk drawer again. Pulling out nothing, as he had suspected would happen, she peered at him and said, "You should have told me about the complicated pregnancy in the first place."

"Would it have made a difference?"

"Yes, it would have," she said. "I'm not a monster, you know. I have feelings for people."

He chuckled. He watched as her gaze roamed around the room and finally landed on him.

"Then that's it. We're done," she said as her voice cracked. "My dream is officially dead," she added, this time opening the drawer and plucking out a handful of tissues. "Don, could you please excuse me. I need to finish a report."

His instinct was to rush to her and provide comfort, but he didn't. She needed to be alone and grieve the loss of her dream, and he understood. His heart was breaking for her, but his resolve was invigorated. Trusting in God's plan and getting off the roller coaster of unforgiveness and perpetual family strife gave him the comfort he needed. He left his mother's office, certain better days were ahead for him and them.

Chapter 48

Don stopped at the cubicle of Abigail's assistant on the way to his office. "Is she in?" he asked, resting against the counter.

"Yes, she is."

"No meeting?"

"Not until later this morning," the assistant replied.

"Perfect," he said and then waltzed into Abigail's office after knocking on the door. "Ms. Gerard, do you have a minute for an old friend?"

Abigail was about to make a call. "Sure. Come on in."

"Oh, I'm sorry. I didn't mean to interrupt," he said, turning to walk out.

"You're fine. Come on in," she said, returning the phone handset to its base. "I can make the call later. No problem."

"Are you sure?"

"Positive," she said, beckoning for him to take a seat. "What's going on?"

Don didn't know where to begin. Abigail was aware of Joel's marriage, but did she know about the pregnancy? Did she know about the tussle over the West Coast division? He didn't want to share information that wasn't his to reveal. On the other hand, Don wanted to chat with his friend and cherished colleague. He respected Abigail's professional aptitude and had relied on her on many occasions. He yearned to lean on her with his recent predicament and get her opinion. He was hoping she'd be objective.

"Did you know Joel and his wife were expecting a baby?"

"No, I didn't," she said without looking away.

Don could have terminated the conversation, but she didn't appear to react adversely. Don was amazed and relieved. He continued, intending to get to his reason for popping into her office. "I'm telling you because Joel and Zarah are having difficulty with the pregnancy."

Abigail cleared her throat and adjusted her position in the chair. "That's awful. I hope things work out for Joel." She opened her laptop. "There's not much I can do except maybe say a prayer for the baby."

"That's kind of you."

"It's what any decent person would do."

"But let's be honest, you're not just *any* person when it comes to Joel. You were in a relationship."

"Ah, ah, ah," she stated with her index finger pointing at him. "According to your brother, we were never in a relationship. At best, we were friends and colleagues, according to him."

"Whatever," Don said in a slightly flippant tone, which surprised even him.

Maybe he'd grown tired of Joel and Abigail's weird relationship. Maybe he was irritated with Abigail's long-term denial. Maybe it was this, or maybe it was that. Bottom line, he wasn't there to define her relationship with Joel. He was in her office for the sole purpose of figuring out how to convince Abigail to stay on board. His reign was coming to an end. With Tamara outright refusing to assume the top spot, Don had to identify a qualified replacement if he wanted to step down. Abigail was the person most suited to run DMI in his absence. As long as she was in charge, he could vacate his CEO position for an extended leave and not feel pressured to return for at least six months.

"I'm over Joel. When he got married, we were done." Don wasn't going to dissect her answer. What she said, he'd assent as her truth. She continued. "There's an entire world outside of DMI for me, one that doesn't require me to run into your little brother." The tone in her voice lightened. "And I'm happy." Don was glad to see her in a content state of mind. He'd been prepared for her reaction to the pregnancy to go in a different direction. Thank goodness it hadn't. "As a matter of fact, I'd like for you to reduce my remaining two-month-notice period to a few weeks."

Don tensed. "Abigail, you're totally blindsiding me. I'm here to ask you to stay longer, and you want to leave sooner." Don was saddened. He sighed repeatedly. "What's the hurry?"

"Dragging out my departure won't change the outcome."

"What can I do to convince you to stay?"

"Nothing—"

"Can I create another senior role for you?"

"Don't be silly. I'm already an executive vice president." She paused and then added, "You were the one who moved me from the fourth floor to executive row as soon as you took over. I appreciate your acknowledging my contributions, but the time has come to walk out."

Don wasn't letting up. His plan would work only if Abigail was on board. There had to be an incentive that would make her consider staying. He had to keep tossing out ideas until he hit the right trigger. "Just tell me what we can do to keep you here at DMI? This is where you belong. Can I change your title, give you a bigger office, hire two more assistants for you, or give you more responsibility? What?" he said, zipping through his idea pool at maximum throttle. Nothing was off-limits.

"The only job above mine is yours as CEO, and the only thing I don't have is a seat on the board of directors," she said.

Her statement reminded him that there were a few areas that were off-limits, and those were two. He'd have difficulty convincing his mother to relinquish either position. Without her endorsement, convincing the board would take some serious work on his end.

"Since you're not offering either of those, there's nothing left for me here."

He didn't want to believe what Abigail was saying, but she might be right.

She went on. "Let's face it. We were a good team while it lasted. We've had a good run, but a lady always leaves the dance before the music stops." She grimaced and added, "It's time for me to take a bow. You know it, and I know it."

"No, I don't," he replied.

"Well, denial never stopped the world from rotating. I love you, my dear friend, but don't make this harder than it has to be for any of us. Let me go. You'll be fine," she told Don. "DMI will be fine, and I will be too."

Don didn't want to be accused of pushing. He was forced to let the discussion rest, but Abigail's time with DMI wasn't over. Not yet. He had one more idea, one that was sure to change her mind about walking out DMI's doors for good. He'd catch up with his mother later to share his plan and get her approval.

Chapter 49

Don trudged to his office, nurturing an idea that was, at best, in its infancy stage. He wasn't overly excited or dejected. How could he be? He'd prayed for direction prior to meeting with his mother and Abigail. Praying and worrying simultaneously burned too much energy. He refused to do both. Since he'd prayed, worrying was out.

There was a photo on his desk that captured Don's attention. It was the one he and Naledi had taken during his last trip to South Africa. He picked up the photo, fixated on her radiance. His soul leapt as he thought about the numerous drives they'd made to the cape, the edge of civilization, where the colossal power and majestic allure of the Indian and Atlantic Oceans clashed. Although the cape's terrain was rocky and difficult to negotiate, the place had an indescribable tranquility and beauty. So it was with the Mitchell clan. Despite their idiosyncrasies, stubbornness, and mean-spiritedness, he saw the compassion in each of them. Often it was buried underneath past hurts, unforgiveness, and mounds of rejection, but compassion and goodness were in each of his family members. Unfortunately, they didn't see it in themselves, which was why Don was convinced his family would continue spiraling aimlessly out of control until the veils of doubt and denial were lifted permanently from them.

Sometimes his heart operated on emotion instead of wisdom. He'd done his part. God had used him to bring the family to the same city. There was hope for further restoration, but Don wasn't sure he was the agent to handle the next phase of it. They'd worn him down, and he was ready to bolt. He drew the framed picture of him and Naledi closer. Regardless of where his heart wanted to be, his spirit, which represented his pure connection with God, was his guide.

As he reflected, Don resigned his desires in order to see the bigger plan fulfilled. If the Lord wanted him in Detroit, then that's where he had to be. On the other hand, if his season in Detroit was over then Don knew he had to go. The only thing worse than doing something God didn't lead him to do was staying in a place longer than required. He didn't intend on bolting too soon or lingering too long, which is why his decisions about DMI were going to be different.

He returned the photo to its rightful spot on his desk. He glanced at the walk clock and saw that it was ten thirty, which was around four thirty in the afternoon in South Africa. Naledi was bound to be in the office. This was the perfect hour to check in. Feeling nostalgic, he dialed her direct line. His emotions soared as he anticipated her voice answering on the other end.

"Good day," she said, inspiring a heartfelt grin from him. It wasn't until she spoke that Don realized how much he missed her. She had been his angel in those early years, right after he fled Detroit and the self-manufactured turmoil swirling around his family. Those days had long passed and were only a memory, void of the sting.

"I'm so glad I was able to catch you in the office. I miss you terribly."

"Yes, and I miss you," she replied, which caused his grin to widen.

Don wished he could snap his fingers and be in Cape Town in the twinkling of an eye, but he wasn't going to ask God for such a miracle. Booking a flight next week, after the Zarah and West Coast division matters settled down, would be a sufficient miracle. He could hold out until then.

"Will you be traveling here soon?" she asked.

"Not soon enough," he wanted to say. "Hopefully next week. We'll see." He traced the frame of their picture. Just in case he couldn't leave, Don was formulating a backup plan. "What about you? Can your schedule accommodate a trip to the States? I really want to see you as soon as possible."

When Don initially returned from South Africa, he was fully committed to restoring DMI and, as a result, had to spend an inordinate amount of time in the United States. Thank goodness Naledi had been able to keep LTI running smoothly with his sporadic visits and remote meetings. Don had to admit, God hadn't let his business lack for anything during his Mitchell family mission trip to Detroit. In the beginning, the distance from Naledi and LTI wasn't much of an issue. That had changed. He desired more personally. Between God's call, the workload of DMI, his mother's plea, and his unresolved feelings for Abigail, Don hadn't allowed himself to think remotely about the possibility of marriage and raising a family. It was time. Maybe the urge stemmed from his recent conversation with Joel. He wanted a family not in five years, but now.

"What do you think?" he asked when she didn't answer his question right away about her ability to travel.

He had to see her, to hold her, and to confess his love to her. He'd waited too long. She was the one he wanted, and there was no justification for waiting. Thinking about Joel and Zarah's ordeal forced Don to acknowledge how fleeting life was. There was no more tugging between old feelings for Abigail and fresh ones for Naledi. He was eager to taste the sweetness of love and marriage.

His future was bright with Naledi in the picture, but roadblocks sprung up. He wasn't quite ready to hop on a plane with a one-way ticket. Detroit wasn't loosening its grip. Steps had to be taken in order to completely free himself from DMI, like divesting their ownership position in Harmonious Energy. He turned his chair to face the windows and peered into the morning sky. Although there was a great deal left to handle, he wasn't worried as long as Naledi was waiting for him at the end of the road. Don was fueled like never before. He continued talking and laughing with her, enjoying a slew of topics. He savored each morsel. Life was good because God was good.

Chapter 50

Tamara's night was restless. She'd tried sleeping but couldn't get Zarah off her mind. She jumped up early, dressed, and was on her way to the hospital. It was close to eleven. She had wanted to go earlier but didn't want to crowd Zarah. She called the car service because the bus and a suburban cab would take too much of her time. She was very anxious. Every traffic light seemed to be red, and the stop signs seemed to multiply. When the car rolled into the hospital lot, she wanted to hop out at the entrance and run the rest of the way. She was able to refrain and waited until the driver parked the car near the visitors' door.

"Should I wait for you, Ms. Mitchell?" her driver asked.

There was no other place she'd rather be. Tamara planned on staying at the hospital most of the day. "No. I'll call later to schedule a ride home."

The car drove off. She dashed inside, prepared to barrel over anyone standing in her path to the maternity ward. She exited the elevator on the fourth floor and zoomed to the room where she'd left Zarah last night. She poked her head in. Her glee was zapped when she found herself staring into Joel's face. She'd hoped he had gone home or gone somewhere, anywhere, except the hospital. He'd established a reputation for being missing in action when it came to Zarah and the pregnancy. She was disappointed when she'd seen him hanging around the house, and now he'd been at the hospital for the second day and counting.

She should have been thrilled for Zarah, but selfishly, she wanted her visit to be uninhibited. She choked up her disdain for Joel and his treatment of Zarah and walked into the room, determined not to argue with Joel. Zarah's well-being was most important, and Tamara would be on her best behavior.

"Tamara, I didn't plan on seeing you here so soon. You were here very late last night."

Why didn't he expect her to be at the hospital? She was Zarah's only friend. She'd been there for his wife when he hadn't. She could have sliced him with a few choice phrases but wasn't going to. She swallowed her attitude and responded, "How's she doing?"

"Better," he said softly. Joel stood and pointed toward the door. He exited the room, and Tamara followed. "She's sleeping off and on due to the medication. I didn't want us to wake her."

"I understand," Tamara replied.

"If you want me to call you later, when she's awake, I can," Joel stated.

Tamara wasn't going anywhere. She had set aside the entire day for Zarah. Tamara understood that the wedge she'd placed between Joel and his wife might prompt him to shut her out. He could demand that she leave, but she hoped he wouldn't. "I'd rather stay until she wakes up."

Joel slid his hands into his pants pockets. "Look here, regardless of what I think about you, I can't deny how much of a friend you've been to Zarah. She likes you."

"And you don't?" she blurted, not screening her reaction.

"Like I said, it doesn't really matter what I think about you. You're here, and Zarah can use as much support as we can give. She would want you here. So I'm glad you came."

"Thank you," Tamara said, perplexed by the compliment coming from Joel.

"I'm running downstairs to get a cup of coffee. I'd appreciate it if you could sit with her while I'm gone. It should only be five or ten minutes."

"Gladly, I'll sit with her." For Zarah's sake, Tamara intended on behaving in a way that didn't threaten Joel. "Um, thanks again for letting me visit."

"Just try to keep the visit short, and don't let her do too much talking if she does wake up. Rest is the medicine for her. Our baby needs as much help as we can give him or her to get here."

"Agreed." Tamara zeroed in on Joel's reference to "our baby." She hadn't heard him speak in such a manner regarding the child. She took note but didn't make the comment an issue for Joel. Besides, it was his baby.

"Zarah has to stay away from stress, and I'm determined to make sure she does."

Tamara liked what she was hearing from Joel. However, she wasn't sold on his sincerity. People could change, but not literally overnight. She wasn't convinced and would have to see more. The main thing was that they had to help Zarah protect the baby. As far as Tamara was concerned, that meant protecting Zarah and the baby from Joel, if necessary. She had her eye on him and wasn't going to blink.

"Does this mean you're going to assume the leadership of Harmonious Energy while she's sick?"

He coughed a few times. "Yes."

"Then I know what this means for me," she stated boldly. "You're keeping the West Coast for yourself?"

Joel stood away from the wall. "Tamara, this isn't the place to discuss business. I have one purpose at this hospital, and that's my wife."

Wow. He was smooth, she acknowledged. She stood there, speechless. Without warning, she was forced to concede their battle over the West Coast division. Joel had ridden in on his gallant horse and had rescued his damsel in distress. The reward for his chivalrous gesture was Zarah's company. She smirked within and swallowed the defeat.

"You're right. Zarah is our reason for being here. Just so you know, she's the only friend I've had in fifteen years." Constantly moving for over a decade didn't lend itself to making friends. "I may seem pushy sometimes, but it's because I believe in loyalty."

"Okay," he said, sounding like he didn't believe Tamara.

She was annoyed but didn't react. He didn't have to believe her. She knew the truth. Zarah had believed in Tamara for who she was, without judgment. For that, Tamara was grateful and wanted to be there for her friend, even if it required putting up with Joel. She'd stay a short while and then leave, not wanting to stress Zarah or make Joel uncomfortable. She figured that was what a friend was supposed to do.

Chapter 51

By that afternoon Joel was approaching a ripe eighteen hours at the hospital. His shirt was pungent, and the grit on his teeth repeatedly annoyed him. Despite his appearance, Joel wasn't going to abandon Zarah under any circumstances. His days of running were over. He leaned against the windowsill as Sherry entered the room. Zarah had finished lunch and slipped into a nap before Tamara left.

"Mom, you should go home. I know you're tired from being here late last night."

Sherry walked over to Joel and kissed him on the cheek. "Oh, don't be silly. You know I have to be here," she said softly. "How's she doing?" Sherry set her purse and jacket on the chair.

"Better, for sure. But I'm still thinking about moving her to Henry Ford. We'll see," he said.

"That's where you were born. They were the best then, and I'm sure they're even better now with all the new technology and stuff," she said, taking a seat. Zarah's tray with her half-eaten lunch hadn't been removed yet. "I see she ate a little. What about you? Have you eaten?"

Joel hadn't thought much about food. "I'm not hungry."

"Well, you have to eat. I can't have two sick children on my hands. Go on and have lunch."

"Nah, I'm good," he said and then changed his mind. "Mom, actually, I need to run home and grab a shower. Do you mind staying for a couple hours? I'll be back by four," he told her since it was just after two o'clock.

She pulled a book of puzzles from her purse. "You take as much time as you need. I'm not going anywhere until six or seven this evening."

Joel thanked his mother, gave Zarah a peck on the forehead, and slipped out of the room. When he got outside, his mind was racing in many directions. He would definitely go home and get refreshed, but that wasn't the only task on his to-do list. He had work to do, otherwise Zarah would return to the same state of chaos and pressure she'd escaped. It was obvious she couldn't maintain a healthy pregnancy while running a high-stress company. Juggling both wasn't a wise move, and fixing the problem was going to be up to him while she was in the hospital. This was his chance to step up.

Upon arriving at the house, he went into his office, dug out Kumar's phone number, and placed a call to the Bengalis' family advisor. It was after midnight in southern India, but Joel made the call, anyway. Kumar generally answered at odd times, for he had learned to manage a mixture of time zones. That was the nature of doing business with people in multiple countries. Fortunately for him, Kumar answered after only two attempts.

"Kumar, it's Joel. I know it's late, but I had to ring you up. It's about Zarah."

"Yes? Is there a problem with Zarah?" Kumar said, sounding kind of groggy.

Joel couldn't take the polite way out and let Kumar get off the phone. In case Zarah came home later today or early tomorrow, Joel had to make some changes on the business front now. She was counting on him, and he wouldn't let her down.

"I wanted you to know that Zarah is pregnant and is having complications."

"This is very disturbing. I didn't know she was pregnant. She hasn't told me such news."

Joel didn't know why she hadn't, but he didn't bother to speculate. "Well, she's in the hospital."

"Thank you for letting me know. I will make arrangements to travel there right away and tend to her."

"Oh no, you won't need to come here. I'm taking care of her."

"But the last conversation we had, you were seeking a divorce and wanted Zarah to return home. How are you tending to her?"

"The divorce is off," Joel told him. "I'll be taking care of her physically, and she also needs my help professionally. I don't know if you're aware of her recent interest in regaining full ownership of Harmonious Energy and running the company as CEO."

"I am aware. She has asked for my help, and I'm assisting her with understanding the company's current state."

"Then I can tell you that she can't assume that role any longer. It's too stressful and not good for the pregnancy. She has to relinquish her involvement if the baby is going to have any chance of living."

"I understand. Joel, why don't you step into the role? Our advisors would endorse you easily and would give you full authority."

The suggestion flowed so seamlessly that Joel didn't have an immediate reply. In the blink of an eye, Joel had what he'd been craving, being back in command of a major company. He mulled over the offer. He became increasingly invigorated the more he reflected on what it meant. This was his chance to get reestablished on the corporate scene, to redeem his failures, and build a better legacy. This was his moment. He should have been leaping with unbridled joy. Yet he wasn't. Oddly, the opportunity didn't settle right in his spirit, primarily because he wasn't able to ignore the truth. Harmonious Energy was not a company that put his God at the forefront of their practices. If Joel was sincere about rekindling a relationship with the Lord, how was he going to run Harmonious Energy when God wasn't a part of the package? The conflict of interest was too great.

Joel plopped into his office chair and acquiesced. Finally, after weeks of searching for spiritual guidance, there was a quiet whisper in his spirit that said no. Stepping into the role would solely be for Joel's glory and would ultimately push him further away from his God. Joel couldn't do it.

"Thank you for the offer, but I have to decline."

"Really? Are you certain?" Kumar asked.

Joel was actually more certain than he had been with any other decision in years. "Someone from the Harmonious Energy advisory board will have to assume leadership of the company," he said.

"Perhaps that will be best for the future, but for now DMI has majority ownership. They will most likely want to maintain majority interest," Kumar said.

Joel doubted what Kumar was saying. He suspected Don wasn't about to get involved in the day-to-day operations of Harmonious Energy. Don had resisted the purchase from the beginning. He had never wanted them to deal with the direct conflict between their core religious beliefs. Joel couldn't hear his brother's pleas a year ago, when the deal was being orchestrated. But there was clarity in the air now, and Joel gulped it down.

"Are you sure it's your desire to pass on the leadership role at Harmonious Energy?" Kumar asked.

"One hundred percent sure."

The conversation continued a little while longer, and then Joel ended the call but held the phone in his hand. He shut his eyelids and leaned his cheek against his closed fist. There was no escaping. He was forced to face his demons of selfishness and pride. The pursuit of success and validation had blinded him for years, but his path to redemption was illuminated. He repented for his decisions, including going against godly advice and arrogantly pursuing Harmonious Energy, along with several other botched expansion projects. Joel cried out, desiring what he used to have: peace, favor, and God's constant presence. Humbled, he realized there was one more thing he had to do.

Chapter 52

The clock was ticking. Joel had showered and jetted to DMI, determined to get there before four o'clock in case someone was cutting out early. He bolted through the lobby, tossing cordial greetings to those who spoke to him. Joel bounced up the stairs and dashed down the executive hallway. He blew past Madeline's assistant and breezed directly into her office. He closed the door and pulled a seat in front of Madeline's desk, drawing her complete attention.

"What are you doing, bursting into my office without an appointment?"

"We need to talk." Joel was extremely familiar with how confrontational Madeline could be. He could tell that she, in typical Madeline fashion, was gearing up for a battle. This time he wasn't giving her ammunition. The purpose of his visit was more important. She had to hear what he had to say while his nerves held out.

"What could you possibly have to tell me?" she asked, briefly peering over the reading glasses that were sitting on the edge of her nose.

"I came to say I'm sorry."

Madeline's gaze zipped up to meet Joel's. "About what?"

"Everything—"

Madeline reared back in her seat, took her glasses off slowly, laid them on the desk, folded her arms, and said nothing. After what seemed like forever, she spoke. "Is this a joke? Because I don't have time for foolishness, Joel."

"This is no joke," he said as layers of strife melted away. "By the way, I heard about Zarah and the baby. How are they doing?"

"Okay for now, but she's got to get plenty of rest."

"I see," she said, putting the glasses back on and pressing a few keys on the laptop. "How do you feel about becoming a father?"

"A little scared, I guess."

"I see."

"Is 'I see' all you're going to say while I'm here?" he said, laughing.

"Well, I don't know what else to say. I'm surprised you're here. It's not like we're buddies who hang out together," she said, cutting her gaze at him.

"No, I guess we're not, but maybe that can change."

Madeline took the glasses off again, laid them in their original spot on the desk, and pulled her chair close to the desk. She folded her arms. "Joel, cut the crap. What are you doing here?"

"I need your help."

"My help?" she questioned.

"Yes, yours. Nobody else on earth can help me. Only you."

"Well, mister, that puts you in a tight position."

"Maybe," he responded as the bantering continued. In the past Joel would have sparred with Madeline for a while and either voluntarily left or had her kick him out. Today was different. "I want back in DMI."

"You're kidding, right?"

"No, I'm dead serious. I want back in the company."

"You know Don is CEO."

"I do."

"Then you know there's no position for you."

"Sure there is. DMI is a big company. I'm not looking for the top job. Seriously, I'm not."

"And I'm supposed to believe you, with the boatload of shenanigans you've pulled over the years?" she said snidely, but he understood.

"I wasn't alone on some of those."

Madeline shrugged her shoulders, which he translated as acknowledgment of her participation in their tenuous relationship. He'd been a worthy opponent, but Joel was ready to toss in the white flag.

"Madeline, I'm not going to sit here and tell you I've changed. You wouldn't believe me, anyway."

"You got that right."

"But I will tell you this. My heart is here at DMI. You know I can impact the bottom line."

"Sure can. You practically drove us into bankruptcy when you bought Harmonious Energy, despite our opposition. Because of you, we lost two key divisions," she stated with a sharp edge in her voice that hadn't been there thus far. "No matter how we pretend, DMI will never be what it used to be when your father was running this place. You ruined the vision."

He had to work quickly to diffuse her escalating emotions or prepare for war. "Maybe, but it doesn't mean we can't establish a new path to success." Madeline eased back in her seat. "You know I can add value. Remember the record sales we realized during my first couple of years as CEO."

"What I remember is how cocky you were back then, trying to make us believe God had given you an extra dose of success and blessings."

"He did."

"What about now?"

"I don't know about the extra blessings, but I definitely know my direction and wisdom have to come from Him.

When I was out there making decisions without Him, my life was a living hell. I don't want to live that way anymore."

"So you've had a come-to-Jesus experience?" she said.

Joel laughed. "I guess you could say so."

"What about your wife? Does she believe in the same God that you do? Because I recall Zarah and her father worshipping light, the sun, and a bunch of other things."

"You're right. We don't have the same religious beliefs."

"How's that going to work in a marriage if you're turning back to God, or so you say?"

"Honestly, I don't know, but for now, she's carrying my baby. She's my wife, and we have to figure this out." Joel was poised to fight for a job at DMI until his knuckles bled. But Zarah was off-limits in the conversation. "I won't abandon her and the baby. Regardless of how we got together, we are married and need to make this work. I pray God helps me figure out what to do."

"Well, you're going to need a miracle if you want a job back here at DMI. It will be difficult to trust that you've changed when your wife practices a different religion. It wouldn't matter in any other company, but you know we sell leadership and financial training curricula to churches and other Christian entities. We lost many sales when our customers found out we'd purchased an Eastern religion–based company."

Joel didn't argue, simply because she was correct. He'd dug a hole, but faith was his answer to climbing out. He'd take it a step at a time, in no hurry to get ahead of God. Not anymore.

"Bringing you back would take a lot of moxie from someone," Madeline added.

"That's why I came to you. No one else on earth can influence the board of directors or Don like you can."

Madeline crossed her hands and laid them on the desk. "What makes you think I'd stick my neck out for you, of all people?"

Joel grinned and laid his hand on top of Madeline's. "I don't know," he said, "but I had to ask."

Madeline gently eased her hand away. "You're a piece of work, Mr. Joel Mitchell, having the guts to come here and to make such an outrageous request of me, of all people."

Joel grinned again. She offered him words of compassion for his wife and baby, hoping for the best. Joel thanked Madeline for listening and left.

Madeline sat there quietly long after Joel had gone, and contemplated his request. A rush of memories, both pleasant and otherwise, flooded her mind. Madeline rewound them to the days when she and Dave were building DMI. That was before she had hired Sherry as her husband's administrative assistant. She remembered those few short years when her four children were young, impressionable, and were running around the house, enjoying what was rightfully theirs, long before Joel was born. Her soul was dampened as she thought about the tragic deaths of her two oldest sons, Sam and Andre. She pulled a tissue from the drawer and dabbed the corners of her eyes. They were gone, and nothing was going to bring them back. So she wouldn't dwell on such a catastrophic loss. Instead, Madeline chose to focus her waning vitality on the two children she had remaining.

As hard as Madeline tried to rid herself of thoughts of Joel's visit, he wasn't easily discarded. There couldn't possibly be anybody crazier or more brazen than he was. Yet Madeline loved his spunk. The more she contemplated the matter, the clearer it became. If she was stepping down, then Don and DMI needed a strong, fiery personality on the team to keep the ambers of progress burning brightly. With the right supervision and reins on his ideas, Joel could be a very effective force at DMI. Maybe he was the missing puzzle piece. He definitely had her thinking.

Chapter 53

Don hadn't moved from his desk. The family bug had been awakened. The allure of having a wife and children was intensifying. He couldn't write the urge off as a passing whim. His soul had confirmed that there was substance in his desire, which he had to pursue while Naledi was fanning the flames of his love. He shut his eyes tightly and wrenched his hands. In order to get to the life he yearned to have, Don had to step down immediately from his post at DMI.

He decided not to fumble around with the inevitable. He had to let his mother know his plans. He imagined her reaction. If he could conceive of the worst possible scenario, Don was certain it wouldn't come close to how his mother was going to respond to his news. He pushed away from the desk. *No sense delaying the chat.* He would go to her now and make his intentions known.

There weren't fireworks lighting his path as he approached Madeline's office. There was mostly respect and sadness for a long history drawing to a bittersweet close. His mother's assistant gave him the okay to enter the office. Madeline was on the phone. He turned to leave.

"Don, take a seat. I'm almost finished," she told him after he watched her push the mute button on the phone.

If he wanted to be spared from the tirade that was sure to come, this was the time to bolt from the office and hide under a rock somewhere. Yet he wasn't the running type. He'd have to stay and face his mother.

"Look, Mr. Young, I've already given you a deep discount. I'm trying to make this a win-win deal for both the Eastern Federation of Free Churches and DMI, but it doesn't feel like you're operating in good faith," she told the prospective client. Don watched his mother's facial expression go from cordial to irritated in a few seconds, which didn't bode well for his revelation.

She went on. "Mr. Young, you have two choices. Agree to the terms I'm offering you or don't, plain and simple. I know we provide the best leadership training program in the country, with a top-notch executive management team, but feel free to try another firm and see how well they do for you. In the meantime, we're moving ahead with the same dedication, quality, and commitment we've had since the inception of DMI."

Don took a seat after reconsidering the notion of bolting. He prayed silently for clarity and grace for his mother. Once he told her he was joining the Tamara bandwagon and would no longer work for DMI, she'd require a ton of prayer.

"You've definitely made the right decision. I'm glad you're going with us," Madeline said, winking at him. "I know you won't regret this," she stated, then got off the phone. "We nabbed EFFC."

"I heard," Don said, easing into position to throw his dagger. "You're the best when it comes to running DMI."

"Flattery will get you everywhere," she told him, then snickered. "This must be my lucky day. I'm seeing you twice in a few hours."

"Is there anything wrong with a son visiting his mother?" Don said, stalling until he could formulate his message and deliver it without shredding his mother's heart into pieces. In less than five minutes, Madeline would learn that neither he nor Tamara would be working at DMI, and her dream would be completely dashed. It was going to be tough for his mother, but she'd get over the transition.

"Mother," he said finally, avoiding eye contact, "I came to tell you I'm stepping down."

She sat quietly, which drove him crazy. He was prepared for her to be outraged and combative. Madeline wasn't, causing him to cringe initially, until he recalled praying for grace. Maybe her tempered reaction was an answer to his prayer. He had to believe it was and continued with that perspective.

"I've been thinking quite a bit about pursuing the relationship with Naledi, settling down, and maybe having children in the next three to five years. What do you think?"

Madeline toyed with a small stack of paper clips. She wouldn't look up at Don, which made him nervous. He continued praying silently for more grace, as the first dose might be wearing off. "Does it matter what I think if you've decided you're out of here?"

No, it really didn't matter, but he would never purposefully disrespect Madeline. He'd take another route to get her to understand his proposition. As far as Don was concerned, God had already spoken and released him from DMI. He'd fulfilled his role as the person tasked with reuniting his family. Once Don had clarity, his mother's validation wasn't necessary. He'd love to have her support, but honoring God would always take precedence.

"Mother, I'm not leaving you forever. I'm just switching gears. Besides, don't you want grandchildren one day?"

She sighed. "Don't even try it. Nothing you say is going to make up for your absence here." So far Don was overjoyed at how well she was taking the news. "Needless to say, DMI will be crushed."

"Talk about flattery," Don replied, intentionally working to keep their discussion pleasant.

"Flattery my behind. It's the truth. We need you."

"You'll be fine without me for a while. God will look out for you, if you let Him," Don told his mother.

"Humph, we're not going there. Let's stick with you. When are you walking out?"

"I don't have a definitive date, but a month would be ideal."

"Too bad I couldn't get Tamara to take over. That would be a perfect transition for us."

Don didn't agree. Tamara wasn't ready. She didn't have sufficient experience. He knew it, and Madeline did too. Since his sister had no interest in the job, he didn't have to voice his disapproval. Instead, he focused on a viable replacement. "What about you, Mother? There's no one more suited for the role of CEO than you. How about it?"

"Oh no, not me. I told you, it's time for me to hang up my briefcase and lie on the beach, sipping on a cool drink of something."

Don scratched his head. "Okay, so Tamara's out and you're out. That puts Abigail at the top of our short list," he said, confident about the recommendation. Abigail had worked for his father, for him, and for Joel. She had DMI oozing from her pores. She was their best option.

"Abigail is a strong successor," she admitted.

"Plus, she's loyal and deserves the job. She's paid her dues several times over."

"She has," Madeline acknowledged. Then she said, "Abigail is good, but I have a better candidate."

"You have to give up on Tamara."

"I'm not talking about Tamara."

Don was startled by her comment. "Then who?"

Madeline's gaze bounced off the wall. "What about Joel?"

Don gave a few coughs. "Joel who?"

Madeline smirked. "Your brother."

"I thought that was who you were referring to. You can't be serious."

"Oh, I'm very serious."

Don chuckled. "Then you'll need to provide an incredible explanation to get my vote."

"Simple. He's smart, charismatic, and has the flare for this job." Don couldn't disagree. "On top of the basics, he's a Mitchell. He has rights and privileges that should elevate him above other candidates."

"But you don't like him, and you've never seen him as a legitimate Mitchell heir."

"I want our company to succeed, which means putting the best people in place."

"But we know Joel has a history."

"Yes, but he came to see me earlier. He apologized for his trifling ways and asked for a job."

"And you're obliged to give him one just like that?"

"Call me crazy, but I have a gut feeling Joel is the one for us. Don't ask me why. I can't explain it. I'm going purely on my gut."

"And I'm going on faith. I say Abigail is the one."

"Then, my son, it looks like we'll have to agree to disagree."

"I guess so," Don replied.

"Well, let the games begin," she told him. "Let me know when you're ready to present your candidate to the board of directors. I'm putting Joel's name on the table."

"Are you sure about this?" Don asked.

"Positive. This should be an interesting fight." She held her hand out and shook Don's. "May the best candidate win."

Chapter 54

Two years ago, Joel couldn't have imagined approaching Madeline with an apology and a request for help. It truly was unimaginable. Yet he had done the unthinkable and didn't feel ashamed or belittled. Truthfully, he was basking in a state of fulfillment. Had Joel known making peace with Madeline would facilitate such contentment, he'd have thrown her an olive branch a long time ago. He was riding high on positivity. The air was light, and so were his worries. He had problems, but they didn't have the same bite. He strolled to his car, letting his thoughts gently flow.

Joel cruised to the hospital around five o'clock, eager to relieve his mother. When he entered the hospital room, he found Zarah sitting up in the bed and talking with Sherry. He was glad.

"You're awake," he said, approaching the bed.

"I'm tired, but I am much better. The baby is good, and I am good," Zarah replied and took a sip of water.

"Well, we're happy you're feeling better. Right, Joel?" Sherry said.

"Most definitely. Have you eaten?" he asked.

Zarah shook her head. "Not yet. I'm not very hungry."

"But you have to eat, my dear," Sherry said, reaching for the water so Zarah wouldn't have to stretch to get it off the tray.

"Joel, did you reschedule my meeting with the board of directors?" Zarah asked.

He didn't want her worrying about work. "It was put on hold," he said, stepping around his mother and taking Zarah's hand. "I want you to put business out of your mind. I'd like you to trust me. Let me take care of those issues for you. I want you to rest, please," he told his wife, peering into her eyes. "Don't worry about a thing. I've spoken to Kumar, and someone will travel from India to help with Harmonious Energy."

"Thank you," Zarah said, and he saw the anxiety begin to melt from her demeanor.

"There's no need to thank me. I'm your husband. It's my job to take care of you."

"Excuse me, but I'd like to grab a bite to eat myself. If you don't mind, I'm running down to the cafeteria," Sherry said.

"Go," Joel said. "And bring me a bottle of water when you come back, please."

"Will do. Can I get you anything, Zarah?"

"Nothing for me," she replied, and Sherry left.

Zarah's radiance was overwhelming. He took pride in comforting his wife. As he held her hand, she touched his heart and melted away any trace of indifference that might have remained. Gazing at her, he reminded himself that she wasn't the woman he'd inherited from a business deal. Joel had to acknowledge Zarah as a living, breathing being with feelings, ones he'd trampled upon and hurt maliciously.

"I truly wanted to run my father's company, but I can't," she stated, tearing up. "The baby comes first."

"I know, and we'll work with the DMI board and Kumar to structure a plan."

"What about you? Can you run Harmonious Energy for me?" she asked, swiping at her tears.

"I can help you, but it's not the company for me in the long run," he said, sliding onto the edge of the bed, next to her. He had to be honest without disrespecting her beliefs. The task wasn't going to be easy, but Joel had to try. "It's based on an Eastern religion, and DMI is founded on Christian principles. I have to go back to what I know works for me. I'm not asking you to convert to my faith, but I can't commit to yours. That's the truth."

"What about the West Coast division? Do you still want it?" Zarah asked.

"No. I'm withdrawing my bid."

The doctor entered, interrupting their candid discussion. Joel wasn't pleased.

"Any updates?" Joel asked.

"When can I go home?" Zarah interjected.

"We got your blood work back. Your test results look fantastic. The baby is stable, which is why I believe you should be able to go home tomorrow, or in two days, at the latest."

"Very good," Zarah responded, beaming.

Joel was thrilled too but maintained his composure. "Should we be concerned after she goes home?"

The doctor came close to the couple. "From what I can tell, a full-term pregnancy is highly possible, but she has to make changes. Rest and relaxation are an absolute must."

Joel and Zarah thanked the doctor, and he excused himself and left the room.

Relieved, Joel caressed her hand. "Zarah, I apologize for not being with you from the beginning of the pregnancy." Becoming a father was a blessing he couldn't discount. "I truly am sorry for my actions, and I'm asking for your forgiveness." Joel did not utter his apology because he was bound by duty or pity. He had faith that God could keep breathing life into his relationship with Zarah.

She was thrilled. They hugged and basked in the tranquility of the moment. He was committed to setting aside their personal and professional challenges. Whatever might come next didn't trump their peaceful moment together. Tomorrow was sure to present complications, but Joel would worry about those problems when they actually materialized. Thankfully, that wasn't today. They could both use a breath of relief.

Joel settled into the embrace. When Zarah attempted to pull away, he held on. There was hope for his wounded marriage as long as they were both committed to making concessions. He was, and he believed she was too. The only question that truly needed to be answered was, how could God save a marriage that had a major spiritual complication? Joel shrugged off the question. The 'how' was for God to determine, not him.

He continued to embrace Zarah. If his heart could be shaped to fit hers, then the possibilities of restoration were endless for others he loved. He even entertained the wild notion that unity resided in his family. Maybe there was hope for the Mitchell clan, Joel thought, imagining layers of strife being shed and hearts softening. Only time would tell.

Reading Guide

MAKES YOU GO "HMMM!"

Now that you have read *Humbled,* consider the following discussion questions.

1. How would you define or label Joel and Sheba's relationship?
2. Joel and Zarah seem to have very little in common. Their most significant disconnect is religion. Ironically, both their fathers based the family business on religion. For DMI, it is Christianity, and for Harmonious Energy, it is an Eastern religion. Do you think Joel and Zarah can or should stay married even though their beliefs differ?
3. Can Joel be a good father without being married to Zarah and living in the same house? If yes, how? If no, why not?
4. Tamara and Zarah have a friendship. Do you believe Tamara sincerely cares about Zarah, or is the friendship based on her ulterior motives? Did you agree with Tamara's advice to Zarah on how to get Joel's attention?
5. In the early pages of the novel, who did you want to end up with the West Coast division? Tamara, so she could gain independence from the family; Joel, so

he could get a fresh start; or Madeline, so she could restore the company?

6. Who do you think should run DMI if Don resigns? Are you siding with Madeline, who has set her sights on Joel, or with Don, who wants Abigail to fill the post?
7. Why do you think Tamara is reluctant to embrace her mother fully and rekindle their relationship?
8. According to Sherry, Joel is repeating the same mistakes his father made. Agree or disagree?
9. Who do you think will get married first? Tamara or Abigail? Why?
10. Do you think Don will leave DMI and go back to South Africa, or will something keep him in Detroit? If he does go back to South Africa, do you think he'll actually marry Naledi after having strong feelings for Abigail over the years?
11. Who's your least favorite character in the novel, and why? (Base your answer solely on *Humbled,* and not on the other stories in the series.)
12. Do you believe Madeline and Joel have truly made peace? Is it possible for them to reconcile after so many years of bitterness?
13. Has Joel really changed, or does he have a hidden agenda?
14. Let's say the Mitchell Family Drama Series is being made into a movie and you are the casting director. Who would you select to play Madeline, Sherry, Don, Joel, and Tamara?
15. At the core of the Mitchell family's discord is an unwillingness to forgive. All the money, power, and influence they possess cannot help them fix their problems, particularly those within the family. Don realizes the freedom that comes from forgiveness early in the series. It looks like others are coming

around too. How about you? Is there anyone you are estranged from or have been unwilling to forgive? Remember that forgiveness is liberating and is the best gift you can give yourself as well as others.

Note: The Mitchell family drama is loosely based on the story of a mighty biblical warrior, King David, who had God's unprecedented favor and a profound purpose. However, King David was also plagued by family problems, personal failures, and sinful mistakes. Because he was able to forgive those who had wronged him and went the extra step of forgetting (letting go of) the pain, the anguish, and the bitterness associated with mistakes of the past, he was at peace and achieved great success regardless of what was going on around him.

Acknowledgments

I thank God for each reader. If *Humbled* brings a smile to your face, entertains at least one person, evokes a laugh, stirs emotion for a character, or provokes you to think about forgiving someone, then my writing will have accomplished its purpose. I pray you will be blessed and encouraged. This book is for you.

There is a long list of family and friends who consistently support me. Although it is humanly impossible for me to personally thank everybody, please know that I am sincerely grateful to those who have contributed in any way to my writing. Even if I don't list your name, we know the Lord knows who you are and has the ability to bless you abundantly, far beyond what I can do.

My circle contains an amazing group of people who I definitely have to acknowledge. My heart beats in unison with that of my beloved husband and best friend, Jeffrey Glass, whom I am incredibly blessed to have as a soul mate. Many thanks to my beautiful, smart, and encouraging daughter (TJ), my nieces and nephews who keep me laughing with their quick wit. I must say thank you to my dear family (Haley, Glass, Tennin, and Moorman), my friends, goddaughters, spiritual parents, god sisters/brothers, my brothers (Rev. Fred, Little Freddy Deon), my cousins who always get the word out about my books (Kattie Starnes, Soror Alesha Russey, Kimberla Lawson Roby, and Kim/Ron Haley Bolden); and my beloved mothers, Fannie Haley Rome and Jeraldine Glass, who keep me covered in love and prayer. With abiding love, I honor the memories of my dad ("Luck"), my brother (Erick), and my father-in-law (Walter).

Special thanks go to my freelance editors, who continuously challenge me to make every book better: Emma (John) Foots, Laurel Robinson, Tammy Lenzy, Dorothy Robinson, and Renée Lenzy. Much love to my publishing editor, Joylynn Ross. You are simply the best. I couldn't ask for a better person to work with in the publishing arena. Thanks to the Urban Christian team, especially Smiley Guirand, for doing such an awesome job with the covers. Thanks to my agent, Andrew Stuart, for making the business aspect easier. I especially have to thank my Delta Sigma Theta Sorority sisters and church families. I'm always grateful to a long list of book clubs, including the Williams Temple COGIC Book Club in Maine, the Bookees in Maryland, media venues, booksellers, and those who continuously support and bless me, such as my beloved family friends Eddie, Regina, Sierra, and Mariah Martin. I also honor a very special person, Mother Peggy Wright at Jones Memorial Baptist Church in Philadelphia, who passed away in July 2013. The love, support, wisdom, and huge smile that she showered upon me year after year, at each book signing, will always be with me.

P.S. Congratulations to Dana Reed and my goddaughters, Nicole Rashida Prothro and Rochelle Patricia Renee Burks, on their college graduations. Congrats to Shantel Haley and Leah Reed on their high school graduations. Happy birthday to Deacon Earl Rome (80th) and Deacon Robert Thomas (85th). Congratulations to my "other parents" on sixty-six years of marriage for Don and Mary Bartel and twenty-eight for Ron and Dottie Fisher. Wow. Much love to the newlyweds: cousins Mike & Marilyn Stapleton and dear friends Larry and Susan Greene. May God's grace and favor always be with each of you.

Author's Note

Dear Readers:

Thank you for reading *Humbled*. I hope you found this addition to the Mitchell Family Drama Series as entertaining as *Anointed, Betrayed, Chosen, Destined,* and *Broken*. Look for *Unforgiving,* the next book in this saga.

I look forward to you joining my mailing list, dropping me a note, or posting a message on my Web site. You can also friend me on Facebook, at Patricia Haley-Glass, or like my Author Patricia Haley fan page.

As always, thank you for the support. Keep reading, and be blessed.

www.patriciahaley.com

UC HIS GLORY BOOK CLUB!

www.uchisglorybookclub.net

UC His Glory Book Club is the spirit-inspired brainchild of Joylynn Ross, an author and the acquisitions editor at Urban Christian, and Kendra Norman-Bellamy, an author for Urban Christian. It is an online book club that hosts authors of Urban Christian. We welcome as members all men and women who have a passion for reading Christian-based fiction.

UC HIS GLORY BOOK CLUB pledges its commitment to providing support, positive feedback, encouragement, and a forum whereby members can openly discuss and review the literary works of Urban Christian authors.

There is no membership fee associated with UC His Glory Book Club; however, we do ask that you support the authors by purchasing their works, encouraging them, providing book reviews, and, of course, offering your prayers. We also ask that you respect our beliefs and follow the guidelines of the book club. We hope to receive your valuable input, opinions, and reviews that build up, rather than tear down, our authors.

What We Believe:

—We believe that Jesus is the Christ, Son of the Living God.

—We believe that the Bible is the true, living Word of God.

—We believe that all Urban Christian authors should use their God-given writing abilities to honor God and share the message of the written word that God has given to each of them uniquely.

—We believe in supporting Urban Christian authors in their literary endeavors by reading their titles, purchasing them, and sharing them with our online community.

—We believe that everything we do in our literary arena should be done in a manner that will lead to God being glorified and honored.

We look forward to online fellowship with you. Please visit us often at *www.uchisglorybookclub.net*

Many Blessing to You!

Shelia E. Lipsey,

President, UC His Glory Book Club

ORDER FORM
URBAN BOOKS, LLC
97 N18th Street
Wyandanch, NY 11798

Name (please print):______________________________

Address: ______________________________

City/State: ______________________________

Zip: ______________________________

QTY	TITLES	PRICE

Shipping and handling-add $3.50 for 1st book, then $1.75 for each additional book.
Please send a check payable to:

Urban Books, LLC

Please allow 4-6 weeks for delivery

ORDER FORM
URBAN BOOKS, LLC
97 N18th Street
Wyandanch, NY 11798

Name (please print):_______________________________________

Address: _______________________________________

City/State: _______________________________________

Zip: _______________________________________

QTY	TITLES	PRICE
	3:57 A.M Timing Is Everything	$14.95
	A Man's Worth	$14.95
	A Woman's Worth	$14.95
	Abundant Rain	$14.95
	After The Feeling	$14.95
	Amaryllis	$14.95
	Anointed	$14.95
	Battle of Jericho	$14.95
	Be Careful What You Pray For	$14.95
	Beautiful Ugly	$14.95
	Been There Prayed That:	$14.95
	Betrayed	$14.95

Shipping and handling-add $3.50 for 1st book, then $1.75 for each additional book.

Please send a check payable to:

Urban Books, LLC

Please allow 4-6 weeks for delivery

ORDER FORM
URBAN BOOKS, LLC
97 N18th Street
Wyandanch, NY 11798

Name(please print):_______________________________

Address: _______________________________

City/State: _______________________________

Zip: _______________________________

QTY	TITLES	PRICE
	By the Grace of God	$14.95
	Confessions Of A Preachers Wife	$14.95
	Dance Into Destiny	$14.95
	Deliver Me From My Enemies	$14.95
	Desperate Decisions	$14.95
	Divorcing the Devil	$14.95
	Faith	$14.95
	First Comes Love	$14.95
	Flaws and All	$14.95
	Forgiven	$14.95
	Former Rain	$14.95
	Forsaken	$14.95

Shipping and handling-add $3.50 for 1st book, then $1.75 for each additional book.
Please send a check payable to:

Urban Books, LLC

Please allow 4-6 weeks for delivery

ORDER FORM
URBAN BOOKS, LLC
97 N18th Street
Wyandanch, NY 11798

Name (please print): ________________________________

Address: ________________________________

City/State: ________________________________

Zip: ________________________________

QTY	TITLES	PRICE
	From Sinner To Saint	$14.95
	From The Extreme	$14.95
	God Is In Love With You	$14.95
	God Speaks To Me	$14.95
	Grace And Mercy	$14.95
	Guilty Of Love	$14.95
	Happily Ever Now	$14.95
	Heaven Bound	$14.95
	His Grace His Mercy	$14.95
	His Woman His Wife His Widow	$14.95
	Illusions	$14.95
	In Green Pastures	$14.95

Shipping and handling-add $3.50 for 1st book, then $1.75 for each additional book.

Please send a check payable to:

Urban Books, LLC

Please allow 4-6 weeks for delivery